Daisy jumped
when the cowboy touched her elbow.

He was so near that she smelled leather.

Coming back to herself, she realized she was clutching her injury. Her face flamed, and she jerked her hand away. "Don't—don't act so familiarly."

"Sorry." He backed up several paces, holding his hands in front of him as if in surrender. "I was just trying to make sure you were okay."

She wasn't all right. She would never be all right. Her eyes burned, but she blinked rapidly. Tried to calm her breathing.

He untied the horse from the post and gathered the reins for her. When he pressed them into her shaking hand, he held on.

She should reprimand him for behaving so familiarly again, but the warmth of his hand wrapped around hers steadied her. She met his eyes, noting again for the second time the unusual shade of gray.

He believed she could do it.

And she would.

Books by Lacy Williams

Love Inspired Historical

Marrying Miss Marshal
The Homesteader's Sweetheart
Counterfeit Cowboy
Roping the Wrangler
Return of the Cowboy Doctor
The Wrangler's Inconvenient Wife
A Cowboy for Christmas

*Wyoming Legacy

LACY WILLIAMS

is a wife and mom from Oklahoma. Her first novel won an ACFW Genesis Award while it was still unpublished. She has loved romance books and movies from a young age and promises readers happy endings in all her stories. Lacy combines her love of dogs with her passion for literacy by volunteering with her therapy dog, Mr. Bingley, in a local Kids Reading to Dogs program.

Lacy loves to hear from readers. You can email her at lacyjwilliams@gmail.com. She also posts short stories and does giveaways at her website, www.lacywilliams.net, and you can follow her on Facebook (lacywilliamsbooks) or Twitter @lacy_williams.

A Cowboy for Christmas

LACY WILLIAMS

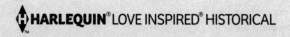

Recycling programs
for this product may
not exist in your area.

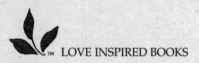

LOVE INSPIRED BOOKS

ISBN-13: 978-0-373-28292-0

A Cowboy for Christmas

www.Harlequin.com

Printed in U.S.A.

Even though I was once a blasphemer and a persecutor and a violent man, I was shown mercy because I acted in ignorance and unbelief. The grace of our Lord was poured out on me abundantly, along with the faith and love that are in Christ Jesus.
—*1 Timothy* 1:13–14

With thanks to Luke and my family
who support me in so many ways.

Also thanks to Mischelle Creager
and Regina Jennings for their input
about my stories, and to OCFW for being
such a supportive group of writing friends.

Lastly, to Martha A. from the ACFW Bookclub
who inspired the idea of a family
sharing an illness over Christmas.

Chapter One

Northeast Wyoming, early December 1900

A wedding was supposed to be a joyful occasion.

But Daisy Richards felt only emptiness as she watched her father and his bride, Audra, stand before the minister in the parlor of the family's ranch house. Audra had her hair pulled back in a simple bun and wore a dark green dress; Papa wore his Sunday suit, and his auburn hair had been slicked back.

They both looked fine and happy as they smiled secretive little smiles at each other.

But Daisy was not fine.

A draft coming in the window beside her ruffled the wisps of curls at her temples and cooled her burning cheeks. She hadn't been around this many folks in months—not since before the accident. And she was as jumpy as a deer during hunting season.

Her father had agreed to have the wedding here on the ranch, but only after a tearful conversation on Daisy's part. It was a second marriage for both her father and his bride. Both of their spouses had passed away years before.

If they'd had a town wedding as they'd initially planned, no doubt they would have had many more guests. As it was, Daisy felt overwhelmed by the small group crowded into the parlor. She could barely breathe.

The ranch house had become her sanctuary. She hadn't ventured outdoors in months, seen her friends or been to church.

She was conscious of too many eyes on her. Audra's twelve-year-old sons kept sneaking glances at her from their position standing on the opposite side of the room. She wanted to duck behind her younger sister, Belinda, at her right side but thought that might draw more attention.

And behind her, back where Daisy couldn't see them without turning her head, were Uncle Ned and the two hired cowboys.

Two young men who had come to work for her father during the late summer. She had never met either of them, had only seen them from afar when looking out her second-story window.

She felt them watching her, their curious gazes like hundreds of tiny needles pricking the back of her neck.

Whether she imagined their curiosity or not, she still felt empty and conspicuous. Exposed.

Daisy wished she hadn't let Belinda pull her hair into the simple bun at the nape of her neck. If her red curls had been down, she might've been able to shield her face and the mottled pink she felt burning her cheeks.

She could only hope that as she stood half hidden behind her sister, the young men couldn't get a glimpse of the empty, pinned-up sleeve on her right side. The dress was slightly out of style. The calico material wasn't really suitable for this winter wedding. And it didn't fit quite right after the weight she'd lost during her recovery and those long summer days she'd spent grieving and found it hard to eat.

Maybe the two men weren't looking at Daisy. Maybe they were looking at Belinda. Daisy's seventeen-year-old sister was beautiful. Her strawberry-blond hair was lighter than Daisy's, and her blue eyes always danced with life. She was trim and petite and had been practicing her charms at every social event since she'd had her birthday earlier in the summer.

Before the accident, Daisy would have been just like her sister—would have welcomed the attention from two cowboys. Worried about the fit and style of her dress.

Been just that shallow.

Now she just wanted to hide in her room until they all went away.

Someone moved behind her with a rustle of clothing, the movement drawing her eyes over her shoulder. One of the cowboys. The man shifted his broad shoulders beneath his worn, pressed white shirt. His head turned slightly toward her, and she had a glimpse of unusual steel-gray eyes and dark blond curls that were wet, as if he'd just washed up.

He'd been there, that night. He was one of the men who had pulled her out of the wreckage. Why had Papa hired him on?

She lowered her eyes before their gazes connected.

Had he seen the pinned-up sleeve on her right side? How humiliating.

Her cheeks burned hotter. Her lungs constricted.

Suddenly, she felt as if the walls closed in on her. As if she was pinned beneath the wagon again. Unable to move, to escape. Acrid smoke choked her.

She couldn't catch her breath.

She must've made some noise of distress, because her father glanced over his shoulder, right at her.

Meeting Papa's eyes brought her fully back into the present. This was her father's wedding day, not that terrible night. She was safe in her family's home.

She tried to summon a smile for him but couldn't.

It wasn't that she begrudged her father happiness. Her mother had passed away when she was thirteen. Seven years ago now. It was high time her father married and found happiness again.

It was more the knowledge that she could never be happy again.

Her momentary lapse into memories had caused her to miss the vows. The small crowd clapped as her father kissed his new bride. She started to join in, hoping no one noticed her inattention and delay.

And then realized all she could do was slap her thigh.

No clapping for her.

A rush of moisture filled her eyes, and she turned away, pretending to gaze out the window until she could steady her breathing and push away the tears.

Her father was living his life, unafraid to remarry even though he'd lost his beloved first wife. Belinda was already caught up in socializing, and no doubt young men would come courting soon.

It was Daisy who was stuck in the mire. Who couldn't move on from the accident that had taken her arm and changed everything.

Daisy ducked into the kitchen, praying for a reprieve,

but everyone seemed to follow her. A sugary-sweet smell wafted into her consciousness.

The cake. She'd forgotten that Audra had asked her to help serve.

Frantic for escape, even if it meant she wouldn't fulfill her promise to her new stepmother, Daisy glanced up to see if she could sneak through the parlor to the stairs in the hall.

Belinda, oblivious, snagged Daisy's good arm and tugged her behind the long preparation counter, where the cake had already been cut and plated. A punch bowl and several cups had been set out to complete the spread. She was thankful Belinda had been tasked with filling the cups.

With the cake already cut, Daisy wasn't needed. Not really.

Belinda blocked her from passing behind the counter in the center of the large kitchen. She could go around the other way—

She felt dizzy, overly hot. As if she might faint.

"Did you see the new cowboy?" Belinda asked in a low voice.

Her question drew Daisy out of the moment, out of herself enough that she could grip the counter with her good hand until her knuckles turned white.

Did she really want to disappoint her stepmother? The woman who would be a fixture in their lives from now on?

All Daisy had to do was shove each piece of cake across the counter to whoever came for them. She didn't even have to speak.

All she had to do was make it through the next few minutes, and then she could escape.

The preacher's approach kept Belinda from saying more, but Daisy supposed her silence wouldn't last long. Her sister was more than interested in the opposite sex. Daisy might've been the same at Belinda's age, but not anymore.

"You look well, Miss Richards," said the preacher.

Daisy startled when her sister jabbed an elbow into her side. Oh. He had apparently been talking to her.

No doubt she looked better than the last time he'd seen her. Her father had summoned him. They'd all thought she'd been on her deathbed until she'd finally fought through the infection that had set in to her arm. And she hadn't been back to town since she'd been brought out here to the ranch to recuperate.

"I hope we'll see you in services soon."

She gave no answer.

Her cheeks burned as she attempted to smile at the man. Several feet behind him, she glimpsed the blond-haired cowboy in conversation with Uncle Ned, her father's right-hand man. Uncle Ned had been on the ranch for nearly as long as she'd been alive. The second cowboy had disappeared. Had he ducked outside instead of staying for cake?

The younger man glanced away from Ned, his slate-gray eyes turning toward Daisy, but she averted her gaze again.

The preacher shifted in front of her. Belinda helped cover the awkward silence by jumping in to talk about the upcoming Christmas program, and Audra approached with her elbows linked to her two towheaded terrors, twelve-year-old twins. Now Daisy's stepbrothers.

Before her convalescence, they'd followed her around

like twin puppies, asking questions about the ranch and jostling and shoving each other whenever they could.

Since the accident, they had seemed unnaturally focused on her missing arm on the few prior occasions she'd seen them.

Daisy shoved three pieces of cake across the counter, the plates scraping loudly against the worn wood. She hoped they would take the cake and leave her alone.

But of course they didn't.

"I'm glad you decided to join us downstairs today, dear," Audra said.

As if she'd been given any choice.

She had overheard Audra and her father arguing several days ago. Audra insisted that Daisy was well enough to begin attending social events again. Her father had cited her improvement since the accident and wanted to give Daisy more time. Audra had accused him of coddling her.

Daisy shivered just thinking about being seen in town, as she was now.

Then yesterday, when she'd been considering whether she could feign an illness as she had done in her younger years to get out of going to school, her father had sat down with her after supper and told her how proud he was of her.

Guilted her into coming to his wedding.

Beneath her calico dress, her legs trembled with the desire to escape.

One of the Twin Terrors nudged the other behind Audra's back. Audra said something to Belinda, her attention flitting to the younger sister.

And Daisy heard Terrance whisper, "Do you think it still hurts?"

Her face flamed. The way both twins' eyes were glued to her, he must be talking about her injury.

Todd whispered right back, "Ask her."

She couldn't do this. She tensed, all her muscles coiling in preparation to run away.

But Audra turned back to the boys, who pushed large bites of cake into their mouths at the same moment, acting as if the whispered conversation hadn't happened.

A selfish part of Daisy wished Papa and Audra had cancelled their honeymoon trip. But they hadn't. She wished for a quiet couple of weeks but didn't hold out much hope. With the twins underfoot and everyone adjusting to the new family, there would be some inevitable growing pains.

And once her father and Audra returned…no doubt her new stepmother would harangue her about leaving the ranch and attending social events that no longer held any appeal.

Daisy would do well to escape the ranch, even though it had been her home for the entirety of her life.

But where would she go when she barely had the gumption to come downstairs?

She was trapped.

Audra and the boys moved back into the parlor, leaving Daisy and Belinda alone, though they could probably still be heard through the open parlor door.

"The new cowboy's good-looking, isn't he?" Belinda asked, as if the interim conversations hadn't happened.

"Shh," Daisy hissed, half afraid he was still within hearing distance. She didn't dare glance up to see. "I hadn't noticed."

Her sister hummed a muffled laugh and twirled away

to join their father, leaving Daisy alone with several slices of cake on plates and only her nerves for company.

Ricky White had never had trouble catching a woman's eye.

Before he'd reformed, most women couldn't stop looking at him.

Until Miss Daisy Richards.

Her fire-bright red curls, tamed in a simple knot behind her head, were a harsh reminder of how everything he touched went up in flames.

But God was behind him now, right? Surely Ricky couldn't mess this up.

Her dark yellow dress matched the autumn leaves on the aspens visible in the distance through the large parlor window.

But her blue eyes skittered around like a cornered animal's might, and that was the whole point, wasn't it?

He was responsible for what had happened to her. He'd been drunk that night in Pattonville, the small town a few miles from their ranch. He'd gotten into a fistfight in the saloon that had spilled out into the street and scared the horses harnessed to her wagon. It had overturned with her inside it, and when the attached lantern had smashed, the fuel spread and caught the wagon on fire. Daisy Richards had been trapped beneath it.

She'd lost her arm because of him.

And with God's help, he was going to make it right. There was no changing the life he'd taken all those years ago, but *this*, he could make right. He had to.

That night had been a wake-up call. He'd thought

the choices he was making as he tried to forget his past mistakes only affected him.

Until he'd been forced to see the truth. And it had saved his life.

Behind that kitchen counter, she trembled like a frightened filly getting a glimpse of her first halter. As if she was about to bolt.

She needed to reclaim her life; he intended to find a way to help her do so. But first he had to speak to her.

He meandered up to the counter, taking in the scent of hot coffee and the warmth emanating from the stove. Pots and utensils hung from hooks on one wall, and a washtub had been built into the counter in front of a large window overlooking the yard between house and barn.

It reminded him of the home he'd left behind.

But he couldn't think about that now.

He reached out for a piece of the cake, even though his stomach flip-flopped in protest. At the last second, he changed from his left hand to his right, realizing she would be able to see the scar on the back of his wrist. Not wanting anything to remind her of that night.

"Howdy, miss."

She didn't look directly at him, just nodded with her eyes on his third button.

"I'm Ricky White. Started working for your pa a couple months ago."

She nodded again.

He'd just seen her talking to her sister. Her voice box must work.

Did she just not want to talk to him? Her shoulders were hunched up around her ears. Either she was shy, or she had taken an instant dislike to him.

He'd never had to try so hard for a single word before. *Before*, he'd seen her around town, known she was someone who would never give a troublemaker like him a second glance.

"It was a nice wedding," he said, scrambling for something to say that might get her to look at him. "Friend of mine had an outdoor wedding a couple of years ago…"

The memory of Sam and Emily's wedding, and Maxwell and Hattie's, several years back…cutting up with his brothers…his pa's affirming hand on his shoulder… all of the memories were a whiplash of hurt that he quickly shook away.

More color rose in her cheeks, but her lips pinched until they were white around the edges. She still didn't say anything. Voices rose and fell in the parlor, but here in the kitchen, he could hear the crackle of the fire in the stove.

Then she turned her profile to him and gave him an unhindered view of her right sleeve, pinned between her shoulder and elbow.

As if to ward him off.

He didn't mind the injury. He'd seen worse as he'd traveled the state, boxing and spending time in saloons and places good girls didn't go.

It certainly didn't detract from her looks.

It was the memory of how it happened, his part in it, that made him wince. He tried to disguise it by chomping a bite of the cake.

He didn't know if she expected him to just walk away, and she didn't know him from Adam, but she'd soon learn he was about the stubbornest cowboy she'd ever meet.

He kept his feet planted right where they were. He'd waited through the last of the summer and all of fall to even get a chance to speak to her.

For once, he was right where he was supposed to be, doing what he was supposed to be doing.

He couldn't mess this up.

She still didn't look directly at him. She looked past him, into the other room. He let his eyes wander over his shoulder and saw her sister in conversation with Ned and Beau, his boss and the cowboy who'd become a close friend during the months they'd worked together.

The fact that she wouldn't say a word to him was starting to make him nervous, and he reached up to stick a finger in the collar of his shirt.

And forgot that it was his burned hand.

Her eyes tracked to the scarring on the back of his wrist. Her face paled.

He saw her lips part and a silent gasp emerge. Her eyes went unfocused, as if she got lost in a memory. And he could guess what she was thinking about. That night. He'd been drunk, gotten into a brawl that had spilled from the saloon out into the street—where he'd spooked the horses tethered to her wagon. The animals had bolted and the wagon had overturned. And she'd been caught beneath it.

Her pa had said she didn't remember everything about that night. She didn't seem to recognize him at all or know that he'd had a part in the accident.

Now she made a sound like a hurt animal, some kind of soft cry.

His gut constricted. What if he'd done the wrong thing, coming in here today? But it would've looked suspicious, him not coming to the boss's wedding when the cowboys were invited.

A glance over his shoulder showed no one from the parlor had even noticed her distress. He didn't know if that was a good or bad thing.

He had to shake her out of the memory, if he could.

He stepped between her and the doorway, giving her a modicum of privacy and asked, as calm as he could, "You want some punch?"

Her panicked eyes rose to meet his, and he tried to give off the same confidence that his older brother Oscar had taught him when they trained horses together.

"Punch?" she asked tremulously.

There. He'd gotten a word out of her. Only the thin sound wasn't exactly what he'd had in mind when he'd come inside the ranch house today.

Still keeping himself between her and a view of everyone else, he stepped up to the counter and used the silver dipper from the punch bowl to get some of the pink liquid into a cup. He pressed it into her hand, and she inhaled, probably because the glass was cold.

But it seemed to break into her thoughts.

She flicked a glance over his shoulder, seemed to calm the slightest bit. Her breathing steadied.

"You okay?" he asked.

And she shook her head slightly. "No. No, I am not okay."

With that, she swept past him and through the parlor. He turned in time to see her skirts swish as she climbed the stairs in the front hallway.

That hadn't gone anything close to the way he'd planned.

Chapter Two

"Daisy?"

Not long after her escape from the cowboy, a knock at her bedroom door startled Daisy as she sat at the small writing desk. Her arm jerked, pushing the nib of the pen in a squiggly line across the paper.

Not that the jagged line looked much better than the childish letters she had painstakingly formed moments before. Frustrated with her inability to make her left hand work the way her right hand had done easily, Daisy smacked several sheets of paper, sending them across the desk and covering her failure.

Shaking, she stood up and turned away from the afternoon sunlight streaming through her bedroom window. The interior of the room was simple. A quilt her mother had made stretched across the bed; a bureau and hanging mirror the only other furniture in the room.

Her father stood in the doorway, expression serious. Had he seen her silent outburst? She couldn't tell. Behind him, through the open doorway, she could hear voices and activity from downstairs. Things were already changing from the quiet life she'd lived here with Papa and Belinda.

She didn't like it.

"Audra and I are leaving now."

She nodded. She knew they planned to stay the night in the hotel in town before taking the train to their final honeymoon destination.

"I'm trusting you to take care of the boys while we're gone."

Why? Daisy wanted to ask. But she didn't dare. Her father was used to running his successful spread. Not used to disobedience.

Daisy forced a faint smile for him. "With Uncle Ned and Belinda to help, I'm certain we'll keep them out of trouble. Somewhat."

He nodded, his gaze passing her to go to the window, where outside the wagon had been loaded.

She couldn't quite say that everything would be fine without him here. She wished she could be certain of it, but nothing had been fine since that night five months ago.

He embraced her, the familiar scent of the horse-radish candies he kept on his desk downstairs bringing tears to her eyes. Not for the first time, she felt the emptiness of a one-armed hug.

Out in the hall there was a rush of footsteps. Over Papa's shoulder she saw two blond heads peering at her from the top of the staircase. The twins.

She must've stiffened, and her papa turned to see why. The boys skittered back down the stairs the way they'd come.

But her stomach knotted.

"If the boys cause too much trouble, send them out to your uncle."

"Mmm-hmm," she agreed. Her mind had already gone to locking her door and keeping them out of her room, her private domain.

Her only solace since the accident.

But her father was asking her to leave her room behind—come outside of herself enough to take care of the two boys. And she didn't want to.

She didn't want to face the twins' scrutiny, the curious gazes. The rude, inevitable questions that only a child could get away with asking.

It couldn't be as difficult as she imagined. Could it?

Three days later, Daisy wished she'd put up more of a fight.

The twins created chaos everywhere. They left muddy boots in the hall and socks strewn up and down the stairs. They frequently dissolved into shouting matches with each other. And the wrestling! They'd nearly broken one of the parlor lamps in one of their grappling contests.

Anytime that Daisy asked them to stop or to pick up after themselves, they balked. Not outright refusing, but sometimes challenging her with a look to see what she'd do if they didn't comply.

They complained all the time. About the taste of the food Belinda had cooked. That they didn't get to see their town friends.

Even now, Todd whined, "I'm bored…" The boy jumped up from the sofa and began circling the parlor.

Terrance looked up from the checkerboard they'd been engrossed in for the past half hour after lunch.

Daisy was not bored. She willed the young man to

sit back down. Of course, he couldn't hear her internal thoughts and kept moving.

Terrance hadn't followed his brother up off his seat but now took a red rubber ball from one pocket and threw it against the wall, right near the fireplace.

"Please don't do that," Daisy chided him. If he missed and the ball flew into the hearth, the burning log could possibly roll out onto the floor and ignite the rug.

The boy pulled a face but didn't throw the ball against the wall again. He tossed it up into the air and caught it. His eyes slid over to Daisy, but she was too weary to protest.

Her patience was worn thin.

She kept her focus on the basket of laundry Belinda had planted at the foot of the couch before she'd flounced off in a huff.

It wasn't Daisy's fault that her missing arm prevented her from doing the things she'd done before. Or that Belinda had had to take over the lion's share of the inside chores.

She would switch in the blink of an eye, if given a chance.

The simple job of sorting and folding the clothes would've been ridiculously easy before the loss of her arm. Now the task had Daisy frustrated, near tears and on edge. With no patience to deal with the Twin Terrors.

She chose a shirt from the basket on the floor and attempted to shake it out. It was smaller than her father's, so no doubt it belonged to one of the two young men in the room right now. The material fluttered but didn't spread the way she wanted it to.

Terrance missed his catch and the ball bounced on

the floor, finally bumping her boot. She strove to ignore him as he scrambled to retrieve it.

Todd passed behind the couch, and his breathing seemed overly loud in the confined room. Was he doing so just to annoy her?

She draped the shirt over the arm of the sofa and folded the two sides of it together. Buttons were beyond her with only one usable hand, so she left them undone. She tucked the arms over the body of the shirt and halved the whole thing, then tucked it up into quarters.

The entire process took much longer than it should've.

"That's not the way Ma folds our shirts," Todd said as his pacing brought him past her, his words perilously like a whine.

She hummed noncommittally and kept her eyes on the next item she pulled from the basket. One of Belinda's dresses.

"Todd!" Terrance whispered from his seat.

She didn't look up to see if the second brother was afraid of getting in trouble or was egging Todd on.

"What?" Todd said, his tone taking on a bit too much innocence. "I think she's doing it wrong a'purpose since she's steamed at us already."

Daisy inhaled sharply and spun to face the child.

He'd paused behind the sofa, too far for her to reach, if she would have even considered the action. His eyes sparked with merriment and perhaps he didn't mean for his teasing to be so cruel, but Daisy's own inadequacies made her sensitive.

"Perhaps you shouldn't talk so about someone unless you have been in their shoes," she said.

"Ma says you're jest being a big baby—"

She gasped.

On the couch, Terrance began to look uncomfortable. Then he thumped the ball against the wall again.

"Do you mind?" she asked, voice shaking as badly as she was. "I'd like to finish this task without interruption. Alone," she clarified.

"Dew yew mind?" Todd mocked her.

"Todd—" Terrance warned.

"What if we *do* mind?" Todd asked.

She couldn't stand his disrespectful, hurtful words another moment.

Tears blinding her, she rushed out of the room. She could hear Belinda above stairs, but she knew her sister would be no help after the way she'd overreacted earlier about *needing a break from the chores*.

Perhaps it was cowardly to run away, but Daisy couldn't face the twins another moment. Where could she find a few moments of peace, of sanctuary?

"Daisy! Don't run off!" came Todd's mocking voice behind her. "C'mon…"

She didn't wait for them to follow but rushed through the kitchen into the yard.

In the barn, Ricky mucked out the horses' stalls with a vengeance. Muscles straining, he huffed with exertion. The task was one he'd done plenty of times at home. The movements were familiar, and he did it almost without thought.

He'd already shed his coat and hung it over one of the interior stalls. The weather had actually warmed up past freezing temperatures today. The big double barn doors were open, allowing fresh air inside and stirring up smells of horse and manure.

But nothing cooled him off.

He'd had the nightmare again. Had every night since he'd talked to Daisy at her pa's wedding. He'd wake up in the darkest part of night, sweating bullets with a cry on his lips, nostrils burning with smoke—ever since the event in his childhood, he *hated* fire—remembering exactly how he'd brawled his way in front of the horses hitched to her wagon, remembering the sight of them barreling down the dark street.

Remembering her tumbling from the wagon seat and the wagon flipping on top of her.

Even now, he shivered beneath the sweat he'd built up with his activity.

He could have killed her.

Instead, he'd just ruined her life. He'd witnessed her panic at the wedding, a small family event that shouldn't have inspired such desperation. He'd wanted to help her but feared her seeing his scar had made it worse.

He needed to make things right for her.

Beau, the cowboy who'd hired on about the same time as him, had comforted Ricky at his most broken. Had told him the same things that Ricky's pa and brothers had, but somehow, because of Ricky's brokenness, it had finally sunk in.

Now Beau daily encouraged him to seek God's will.

Ricky was trying, but why did it have to be so difficult to hear? Surely God wanted Daisy to heal, too, didn't He?

"What do you think, old girl?" he asked the huge black dog lying in an empty stall beside where he worked. "Have I lost all my charm?"

The dog didn't answer, of course, only panted through a wide doggy smile, tail flopping against the hay-strewn floor. Horses shifted in their stalls, sometimes softly whickering to a neighbor. None of them answered about Ricky's charms, either.

The women, too many young women, had been a distraction from the pain of Ricky's past. Only each dalliance had proved a temporary diversion.

Now he knew there was nothing to take away the pain. Nothing but the Lord, and he was still learning to trust Him.

It seemed the Lord was on his side today, because as Ricky mucked out the stalls, a glance out the open doors revealed the flaming head of hair that could only belong to Daisy, who was crossing the yard between the house and barn. Heading straight for him.

Heart thudding, he pretended casualness and kept on shoveling.

She swept inside the door.

"Morning, miss."

She startled, raising her hand above her eyes as they must've been adjusting to the lower light inside of the barn. "Oh."

She hesitated, looked unsure if she wanted to come or go.

There were shouts from outside, near the house, and she ducked into the first stall, disappearing from sight as she crouched inside it.

What was she doing? His lips twitched, and a punch of curiosity hit him squarely in the gut.

Her head popped up briefly. "I'm not here," she whispered.

Then she disappeared again.

And he very quickly found out why.

"Daisy!"

"Oh, sister…"

Two active twelve-year-old towheads rushed into the barn, looking around. One whistled, causing the nearest horse, a buckskin gelding, to bob its head and nicker.

"Boys," he warned.

One had a smudge of something left over from lunch beside his mouth. It was the only discernible difference Ricky could see. They both had trousers that were an inch too short—likely they'd had a growth spurt and their ma hadn't gotten around to sewing them each a new pair yet.

Had they been harassing Daisy in the house? Then chased her out here? No wonder she'd hidden. Being an ornery male himself, he remembered plenty of times during his childhood with Jonas and Penny when he'd irritated the fire out of his ma.

But that didn't mean he wanted them bothering Daisy.

"Did Daisy come in here?" one of them asked.

"We thought we saw her…" The other one peeked over the top of a stall. Blessedly, he was on the opposite side from where she'd hidden.

Several more horses began shifting in their stalls.

"Hold it!" Ricky moved between the boys and clapped a hand on each of their shoulders.

They froze, mouths gaping open at him.

"What d'you think you're doing?" he demanded in a firm voice that might just be an echo of his pa's.

The irony was not lost on him.

"We were just—" one started.

"—looking for Daisy," the other twin finished.

"You see her anywhere?" Ricky asked.

Their eyes darted around, starting to look a little wild, like an unbroken colt under his first saddle.

"No," one mumbled.

"You see these horses?" he asked.

"Y-yes, sir."

"You're spooking them."

The boys looked a little bewildered.

"You know what that means?"

One of the boys shook free of Ricky's hold, and the other quickly followed suit. They looked miffed.

"It means you're scaring them with your shouting and flailing around. When your new step-pa gets back, do you really want to have to explain how you got his horses excited in the barn, 'specially if one of 'em hurts itself?"

One of the boys crossed his arms over his chest, belligerent.

But the other looked slightly chastened.

"What's your name?" Ricky asked, going back to his pitchfork.

"Terrance," came the quiet reply, with a glance over his shoulder at the second brother, who was peering over the edge of the stall where the black dog lay. "That's Todd. What're you doing that for?"

"Would you like to stand around in your own mess all day?"

The boy wrinkled his nose in consideration of the question.

"C'mon, Terry!" the other brother called out. "Maybe she went around the house the other way."

Terrance watched Ricky for another moment, almost looking as if he wanted to ask another question, but then followed his brother out the double doors the way they'd come.

Had Ricky's distraction earned him any goodwill from the woman he wanted to speak to? He could only hope.

The cowboy had saved her.

Oh, it was only from the Twin Terrors, but still...

She found herself hesitating when she should've been kicking up her heels out of the barn. She poked her head above the stall to make sure the twins were really gone.

Then when her feet should've taken her back toward the house, instead she slowly wandered toward him, hand trailing along the side of the stalls. New, freshly spread hay crunched under her boots, sending its sweet smell wafting up to her.

She still didn't quite dare look at him.

"If you're aiming to take a walk, I'd recommend sneaking down by the pond," he said, still mucking out the stall and not really paying attention to her.

His inattention gave her the courage to say, "Thank you."

He nodded. She didn't know if that meant he understood that her thanks was for the advice or for handling the boys.

It had been such a long time since she'd spoken to someone outside of her family, save the preacher at her father's wedding days ago. And she'd embarrassed herself in front of this man at the same time. But he didn't seem affected. He just kept working.

For the first time in a long time, she wanted to say something. But she didn't know what. She thought to turn and go back to the house—and perhaps lock the exterior doors to keep the Terrors out—but before she had even moved, something cold and wet burrowed into her hand.

Gasping, Daisy looked down on a great black beast of a dog. One of three that usually rotated between being out with the flock and living in the barn. This one had been Daisy's favorite for years.

"Matilda," Daisy breathed. Her hand smoothed along the curly hair along the dog's back—nearly to Daisy's waist. Her hand paused along the dog's swollen midsection.

"You're…"

"Getting ready to have pups," said the man nearby.

The cowboy had set aside his pitchfork, leaned it against a nearby stall door. He squatted, and Matilda, usually notorious for despising strangers, waddled over and nosed his chest. "You doin' all right today, old girl?"

Daisy watched, dumbfounded, as the animal consented to having the fur beneath her chin scratched, even sitting on her haunches.

"Do you know when?" Daisy glanced at the cowboy.

His eyes were warm, open and friendly.

It surprised her.

Her curiosity about the animal, one who had been Daisy's companion since just after her mother passed away, propelled her forward. She ducked her chin and scratched the dog's back, kept her focus there. Matilda was *her* dog. Not his.

"Hard to say, exactly, but your uncle thinks maybe within a week or so."

And she'd missed the dog's entire pregnancy. Stuck in her room for five months. Afraid of coming outdoors, of being seen.

A whicker from nearby brought Daisy's gaze up to the large head above the next stall door over. "Prince."

She stood on wobbly legs.

The Appaloosa gelding blew a warm puff of air against her cheek. It was natural for her to reach up and rub beneath his forelock. He'd been her horse since her tenth birthday. Often, he seemed to share her thoughts, and now was no exception. He remained still as she allowed her forehead to rest against his nose, breathing in the familiar horse's scent and just being with an old friend she hadn't seen since the accident. Remembering how things had been before.

"Seems like your friends out here have missed you."

She looked over at the cowboy's words. He'd picked up his pitchfork, and again, his attention was diverted. Matilda had lain down and now rested her chin across Daisy's boot.

Daisy's throat burned.

She'd missed her animal friends, too.

Prince nibbled the shoulder of her coat, reminding her of his presence. She scratched beneath his chin.

The last time she'd ridden him, they'd raced across her father's patch of prairie, warm summer wind blowing through her hair and exhilaration flying high.

Her cheeks twinged—an unfamiliar feeling. And she realized she was smiling.

"If you want to ride out, I'll saddle him for you."

The cowboy's shoulders flexed beneath the worn woolen shirt as he kept working. Belinda was right. He *was* handsome. Tall, broad-shouldered, blond curls peeking from beneath his Stetson.

"I can't."

"Why not?" His frank question put her on the defensive.

"Isn't it obvious?" she said, turning her empty arm to him.

He didn't even look up from the work, irritating man.

He shrugged. "Seems like your legs do most of the talking in the saddle. You've got a hand for the reins." Now he looked at her, raking her with a glance. "Doesn't seem to be affecting your balance much."

His frank acceptance of her injury was so unexpected, so simple, that it brought immediate tears to her eyes.

She turned away quickly, dashing at the offending moisture with her wrist.

"Not today," she said quickly.

And she escaped back to the main house without even looking out for her stepbrothers.

Chapter Three

"This is going to be harder than I thought," Ricky said to the dog. Daisy had run off before he could muster an apology for making her cry.

He took off his hat and ran a hand through his sweat-matted curls. The barn was quiet around him, some animals moving in their stalls, the outside breeze causing the occasional quake or groan from the building.

Seeing tears in her eyes unmanned him.

He stuffed his hat back on his head and slapped the heel of one hand against the nearest stall door.

It didn't help.

He'd thought to come here to her pa's ranch and help her get back on her feet, as it were, and move on.

But her hurt ran deep. Deeper than he'd wanted to believe.

His actions of one night had been more far-reaching than he'd intended.

The guilt was strangling him.

He rested both hands on top of the stall and lowered his head between his arms. The weight was so heavy...

What if he couldn't fix things for her? He wasn't a man

to give up, but this task he'd set for himself… It wasn't going to be easy. If he got involved with her, became her friend… Well, he wasn't even sure he could do that.

He didn't have a good history with women. More like a string of broken hearts left behind.

"What's happened? Was that Daisy I saw running back to the house?"

Ricky looked up to find Ned and Beau leading their mounts into the barn, one of which had a sheep tied across its back.

Ned's question held a tone of suspicion. Ricky couldn't pretend to be working when the pitchfork leaned against the wall and wasn't in his hands.

"The twins chased her out here."

Ricky didn't mention his own part in upsetting her. Saw no reason to.

Ned's face cleared—a bit—but his eyes remained narrowed on Ricky. "I've a mind to give them both a good lickin'," the older man grumbled. The unspoken challenge was that he could lick Ricky, too, if the cowboy stepped out of line.

Ricky cleared his throat and stuffed his hat back on.

"You help Beau with this ewe. She got tangled up in some wire," Ned said. "I'm going back out to check the back fence where we found her."

"Sure thing, boss," Ricky responded. He met the other young man and saw the reason they'd brought in the ewe. One of her legs had been badly cut, several inches above the hoof.

"You have to wrestle her down?" he asked the other man.

Beau just grunted as he started to untie the animal from the saddle.

"Leave her feet until we can get her doctored, yeah?" Ricky asked.

The other man nodded.

He'd grown used to Beau's quiet nature. Beau sort of reminded him of his older brother Maxwell, who he'd seen only a few times the past few years as Maxwell worked on his education finishing university and medical school.

Ricky didn't want to think about home or his brothers. He forced his thoughts to the task before him.

They worked in companionable silence to get the ewe into one of the stalls. Beau ran off to grab the few things that qualified for a medical kit from the tack room.

Thinking about his family always upset Ricky. But he had a history of ruining the things he cared about. He'd almost messed up with his brother Edgar's wife. He'd gotten drunk and thrown in jail for destroying property in a barroom brawl when a couple of bad guys had been on Fran and her sister Emma's trail. The men tracking them could've used the opportunity to snatch the young women and might've except for Edgar's quick thinking and planning. That was when Ricky had known he had to leave. He'd been trying to outrun his past, but that hadn't worked out. Impossible to outrun something that lives on inside of you.

He ran one palm over his face, wishing he could wipe away the memories.

"You all right?" Beau asked, returning to the stall and kneeling over the sheep.

"Yeah."

"Ya sure? Something happen with Daisy?"

Were his feelings so visible on his face? Although he'd shared some with Beau, he hadn't told the kid the real reason he was here. He had told Daisy's pa when he'd hired on, but no one else knew. The older man had been willing to try anything to help his daughter, but had also cautioned Ricky that he would be watching.

"I came here to…" Ricky couldn't admit it. Just as he'd never told his pa, Jonas, the truth about why he'd run away with his brother Davy, back when they were kids.

Beau had a rudimentary respect for him; Ricky's pa loved him. He was chicken to change their opinions about him.

"I guess I'm wondering why things have to be so hard," he said cryptically. He pressed most of his weight down on the animal as it struggled while Beau applied some stinky-smelling antibiotic and went for a bandage. "I thought I was following the Lord's will, but…"

Beau grunted. "I guess the Good Lord told you that what He wanted from you would be easy? Provide a nice, clear path for you?"

Ricky shot a look at his friend.

Beau didn't say anything more. He didn't have to.

Ricky got it.

If he was really following God's leading, he would finish this task, no matter if it was difficult or not.

He'd made a promise, not knowing how difficult it would be to fulfill it.

He wasn't entirely sure he could do it.

He'd have to be extra careful to protect Daisy from himself. Not only from his reputation—which was why he'd been steering clear of town—but also from him making any overtures that could be misconstrued as something other than friendship. He knew how easy it was to play with a woman's emotions and had promised himself he wouldn't do so again.

Could he really be just her friend? He would have to try.

Days after hiding from the twins in the barn, Daisy slipped from the house, struggling to get her coat on one-handed. Heart thundering in her ears, her hair flew wild around her face, blowing in the cold wind, as she crossed the yard. She ran as quickly as she could move without tripping over her own feet.

How could the sun be shining on such a dreadful day?

She slipped into the barn, hoping against hope that it would be empty of cowboys, but she was disappointed and stopped in the doorway, the sunlight slanting in behind her and casting her shadow on the dirt-packed floor.

Ricky White was there, brushing down her Prince, who was tied off to a post and standing placidly. The sharp smell of the animals and manure bit her nose. She brushed her wind-blown hair back out of her face. Some of the horses nearby stamped their feet inside their stalls, clearly agitated by her rushing into the barn as she had.

But not the cowboy. He looked up, doffed his hat at her. "Morning, miss."

Polite, as he'd been during their two previous interactions.

She didn't have time for politeness. Not today. "Can you close the barn doors?"

With the double doors open, she could possibly be spotted from the house.

He didn't move from his spot on the opposite side of the horse, didn't stop the steady brushing motion. "Something chasing you?"

An apt question.

"The boys again?" he went on to ask. So calmly that she wanted to…shake him or something.

"Not them," she muttered.

He kept on at his task. As if he was waiting on her to answer.

"Two of my friends from town have come calling," she finally said. "They're coming up the drive in a carriage."

His eyebrows went up, disappearing beneath the brim of his hat. But he didn't say anything.

And she felt obliged to fill the silence that was rapidly becoming uncomfortable. "I haven't seen anyone since the accident," she burst out. "Since I lost my arm."

She rushed past him, toward the back corner of the barn, the smell of hay more stale here where there was less activity. Could she hide back here? It was a simple setup, and she could duck into one of the stalls as she had the other day hiding from the twins. Unless the cowboy ratted her out.

"Seems like a real friend wouldn't care about your arm." Ricky said the words placidly, as calm as the horse he was brushing down.

She gritted her teeth.

Perhaps not. But *she* cared.

She'd missed the birth of her best friend, Ethel's, baby, although she'd sent a note of apology. She couldn't bear seeing her friend so happy when all of her own dreams had been shattered with no hope of ever achieving them.

It might be shallow of her, but she just couldn't face them yet.

"Please, can you close the doors?" she asked again, this time her irritation leaking into her voice.

"I suppose if your friends got tired of you avoiding them—tired enough to drive all the way out here—a closed door might not stop them."

He was right.

What was she going to do?

Panic clawed at her throat. Her skin prickled like tiny bee stings all over her body. Her vision began to darken, turning black at the edges.

"Hey."

She jumped when the cowboy touched her elbow, so near that she smelled leather and horse.

Coming back to herself, she realized she was clutching her stump of an arm, her injury. Her face flamed, and she jerked her elbow away from his touch. "Don't— don't act so familiarly."

"Sorry. Sorry." He backed up several paces, holding his hands in front of him as if in surrender. "I was just trying to make sure you were okay."

She wasn't all right. She would never be all right. Her eyes burned, but she blinked rapidly. Tried to calm her breathing.

"If your friends care enough to come all the way out here to the ranch, surely it won't matter what your arm looks like," he said.

He was such a *man*. He didn't get it.

She shook her head, emotion clogging her throat, making her unable to speak. She *couldn't*.

"Look…" He sighed. "If you really can't—if you

really need to be away from the house, I'll saddle this old boy up for you."

She'd thought of little else since their conversation in the barn days ago. There were many things she was unable to do thanks to her injury, but his suggestion that she could still ride had stuck with her.

He seemed to take her silence for agreement, because he went to the small tack room and emerged with a saddle and blanket and began getting the horse ready.

"Will you…ride with me?" She hated the vulnerable note in her voice but was unable to call the words back.

He considered her for a long moment. She hated that he saw her weakness. He was no one to her, someone who worked for her father, but in contrast to who she had been before the accident…she hated it.

"Ned's expecting me to finish with the horses," he said, an apologetic tone to his voice. "You sure you don't want to stay and meet with your friends?"

Oh, yes. She was certain.

She lifted her chin. How many times had she ridden this horse? She'd ridden when she was sick and hale, as young as eight years old.

The horse was a gentleman.

She could do it.

She must do it.

Ricky finished cinching the saddle, and she joined him at the horse's side. Her hand shook as she reached for the saddle horn.

She would've been able to mount without assistance, before the accident. But when he offered his help, she gladly surrendered.

She put her booted foot into his cupped palms and

steadied herself with her hand as he boosted her into the saddle.

Leather creaked as she settled into the seat. She gripped Prince's mane. Being so far off the ground had her head swimming. She squeezed her eyes closed. She could do this. She had to do this.

She felt the cowboy's sure, steady movements as he adjusted her stirrup on one side and then ducked beneath the horse's head for the other side.

"You sure you're all right?"

"Yes." And her voice only shook slightly as she said the word.

He untied the horse from the post and gathered the reins for her. When he pressed them into her shaking hand, he held on.

She should reprimand him for behaving so familiarly again, but the warmth of his hand wrapped around hers steadied her. She met his eyes, noting again the unusual shade of gray.

The steady confidence in his gaze told her he believed she could do it.

And she would.

She turned the horse with only a slight tremble in her legs.

The movements so familiar before, different now without her right arm. But the familiarity was a comfort and by the time she'd walked Prince around the side of the barn, she felt confident enough to lean into a trot as she crested the first hill.

Ricky followed Daisy's Appaloosa on foot until she outpaced him and disappeared over the horizon. She'd been so distracted and upset he didn't think she even noticed. She never turned back.

He crossed his arms in front of him, the wind chilling him without his coat, but he still stood squinting in the bright morning sun, staring after where she'd disappeared.

He'd been torn when she'd asked him to ride with her. She'd been overreacting to her friends' surprise visit. Had to be.

He couldn't imagine any of his brothers giving up on him, just because he'd lost a limb. After interacting with her just a handful of times, he didn't even notice anymore.

But she was a female, and he knew females weren't always the most rational of creatures.

She wasn't ready to face her friends, even though she was totally recovered, as far as he knew.

It was another thing to add to his list of ways he had to help her. Another fear to chalk up to his mistake.

But not today.

Today's small victory was getting her on the back of that horse.

He'd sensed the strength in her. He knew she could do it alone—but she didn't know that. And wouldn't until she tried.

And he'd guessed right. As she'd ridden off, she'd leaned into the saddle, comfortable as only someone with a long history of riding could be. She and the horse had moved as one; her red hair had flown out behind her like a flag.

He'd known she was pretty all along. But this morning, seeing the determination enter her blue eyes had shown her true internal beauty.

She could heal.

And maybe he could help her.

Daisy flew over the rolling hills of her father's property, passing the aspens that clung to their last golden leaves.

Each thud of Prince's hooves reverberated through her as they traversed the moisture-softened ground and the occasional pocket of unmelted snow. Together.

The cold wind rushed through her hair, which was falling loose behind her. She always needed assistance putting it up now. Usually Belinda helped her with a simple bun or braid, but there hadn't been time this morning before she'd spotted the quick-moving wagon out her bedroom window.

It was exhilarating. She felt free. Riding Prince was like coming home, like being whole again.

She was doing it on her own. One of the few things she could do without help anymore.

She guided the horse past a dry creek bed and nudged the horse with her heels to spur it into a gallop.

If she could ride Prince…maybe there were other things she could do.

Maybe she didn't have to be confined to her room or the ranch house.

Her old dreams, before the accident had happened, had included her taking over her father's ranch, along with the husband she could no longer hope for.

What if… What if she could still run the ranch?

She pulled up at the crest of a hill, looking down on the winter-sun-drenched fields below, dotted with sheep.

Her heart beat loudly, painfully, in her chest as the dream grew.

What if she could still work the ranch?

And then the dream came crashing down around her ears.

When she returned to the barn, she wouldn't be able to unsaddle Prince.

She could brush him. She could pour oats for him from the bin.

But she couldn't fork hay for him. She doubted she could bridle him with only one hand.

What was she thinking? Her shoulders drooped as the reality of her situation hit her, hard.

This morning was a nice diversion, and that was all.

All the confidence that had been building since she'd gotten on Prince's back? Gone.

How had the cowboy known she would be able to ride?

And more important, why did he care? She didn't know him, other than he'd been a part of getting her out when she'd been trapped beneath the wagon. Her father must have some level of trust for him, or he wouldn't have let him hire on.

And he seemed to work well with Uncle Ned and the other cowboy.

But if he felt sorry for her…well, she would let him know she had no room for anyone else's pity. She had enough of her own.

She rode toward the barnyard, satisfied to see that the wagon was no longer there. She guided the horse all the way into the barn, intending to tell the cowboy what she thought of his interference.

Only to find it quiet and empty of any human inhabitants, the still warmth inside bringing an immediate flush to her cheeks in contrast to the wind outside. Several of the horses looked up, shifted in agitation at Prince's abrupt stop as she reined him in.

She clucked to the animal. "Sorry, boy." No reason he should feel the brunt of her annoyance.

Then she realized there was no one around to help her dismount. In her *before* life, she never would have considered getting off a horse a problem, but with only one hand to balance and steady herself...

It took her two tries. Prince remained placidly in place until she finally got her boots on the ground with an *oomph!*

She was shaking with the last vestiges of adrenaline. She apologized to the horse as she tied him off where he'd been before she'd ridden out. The cowboy would have to come and unsaddle him and brush him down. She hadn't ridden him hard, so the animal should be all right.

But she wasn't.

Her dreams were gone. And even the thought of finding new dreams had been stolen from her.

She would never be all right again.

Chapter Four

Nearly a week after riding out on Prince, Daisy was sequestered in the ranch house again.

It was quiet. Unusually so.

Uncle Ned and Belinda had taken the boys to town for Sunday services. She'd been invited. First Belinda had applied a liberal dose of guilt. Then she'd tried cajoling.

But Daisy wasn't ready. She couldn't bear the stares she knew she would receive. Nor the things her friends must think of her after she'd avoided their visit. Yes, the twins had given a full report, gleefully retelling how disappointed Ethel and Mary had been.

Now, a half hour after everyone had left in a flurry of scarves and mittens, Daisy wandered through the house, idling away the morning.

She paced the upstairs hallway.

She tarried in the hall outside her father's office, then slipped inside.

And gasped.

It looked as if it had been ransacked, and she could only suspect the twins had been *bored* and done this damage. Papers were strewn across the massive oak desk. Books had been removed from the tall library shelf along one wall and stacked every which way. Behind the desk, drawers stood half-open; their contents obviously had been rifled through.

Daisy set about restoring the room, hand trembling with the force of her anger. Those two had no respect for others' property! They were a complete annoyance.

Would they act the same when Audra and Papa returned? Or was this a special form of torture for Daisy and Belinda alone?

After a half hour of fuming and resetting the room, Daisy finally allowed herself to stop behind her papa's upholstered chair and look at what she'd done, letting her fingers slide across the back of the chair. The room smelled of him, of leather and the horseradish candies he hid in one of the desk drawers.

She missed him. The house was different without her father's boisterous voice booming through its corridors.

The large window behind the desk looked out on his fields, the mountains in the far distance. Fresh snow covered the ground from a snowfall overnight, the landscape dotted with woolly animals.

She squinted, looking for a cowboy out there with them, but she didn't see either Ricky or the quieter young man she hadn't met at her father's wedding. Her sister had spoken of nothing but Beau for several days after.

Daisy couldn't really picture him. She'd been so self-conscious that day, her first time after the accident being around people other than her immediate family. All she knew was he was dark-haired and quiet.

His coworker, on the other hand…

She couldn't seem to stop thinking about the blond-haired, gray-eyed cowboy. Ricky had looked at her. Seen her.

Challenged her to ride Prince.

The past few days, she'd been too afraid to step foot out of the house. She should tell him that she wasn't interested in someone feeling sorry for her.

But she was chicken.

She turned away from the window, not wanting to spend another moment trying to identify the cowboy.

Wandering into the kitchen, she turned away from the preparation counter and its painful memories. Belinda had pushed her to try just yesterday. Daisy had dumped a pitcherful of tea across the table trying to pour a glass for herself. She'd broken a crock—one of her mother's dishes!—trying to help get supper on the table.

She was a failure. Because of her injury.

Back into the parlor. And instead of the pine boughs and bright ribbons Daisy's mother would have had draped over the mantel, there were two pairs of dingy socks, two pairs of muddy boots, checkers scattered across the floor and one of the books from her papa's office opened and turned facedown on the sofa.

She shrieked, the frustration boiling over.

She couldn't stand being inside one second longer, not with the mess those irresponsible twins had left.

Ricky didn't know if something had happened on Daisy's solo ride, but she hadn't been back out to the barn to visit her horse in five days.

Maybe his spur-of-the-moment plan had backfired. He was fighting discouragement and tossing hay bales down from the barn loft into the aisle between the two rows of stalls when she stomped into the barn. She was riled up about something, because instead of going to Prince's stall—the horse had peeked his head over his stall door when she'd come in—she paced up the aisle, skirting the bales he'd already thrown down and then heading back.

And it sounded as if she was talking to herself, though he was too far away, and she was talking too soft, to make out the words. She was clearly agitated, gesticulating and pink-cheeked.

"Watch out below!" he called out, before he tossed the last of the bales down.

They landed in a cloud of dust and by the time he'd scaled the ladder, she was staring at him with big blue eyes. She looked away and wandered over to Prince's stall, as if she hadn't just been on a private tirade. She reached her hand beneath the horse's neck and scratched his chin.

"Morning, miss," Ricky said with a doff of his hat.

"Good morning," she murmured. "I didn't realize anyone was out here." The bloom of pink in her cheeks darkened. Was she embarrassed that he'd overheard her?

"Your uncle and Beau went to services with the others." He started hauling the hay to stack it near the back wall. "Didn't mean to interrupt your little…talk."

Now she ducked her head, ostensibly to give affection to the horse, but he suspected she was blushing even more.

"You heard that?"

"Mmm-hmm." He hefted and moved another hay bale while she stayed by the horse, petting its nose. "Something wrong?" he half grunted the words as he hefted the bale onto the growing stack. Having a supply of bales at the lower level would make it more convenient when they needed to load up the wagon over the next few days.

"Not really," she said quietly, her attention still on the horse. "It's just…the twins."

"Thought they went to town with the rest of 'em."

"They did. But they left the house a wreck. Boots and socks all over the place—you'd think they'd never been asked to tidy up after themselves before."

He bent to grab the next bale, and it gave him the opportunity to hide his smile down in his shoulder. Sounded about like Ricky's childhood bedrooms and even the bunkhouse at times.

She blew out a frustrated breath, whirling from the horse, her hand flipping up in the air. With the swirling dust motes around her from the hay he was moving and the motion of her dress, she almost seemed… magical. "It's not just that," she said. "They argue with *everything* I ask of them. One day they don't want to haul in firewood, the next…"

"They're what…twelve?" He huffed, picking up the last bale. "No twelve-year-old likes to be told what to do. Ask the schoolteacher in town, she'll tell you."

She shook her head, hand parking on her hip. "You'd think they would try a little harder to fit into this new family. It isn't as if I *want* them underfoot, either!"

Again he had a strong urge to smile and again he tried to hide it, but he was at an angle to her and she must've seen it, because she demanded, "What?"

"You're just reminding me of when my brother Matty came to live with us—I've got six adopted brothers and an adopted sister."

Daisy had completely turned from the horse now, listening to his story. The black dog Matilda wandered into the barn from who knows where and sidled up to her human friend. Daisy absently stroked her head, still listening. So he went on.

"Matty's parents had died of some sickness, and he had no one else. So my pa brings him home and he just walks right into the bedroom and puts his satchel on one of the beds—my bed—claiming it as his. Belligerent as can be, daring somebody to tell him he couldn't have the bed he wanted. Boys don't talk about their feelings, but every one of us brothers knew he was feeling sad and lonely. Not sure where he fit in."

He'd finished stacking his hay bales and now stood with one gloved hand leaning against the pile.

"Did you give him your bed?"

"No. We got into a wrestling match and by the time we'd given each other a few bruises, we'd sorted out that he fit right in with the rest of us."

He couldn't help the smile that spread over his face when he finished the telling. His brothers were something, all of them.

She looked puzzled, as if the story he'd told her didn't make any sense. Maybe it didn't to a girl.

"So the moral of the story is I should…wrestle them into compliance?"

He laughed, a sharp bark of sound that surprised him. She didn't look as if she thought it was all that funny.

So he stifled his smile the best he could and shrugged. "Sometimes it takes a little time to adjust to a new family situation."

She narrowed her eyes at him, and he felt the weight

of her questioning gaze. And then she turned her focus down to the dog.

"Did you want me to saddle up your horse?" he asked when the silence stretched between them.

She hesitated. "No, I… No. Not today."

There was something deeper behind her hesitation. It was as if she didn't want to go riding, but she didn't want to go back to the house, either. His mind spun, trying to figure a reason to keep her from retreating.

"It's not just the twins," she said before he'd figured it out.

He waited, just listening. Letting her talk at her pace. "The house isn't right."

"What do you mean?"

She looked up momentarily, then back down at the dog. "If my mother was still alive, she'd have brought in pine boughs and wrapped them with ribbons. She'd have had my papa cut a tree and had it decorated. She loved Christmas…"

The sadness buried in her voice resonated with him. He'd lost his mother at age nine. She hadn't been the best ma—she'd been a saloon girl and he'd mostly been raised in the back rooms of a bordello—but they'd had their own Christmas tradition of spending the quiet night eating a special supper and reading a book by the fire. Usually one of Dickens's stories.

He shook himself out of the memories. It wasn't a good idea to dwell on his past. The things he'd done… He knew God had forgiven him, but he didn't know how to forgive himself.

Daisy ruffled the dog's ears, and the canine looked up at her as if she was everything good.

"What's stopping you?" he asked, kicking off of the stacked hay.

She looked up at him, brow wrinkled. "What?"

"What's stopping you from going and getting some pine boughs—and a tree, right?—and decorating the house the way you want it?"

She frowned. "I suppose when Belinda gets back…"

He took off his gloves and slapped them together. "Not them. You."

She turned around, visibly bristling. "I'm certain you can see why—"

He shrugged. "Seems like if you can still ride a horse, you can decorate a house."

"What do you care anyway?" she burst out, coming closer, her cheeks reddening.

He held up one hand before him. The bad one, the ugly red scar covering the back of his hand visible until his skin met his shirtsleeve.

Seeing it seemed to stall her. He quickly tucked it back behind his waist. He didn't want her to remember that night, even if she didn't know about his part in it.

"If you pity me—"

"I don't," he interrupted. And he really didn't. His regret was so much deeper… Tied up in regrets about the things he'd done after his mother died, all those young women he'd hurt…but mostly about causing the accident.

"If you want to go cut some pine boughs, I'll hitch up the sleigh. We can get a tree, as well."

He put his gloves back on without waiting for an affirmative answer. He figured she wouldn't have brought it up if she didn't want to go.

It took only a few minutes to hitch two of the horses

up to the sleigh. The animals stamped their impatience into the snowy ground, blowing puffs of steamy air and bobbing their heads, while Daisy hesitated in the doorway.

"If you don't feel sorry for me, then why are you helping me?" she finally asked, eyes appraising.

He couldn't tell her the real reason. Not yet.

"Your pa told me and the boys to take care of you and Belinda and the twins. I'm just doing my job."

She scrutinized him for moments longer but finally seemed to accept his answer.

Daisy was really doing this. Getting into the sleigh behind two of the draft horses and with a cowboy at her side. He bundled her in a lap blanket. The heavy coat and scarf she'd managed to get into would help keep her warm.

But she was tired of feeling helpless. How long had it been since she'd bundled into a sleigh and gone somewhere, even on her papa's property?

And the cowboy was right. This was something she could do. She needed to find her feet if she was to have a hope of standing up to Audra when the other woman arrived home, ready to be the mistress of the house.

She directed him toward the grove of firs on the other side of her father's property and he turned the horses that way. The clink and jingle of their harnesses and the swish of the runners were comforting sounds.

She breathed in deeply of the crisp winter air. With snow covering the landscape, everything was fresh and new.

"Beautiful, ain't it?"

"Mmm-hmm," she agreed.

"You didn't want to go to church with your sister and the boys?"

She glanced at him from the corner of her eye. It wasn't his business. "You didn't attend, either."

It might be her imagination, but there appeared to be red creeping up his neck. It sparked her curiosity. Back in the barn, she'd found that talking to him wasn't as hard as it had been that first day, at Papa's wedding.

"What?" she asked, giving in to her curiosity.

He squinted beneath the brim of his hat, his eyes focused in front of the horses. "I was just thinking that my ma would have my hide if she knew I was skipping Sunday worship."

Perhaps it was too dangerous to ask why he had. She chose the safer route of questioning instead.

"Where do you hail from?"

"Little town called Bear Creek. East of the Laramie Mountains, about thirty miles from Cheyenne."

Silence lagged between them. She'd had several young men come calling, and never had she felt as awkward as she did in this moment. A glance at the cowboy beside her didn't reveal that he felt any such thing. He seemed content, watching the landscape and his attention on the horses.

She coughed. "Does your family raise sheep, as well?"

"Cattle," came his steady response. "One of my older brothers breeds horses."

Aha. Here was a conversational thread she could follow. "You said there were eight of you altogether?"

It couldn't be much longer to the pine grove. She didn't remember the trip ever taking this long when she and Belinda had come with Papa. She was intensely aware of the man beside her, his warmth, his height and the breadth of his shoulders.

"Eleven now, including my pa's natural kids. Eight brothers. And two sisters."

He must've read the shock in her expression because he chuckled. "You think the twins are troublesome? You should meet my brothers. And Breanna—our sister—isn't much better."

His expression drifted far away, one corner of his mouth quirked up in a soft smile.

"You must miss them," she said. "Will you go home for Christmas?"

His expression darkened, closed off. "No."

There was a finality to the word that aroused her curiosity. It would be impolite to ask. But she couldn't help wondering why he would choose to stay away from his family.

They were silent for a time.

When she couldn't stand it any longer, she asked, "Did you and your brothers play pranks on each other, like the twins do?" She couldn't imagine what he would've been like at that age. He was such a contradiction now. Helpful. But challenging her.

"Hmm." She didn't know if his hum was agreement or what. "My pa would say they need direction. A job to do."

"What do you think?" she asked, honestly wanting to know. She didn't know how to deal with her new stepbrothers.

"I think my pa is usually right."

His simple words touched her. He sounded as if he respected the man. She wanted to ask more, but wasn't sure she dared.

She looked up and out and realized they were coming up to the grove. Joy raced through her, but she tried to temper it. Even though she was here to help, she wouldn't be able to do things as she had in the past.

Ricky reined in the horses and hopped out, boots sinking into the snow that had drifted more here than it would have in the open fields. She expected him to walk around the sleigh and help her out, but he had his back turned as he scanned the trees before them.

A little miffed, Daisy threw off the lap blanket and gripped the side of the sleigh, carefully steadying herself as her own boots also sank into the snow.

He turned and bent to remove the small ax and handsaw he'd put beneath their feet on the floorboards of the sleigh.

"All right?" he asked, finally glancing up at her.

Temper sparking to cover the uncertainty she felt, she gritted her teeth and nodded. What choice did she have?

Daisy looked like a newborn foal on wobbly legs as she walked around the back of the sleigh to join him.

Where she'd been confident on the horse's back days ago, now she picked her way gingerly through the snow, which was only inches deep, keeping a grip on the back of the sleigh.

Her tentativeness made his gut contract, a reminder of why he was really out here: to help her find her confidence again.

The cold winter air felt sharper on his side where she'd been tucked in beside him.

And then he noticed her ungloved hand. He moved forward and met her behind the sleigh, allowing the ax and saw to drop, head down, and lean against the conveyance. "Don't you have a mitten or something?" His guilt made the words a bit sharper than he had intended.

She glared up at him. "Of course I do." She pulled a red one from the pocket of her coat. "But I couldn't get it on by myself."

He snatched it from her fingers. "You'll give yourself frostbite, and then your pa will have my hide…"

Of course it was no worse than he deserved.

He couldn't get a good grasp on the small bit of yarn with his own gloves on, so he shucked them and stuffed them into his coat pocket. His big paw still fumbled with the small mitten until he got two fingers into it and held it open, all the while conscious of the crown of her head just inches from his chin as she stood directly in front of him.

"Won't hurt ya none to ask for help," he grumbled beneath his breath, the words puffing into a white cloud in the space between them.

"Do you like asking for help?" she asked, blue eyes sparking up at him.

And he found himself grinning down at her. "Not particularly."

Her tiny hand slid between his fingers and into the mitten. She looked down, and he worried she would see the scarring on his hand, so he stuffed his hands back into his gloves and picked up the ax. He motioned toward the trees. "How many branches do you want? And which tree?"

She followed slightly behind as they walked amid the snow-covered trees.

She chose a four-foot tree, and he set about chopping it down, allowing his frustration with himself to fuel each stroke of the ax to release some of the tension that coiled him too tight.

He knelt to examine the cut and make sure it was going to fall the way he wanted it, and as his shoulder brushed against the tree's lower branches, snow slid down the back of his coat beneath the brim of his hat.

He jumped at the icy sensation against his neck.

Daisy laughed.

He looked over his shoulder to find her attempting to stifle her smile behind the red mitten.

And her giggle gave him an idea.

He pretended to lean closer to the tree, resting on one hand. He used the hand on the ground to scoop up a handful of snow. He didn't take time to pack it, it was really too fine to pack together anyway, but turned and launched it at her, showering her in the fine white powder.

She gasped, releasing a puff of white breath.

He froze, afraid he'd made her mad.

But her lips set in determination and she knelt to scoop a handful of her own.

A snowball fight ensued.

He allowed her to get in several strikes, the small balls pelting against the shoulders of his coat, before he chucked a fist-sized snowball that hit her directly in the stomach.

She huffed out a startled breath. Then growled and knelt to scoop more snow. He bent to find some of his own, but she advanced on him too quickly and knocked off his hat, pressing a handful of wet snow into his hair.

The move surprised and startled him into falling on his rump, further chilling him.

He mock-glared up at her; her eyes popped bright

against the blue sky behind her. She shrieked and darted behind the tree. He scrambled to get off the ground and chased her.

She'd forgotten about her tentativeness, forgotten to be careful as she darted between the trees, often ducking to scoop up more snow and lob it at him.

He thought to sneak around a tree and surprise her, but it was him who was surprised when she came behind him and dumped a branch's load of snow on his bare head.

"Truce!" he cried, putting both hands up before himself. He was freezing. His hands were cold and wet, and shivers were snaking down his spine from the flakes that had snuck down the collar of his shirt. His hat remained where it had fallen, next to her Christmas tree.

But his heart was pounding, hammering against the inside of his sternum with each beat.

Her cheeks were rosy and her eyes were sparkling. If she had been one of the young women he'd met before, he would have pulled her into his embrace and maybe even kissed her.

But she wasn't one of those young women.

And he wasn't the same man he'd been before, either.

The merriment faded between them, leaving an awkward silence as he scratched the back of his head.

"I suppose your beau doesn't stand a chance in a snowball fight against you." He blurted the first thing he could think of to put a bit of distance between them.

"I don't have a beau," she said quickly, sharply.

He knew that.

She turned away, her arm coming around her midsection. Of course he'd said just the wrong thing—but he'd never tried to distance himself from a girl he'd liked before. What could he say to lighten the sting he'd delivered?

"Well, you'd better give a future suitor fair warning before you pick a fight with him."

She began stomping back toward the sleigh, struggling in a snowdrift, her movements jerky and uncoordinated, in contrast to the ease with which she'd been jumping and darting through the snow moments ago. She sent him a scathing look over her shoulder. "Just what kind of man do you imagine would want to come courting someone like *me*?"

"Any kind who takes a good look at your pretty face." The words were out before he'd really thought about them, an immediate response to her self-deprecating statement.

But this time she didn't look over her shoulder to reprimand him for the familiar, almost flirting words.

She was quiet, too quiet, as he finished knocking down the tree and worked at tying it off behind the sleigh.

He hadn't meant to blunder like that. He'd been afraid of the thoughts whirling through his head. He was attracted to her and not because of his guilt or the situation. She was a beautiful young woman.

How could he make this right now?

Chapter Five

Perhaps Daisy had been a bit overzealous choosing the boughs to decorate the ranch house, because when the greenery was stacked at their feet and beside her on the bench seat, she found herself uncomfortably close to the cowboy beside her. Their exertions playing in the snow had warmed them both, and she was intensely aware of the smell of his soap and something uniquely him even over the sharp pine scent.

But she was even more aware of her empty coat sleeve between them as the sleigh jostled to a start and her shoulder bumped his arm.

She leaned as far away as she could, until her opposite shoulder pressed into the fragrant boughs piled on the seat beside her. "S-sorry."

He looked pointedly at the space between them. "It doesn't bother me."

But his statement was belied by his white-knuckled grip on the reins.

She set her back teeth and fixed her eyes on the horizon. The sooner they arrived back at the ranch house, the sooner she could be away from him. For moments, the swish of the sleigh runners against the snow was the only sound.

"Look." He sighed. "I'm sorry if I offended you back there. You are easy on the eyes—"

She shook her head, denying his claim. The overhead sun felt as if it burned her cheeks. Or maybe the burn came from inside.

She knew exactly what she looked like. She'd spent far too many hours before a looking glass, her eyes tracking over the missing arm time and again.

"Are you calling me a liar?" His voice remained low but now had a dangerous tone to it.

She looked off into the far distance, not wanting him to see how hurtful it was to think of, even now that she'd had months to get used to it. All the warmth and camaraderie she'd felt moments ago, playing in the snow with him, had faded to the cold that seemed to constantly surround her.

He reached across and touched her mittened hand where it lay fisted in her lap, shocking her into looking at him.

"You are beautiful," he said, quietly, seriously. His gaze was straightforward, and she found she could almost believe him.

She wanted to believe him.

But she didn't dare.

She blinked the sudden moisture pooling in her eyes and cut her head in the other direction. She squeezed her eyes closed tightly, hoping to stave off further tears.

He was silent again. She focused on the sounds of the wind in her ears, the slight jingle of the horses' harnesses.

Finally he said, "When you find the right man, he

ain't going to mind that you're missing an arm. Everybody's got something about themselves they don't like."

She looked at him, brows raised with disbelief. A little surprised that he would say—and believe—such a romantic-sounding statement.

"Even me," he said levelly.

"What?" she demanded. Perhaps it was rude and presumptive to ask, but her injury was out there for him to see and she wanted recompense.

He hesitated for so long that she thought he wouldn't answer. Until he said quietly, "I've done some things in my past I'm not proud of."

For a moment, it seemed he would say more. But he didn't.

The shadows behind his eyes, the ones she'd noticed before, touched her heart. She wasn't the only one with regrets. There was something deeper in the cowboy's life, as well. Whatever it was, was it the thing that kept him from his family?

They rode the rest of the way in silence, fraught with tension that remained.

He helped her haul the boughs into the front hallway, then told her he'd return when he'd fastened cross boards to the tree's trunk. She watched from the kitchen window as he pulled the tree across the yard and into the barn.

There was something about the enigmatic cowboy. Not just his physical presence, though she could hardly ignore it. She'd seen his strength in each chop of the ax today. But there was also something beneath the surface. Were they kindred spirits? Had he suffered the same crushing pain she had?

She didn't know. She did know she was drawn to him.

But she imagined that he was attracted to her. Even if he *was*, she couldn't entertain thoughts of being a wife, a mother. She would be dependent on others for the rest of her life. As evidenced by the mitten. She couldn't perform the simplest tasks.

The cowboy was kind, but she should discourage any further time together.

And she would, when he brought her tree back. She passed through the downstairs, gathering the twins' things to take to their room, and grumbling beneath her breath when she had to take multiple trips because she had only one working arm.

When she was finished cleaning up their mess, she tucked the fragrant boughs between the spokes on the banister and draped several across the mantel in the parlor.

She held on to her emotions all the way up until she found her mother's red velvet ribbons tucked in a box in one corner of an upstairs closet. When she opened the box, the smell of her mother's rose water brought the prick of hot tears to her eyes.

She sat down right there, half in and half out of the closet, hugging her knees close to her chest and trying to stifle the tears—constant tears. Why did things have to be so hard? She wanted her *mother*.

But Mama wasn't here. And after a while, Daisy made herself stand up and bring the box downstairs. She wound the ribbons through the branches she'd already placed, thinking of her mother as she did so.

The result wasn't the same as when Mama had been alive, but it was festive enough.

Belinda would be surprised. And the task had distracted Daisy from thoughts of the cowboy for a little while, at least.

She had accomplished one small thing. And was sweating and exhausted from the efforts of the morning, with small strands of hair plastered to her temples.

How could she even think of keeping her own home?

She couldn't.

Yes, keeping her distance from the cowboy was the right thing to do.

But when he'd manhandled the tree into the parlor, she found herself asking him whether he would come in for dinner.

He'd been rescued by the arrival of Daisy's family and the other cowhands. Belinda had overheard Daisy's invitation as she'd burst into the house in a flurry of energy and somehow all three men had been wrangled into eating lunch.

So now Ricky found himself crowded between Daisy and Beau at the corner of the table. Her sister sat across, the twins kitty-corner to his left, and Ned rounding out the table, reading a newspaper and ignoring the younger people for the most part.

With the twins chattering about the friends they'd seen at church, it almost felt like home, and the pang of homesickness that cinched his gut was almost enough to make him lose his appetite.

Except trudging through the snow all morning had made him hungrier than usual, and the smell of roast and fresh bread had his stomach gurgling. The hot coffee helped warm those parts of him still chilled from the earlier snowball fight.

Belinda leaned close, whispering to Daisy, and he

watched the redhead's cheeks fill with color again. Both girls' eyes flashed to Beau, whose face was about as red as Daisy's hair.

The idea had come to Ricky as he'd been constructing the tree stand out in the barn.

Daisy didn't think she was attractive any longer. Didn't expect to have any beaus or find someone to marry.

So he could find someone for her.

As he'd gotten to know the quiet cowboy over the past couple of weeks, he'd found Beau to be steady and reliable, if a bit quiet. Or maybe Ricky only thought that because he missed his boisterous brothers. All of them, even Edgar, who tended to ride him hard about family responsibility.

Beau had changed Ricky's life. He was a good Christian. A good person. Not like Ricky.

Beau was perfect for Daisy. And this lunch was as good a time as any to start introducing the idea to the both of them.

But Ricky saw Daisy's shoulders tense when her sister had to cut the meat on her plate, as if she was a little child again.

He cleared his throat and leaned close to the cowboy at his elbow, attempting to distract the man and ease Daisy's discomfort. "How'd ya like Miss Daisy's decorating?"

The other cowboy looked startled for a moment, almost surprised that Ricky had spoken to him. "Oh, ah…" His head swiveled to glance through the doorway into the parlor. "It's…very nice."

Belinda seemed to understand Ricky's intentions to move the attention off her sister, because she chimed in,

"Our mother used to do the very same, every Christmas. It reminds me of her." She smiled sweetly. "Does your family have any Christmas traditions?" She directed her question to the both of them.

The kid had gone even redder, if that was possible. He seemed to be having a hard time getting any words out, so Ricky laid down his knife and answered.

"We've got a big family, so my ma always draws names for each of the kids. Sort of a secret surprise for that person. We pick out something we think the other will like."

He paused. Waited for the kid to chime in with something of his own Christmases, but nothing came.

"'Course, it always seems like some of the cattle always choose that day in particular to wander off. I can't tell you how many times my brothers and I have had to ride out in nasty weather to get them."

Still nothing from the cowboy beside him, except the clink of his silverware against his plate. Ricky nudged the other man's arm.

"Same for you, Beau?"

"Oh, uh…yeah, I guess."

Great conversationalist. Ricky ground his back teeth. How was Daisy going to find out what a catch Beau was if the other man wouldn't even talk? Of course, Beau wasn't exactly in on Ricky's plan. Yet.

But a glance across the table revealed Belinda's interested look.

"Beau aims to get a spread started in this area," Ricky said, slapping the other man's shoulder.

Beau lost his hold on his fork and it rattled on the table. He winced. Ricky did, too.

"Not anytime soon. I got to have some start-up cash first."

Belinda smiled at the man. She nudged Daisy's arm. "Our father started this ranch with a homestead and not much more than the clothes on his back."

"Is that right?" asked Ricky.

"Mmm-hmm," Daisy said. She seemed focused on her food, her cheeks still pink. Still embarrassed?

"Papa always says how it was God and our ma who gave him the gumption to make this place what it is," Belinda said.

"Well, then maybe you should be looking for a wife," Ricky said with another pat on Beau's shoulder.

The younger man choked on his food.

Ricky slapped him on the back until he finally cleared what had lodged in his craw and reached for his water glass.

Ned cleared out, grumbling about young people and unnecessary days off.

Quiet from the other end of the table drew Ricky's attention down that way. The twins had their heads tucked together, whispering. Most of the food on their plates had disappeared.

Ricky knew that whenever he and his brothers got quiet, things got dangerous. It usually meant mischief was being planned.

And he didn't want anything interrupting this chance for Beau to make a good showing with Daisy.

He stood up, bringing his mostly empty plate with him. And stopped behind their chairs.

"Boys, the gals made this nice meal for us. Why don't we say thanks by clearing the table."

His voice made it less of a question and more of a

command. They looked at him, looked at each other, then back at him.

He kept his expression serious, channeling his pa or Edgar, he was sure.

They reluctantly took to their feet and followed him to the kitchen, where the warmth of the stove and the scent of the meal they'd just eaten still lingered.

Ricky's adopted ma, Penny, had grown up in a well-off family and when she had married Jonas, she hadn't known her way around a kitchen much at all. Most of the kitchen chores and cooking had fallen to Ricky's pa and brothers—that was okay, they'd been doing it before her arrival. And teaching her had provided some hilarious moments for the family.

Because Ricky knew his way around a kitchen, he quickly spotted the scrap bucket.

He set Terrance to scraping plates. Todd he kept with him as he went back to the table for the serving dishes. Todd seemed the more ornery of the two—likely the instigator—and needed keeping an eye on.

From this end of the table Ricky witnessed that Belinda seemed to be the only one talking. Beau was red-faced, staring down at his plate but with his head bobbing to show he was listening.

Daisy had her eyes on the window past the other cowboy. Not paying any attention.

Ricky must've made some noise because her eyes flitted to him. He had the strangest urge to wink at her.

Which was totally inappropriate. He was a new man.

Why did he still want to flirt with her?

The boy at his elbow grumbled. "Don't see why we have to clean up. Ma never makes us. It's a woman's job anyway—"

"A woman appreciates a man who helps her out." The teasing words were out before he really thought about it.

And he made the mistake of looking up. Daisy's eyes were still locked on him, and sure enough…he thought he saw the echo of appreciation in their depths.

What had he done?

Not long after eating, Ricky tossed his hat onto his bunk in the small barn loft Richards had turned into a bunkhouse of sorts. He and Ned and Beau shared the space, with one empty bunk in the back corner. A table was wedged between the two bunks on one side. They stowed their personal belongings beneath the bunks or on hooks on the opposite wall. The space wasn't heated—couldn't have a stove with all the flammable hay just behind the wall separating the open loft from this area—but retained enough warmth from the animals below that it wasn't too bad when they bundled up in their bedrolls at night.

He paced the enclosed space, trying to figure out what was wrong with him.

Something had happened between the snowball fight, talking in the sleigh and the teasing at the table.

Some small connection had been made between him and Daisy. He'd seen it in her eyes. He felt it.

He hadn't meant for it to happen. He didn't want to hurt her, not as all those other girls had been hurt when he'd flirted, and more, with them. And then walked away. Staying in Pattonville had never been in his plans.

He had to keep his distance.

But he also needed to make things right. Including finding her a husband.

And if there was some *connection* between her and Ricky, that might interfere.

He liked her.

"You want to tell me why you embarrassed me at the meal?"

Beau burst into the room, and it instantly felt confining. There wasn't much space between the bunks already and with the two of them in there it was even tighter. Hard to dodge a swing if the other cowboy was so inclined.

And Ricky had never seen the quiet cowboy so riled before.

Again, it reminded him of his brother Maxwell.

Beau didn't take kindly to Ricky's smile, and his fists clenched at his sides. Ricky backpedaled, raising both hands in front of himself.

"We've become friends over the last coupla weeks, haven't we?"

The other cowboy took a breath, seemed to calm some. Nodded.

"And I've been trying to make friends with Miss Daisy." Here's where he needed to finesse the words a little bit.

"Now that I know the both of you a little better, I think you'd make a right nice match."

Something tightened in his gut as he said the words. He ignored it.

"You do?" Beau appeared flummoxed. He sat down on the nearer bunk, Ned's bunk, and took his hat in his hands, flipping the brim one way and then another.

The other cowboy was going to ruin his hat if he kept it up, but he didn't even seem to realize he was doing it.

"I don't know…"

Ricky propped one shoulder against his top bunk, settling in now that Beau didn't seem to want to punch him anymore. "What do you have against her? Her arm?"

The other cowboy looked up and appeared a little afraid of the growl in Ricky's voice. He'd scared himself a little, in fact, and worked at making his voice sound more normal. "She's working at getting over it." Sort of.

"It ain't that," said the other man, now rubbing his knee. "You might've noticed I'm not the best at talking to fillies…"

No kidding.

"And she's from—well, her pops has got this fine place…" Beau motioned in a circle around them.

Sure, it was a nice spread. Same as Jonas's.

The pang of homesickness hit Ricky hard in the gut. But maybe he could use it.

"Look," he said, quieter. "You sorta remind me of one of my brothers. I'm just trying to look out for you. And I think you and Miss Daisy could really have something."

There was that pain in his midsection again at the words.

Daisy needed someone kind. Someone patient, like the other cowboy. If Ricky could make them both see it, he would be on his way to redeeming himself and the situation.

"Will you at least think about it?" he asked.

Beau still looked skeptical but finally nodded gravely.

Good.

So why did Ricky feel a little as if he was going to lose his lunch?

Chapter Six

Several days later, Ricky rode back into the barnyard, huddled in his slicker and half frozen from a long morning of checking on the flock. He'd never been so happy to see the barn.

Two of the woolly beasts had decided to hide in a brushy canyon, and he'd had to spend extra time locating them. The winter weather didn't stop predators, although Ned had two farm dogs trained to stay out with the sheep and protect them. It was important to keep watch over the flock.

Ricky was used to being out in inclement weather. On his pa's spread, it seemed as if the cows always picked the worst weather to give birth in. He'd been out in near-blizzard conditions, ice, freezing rain... But never alone. Always with one of his brothers at his side.

But his family troubles weren't the burr under his saddle today.

He was full of pent-up emotion. Frustration. Guilt. He'd had the nightmare about Daisy again this morning, woke up with his nostrils burning from smoke, the back of his wrist on fire.

Shaking.

He might've even cried out, but he couldn't be sure because the loft had been empty, Beau out on a night watch and Ned blessedly gone.

Now his breath puffed out in front of him in a white cloud as he dismounted outside the barn and pushed open the door to let the animal inside.

He cared for his horse first, finally warming up enough to unbutton his coat in the barn.

When the animal had been tucked away, Ricky went back to the project he'd been working on these past few days. He hadn't been able to see Daisy or figure more ways to push her and Beau together, but this he could do.

And he had a couple of hours before he had to hitch up and go to town to pick up the boss and his new wife. Beau and Ned were still out delivering a wagonload of hay to the sheep, a job they had to do every couple of days to supplement what the animals could forage in the winter, what with the grass covered in snow.

He hadn't seen Daisy in several days. He was missing her. It wasn't right, not when he wasn't good for her, but that was how he felt.

Yesterday, he'd strung two hooks from a rafter in the back of the barn. But the leather straps Ricky had looped through the hooks hadn't been long enough for what he had in mind.

Now he shucked his coat so it wouldn't hinder him. Then he clambered up onto one of the stall dividers, holding on to a post for balance. Stretching until he reached the first strap and disengaged it from the hook.

He was fighting with the second strap—it had gotten tangled in the hook somehow—when he felt a rush of cool air and the barn's dim interior lightened momentarily. Then it went still and dim again. Someone must've opened the door and come in. Ricky couldn't look away from what he was doing, afraid he'd lose his concentration and fall.

Figuring it was Beau or Ned, he kept at what he was attempting. He almost had that loop...

It slipped loose and he cried out. Success.

"What are you doing up there?"

The feminine voice had his head jerking around and he wobbled perilously, grabbing the post with one arm.

Daisy. She looked up at him, a mixture of curiosity and wariness on her expressive face.

She'd come out of the house.

She was pretty as a peach, her hair down around her shoulders, and he felt nine feet tall—or maybe he just felt that way because he was standing on the stall.

"Help ya, miss?" he asked with a charming grin.

"*What* are you doing up there?" she asked again. She stood several yards away, and didn't come any closer.

"Working on something." He grinned again. Had she sought him out? The thought warmed him up from the inside.

He grabbed one of the longer straps from where he'd thrown it over his shoulder and, still holding on to his post with one arm, reached up to loop it through the hook.

"I grew up on this ranch. When we've been short on hands, I've done just about every job there is to do around here. But I still can't even fathom a guess at what you're doing this very moment."

He grinned. It was supposed to be a surprise for her, but now that she'd caught him, maybe he should fess up. And he would, once he got down.

"What's your favorite chore?" he asked. He tucked the second strap through its hook and straightened the pair of them. Yes, that looked as if it should reach where he needed it much better.

She hesitated only a moment, then murmured, "I liked driving the hay wagon at harvest."

He steadied himself with his hand against the post and bent his knees, then jumped off the stall wall into the soft hay below, landing with a wobble and a thump. He lifted his head and grinned at her.

"Harvesting? The long, boring days... It's always so hot..."

"The sweet smell of the hay, the sense of satisfaction when the fields are bare," she countered. "The knowledge that you've provided for the winter ahead."

She looked from him to the two straps hanging from his hooks in the rafter overhead. "What is that?"

"Well, it's not done yet. A better question is, what is it going to be?" From his hip pocket, he pulled a sheet of paper, folded into quarters, and held it out to her.

The paper crinkled as she spread it out. He knew what she would see. It was a rough sketch of his idea to hang a bridle about at the height of the horse's head. He'd spent several hours over the past few days piecing together a square metal rigging with two hooks—one shorter and one longer—that hung down.

"Is that a...bridle?"

"Yep. The way I figure it, your boy—" he nodded to her horse, stalled in the middle of the barn "—is docile enough, you could train him to step into his bridle, and if you use this, if it works, you can bridle him yourself."

She looked skeptical, frowning, her eyes trained on the single page.

Daisy kept her eyes focused on the cowboy's sketch, as her heart thundered in her ears. The man's presence was simply...overwhelming.

He'd come up with this...somewhat elaborate plan for her to be able to bridle Prince on her own. For a moment, hope soared but she stuffed it down inside.

"And what about a saddle?" she asked, the words expelled on a painful breath. "How shall I lift and secure the saddle with only one arm?" She extended the drawing back to him.

He watched her, those slate-gray eyes probably seeing too much. He didn't reach out to take the paper.

"You don't always have to have a saddle," he said softly. "Or if there's someone around to help ya, you could ask."

She hated having to ask for help. Hated the helplessness of her condition. And yet, she'd come out here to do just that.

"And if the horse refuses to be trained?" she asked. Then she waved off the question. "Never mind. I came out here for another reason."

"The pleasure of my company?" he teased. "Or to escape your Terrors?"

The boys' behavior had not improved over the past few days. Daisy was ashamed that she'd locked herself in her room several times when her patience had run out. Once they'd attempted to pick the lock, and she'd *almost* thought about climbing out the window.

She wasn't their mother; she couldn't demand that they attend to chores on the ranch. Once he got home, her father would likely insist on it, so she'd made do and hoped that things would get better once her father and new stepmother returned.

"Neither," she said stiffly. Because he left her no choice, she refolded his paper with some difficulty, her fingers stiff from the cold. She stuffed it in the pocket of her working dress and pulled out the paper she'd stowed there before leaving the house.

"This is a list of items I would like you to procure from the mercantile. I thought—since you would be in town anyway, to pick up my father and Audra—perhaps you wouldn't mind doing me the favor." It was the closest she could come to asking for his assistance. She rushed on, "The mercantile may not have some of the items in stock. If that is the case, please ask the owner to order them."

He raised his brows at her. "Any reason you haven't sent your uncle on this errand?"

Her cheeks warmed. "These are…Christmas gifts for my family. I can't exactly craft anything homemade this year." She was aware of the bitter note in her voice, but couldn't do anything to quell it.

Now he took the paper from her hand, eyes softening the slightest bit. She didn't want his pity, and stiffened her spine.

He tucked the paper into his pocket. "Why don't you go into town with me? Surprise your pa at the train station."

She thought about it. She honestly did, picturing her papa happy to see her. But she couldn't get past the thought of other people on the streets, at the station—

"No, thank you," she said stiffly.

He nodded. And maybe she imagined the flicker of disappointment in his eyes.

She rushed on, "I haven't got the money right now, but I believe the proprietor will extend me the credit. My family has always been a good customer."

She hadn't had pocket money since early in the summer, and hadn't seen any reason to ask her father for any, since she never left the ranch. Until now. She would find a way to make some money before the holiday, though.

But what if the store wouldn't order her gifts without money up front?

"I'll handle it," the cowboy said.

"Thank you," she returned stiffly. She spun on her heel to make for the door.

"If you change your mind about helping me train old Prince-boy, I'll probably have this contraption fixed up by suppertime," he called after her.

Even after she'd gone inside and checked on Belinda's supper preparations and sequestered herself in her room, she couldn't stop thinking about his contraption. Why would he do that?

She didn't want his pity...but the project didn't particularly smack of pity. He had thought of and created a way for her to learn to do a previously familiar task on her own.

But his idea was ridiculous. Wasn't it?

She couldn't go back to being the girl she was before.

But could she go on from here?

Hours later, Ricky stopped the sleigh in front of the mercantile in town and tied off the horses. The bitter wind had turned from the north and he had a gut feeling they were in for a storm. He hoped the train was on time and he could get the boss home before the storm arrived.

But first, Daisy's errand.

He had to tear himself away from the urge to stare at the dirt-packed street, the scene of his recurring nightmare, and force his feet to move. He tipped his hat to a couple on the boardwalk, but they snubbed him by turning their faces the other direction. He stifled the ugly feeling that rose in him.

He ducked into the store, thankful for the chance to warm up near the potbellied stove. The mix of smells—coffee beans, textiles, leather, metals, the tang of fresh oranges—always made him think of Penny's brother Sam and the family store he and his wife helped run back home in Bear Creek.

He cupped his hands over the stove, trying to retain some warmth. He nodded to the two old codgers playing checkers at a narrow table nearby. They watched him, neither nodding nor outright ignoring him.

He noticed a couple of gals in the corner of the store where all the feminine frills were housed. He didn't recognize either of them, but they whispered behind gloved hands and kept shooting glances at him.

Heat crept up the back of his neck. No doubt they'd heard of his reputation. He hadn't been back to town much since he'd taken the job cowboying for Richards. And this was why. What he knew about small towns was they had a long memory.

He didn't want Daisy to be hurt by having her name attached to his.

And so he waited to make her purchases.

He dawdled by the stove, turned to warm his backside, and his eye caught on a lovely brooch in a glass display case. It was pretty, pretty enough for Daisy.

What was he thinking? He didn't have any business even *thinking* about getting her a gift like that.

His distraction had kept him from noticing that the two gals had wandered closer. One of them stepped into his line of sight. "Are you Ricky White? I'm Adelaide."

He nodded, but didn't smile, didn't speak. Didn't want to encourage her.

Behind her, he saw the old men at the checkerboard frown and glance back at him again.

He gave another nod to the young women, trying not to be rude, and moved away, pretending to be interested in a display of belt buckles.

They tittered and whispered for another ten minutes before they finally left the store. He'd made a half circle and ended up across the store from where he'd started. Now he looked back at the codgers. They were still involved in their game, although he had a suspicion they were keeping tabs on him, as well. It was obvious they weren't leaving, so he sighed and approached the proprietor. He hated the feeling of being watched. And *judged*.

The man listened to Ricky's explanation, but was hesitant to extend credit for Daisy, who hadn't been seen in town since the accident. Ricky had drunk away most of his pay from before this job but had saved up some since working for Richards. He agreed to pay for the items on Daisy's behalf. She probably wouldn't like it but she could pay him back just as easily as she could the mercantile.

Then they looked at her list. It was made up of two columns, the words mostly neat but with some letters slightly larger than the others. Dress fabric for Belinda. For her pa and stepma, a specific mantel clock she'd picked out from a catalog. A small gift for her uncle. It was the two books she had listed for the twins that he got hung up on.

Books?

For those active, troublemaking boys?

He could well imagine their expressions of dismay on Christmas morning.

He knew Daisy's relationship with them was on shaky ground. If she bought them books for Christmas, he could only guess that their teasing would get worse. It's what he would have done at that age.

Likely their ma would purchase or make some necessities, like new trousers or boots.

Daisy should get them something completely frivolous. Not the books. They wouldn't appreciate those.

And the shopkeeper was quick to agree with him.

But what? What would he have wanted at that age? What would he have gotten for one of his brothers?

And then he saw the perfect gift as he flipped through a catalog the man pulled from beneath the counter.

She might be angry if he bought something that wasn't on her list.

But it might be worth it, to help ease her relationship with the twins, just a little.

"Papa!" Belinda flung herself at the man as he shouldered open the door. He laughed and caught her and pushed her inside so Audra could follow.

"It's cold out!"

The twins accosted Audra, bombarding her with questions, as Daisy hung back in the parlor doorway.

The noise and bustle made Daisy's head hurt, but she still found a smile for her father. She was so grateful they'd made it home safely. Maybe now things could go back to some semblance of normalcy.

The back door opened again, and Ricky pushed his way inside, loaded with luggage. He nodded to her as he passed by toward the stairs; their eyes caught and held for a second too long.

She hoped he wouldn't mention anything about the Christmas gifts, and he didn't, just nodded before he went back out on a gust of cold wind.

"Look at the Christmas decorations. Oh, it's lovely!"

At her stepmother's words, Daisy realized she'd been staring after the cowboy. She made herself smile as Belinda said, "Daisy put them up. Aren't they pretty?"

Papa came to Daisy's side and drew her against his side in a hug. "Reminds me of your mother," he said, voice a little gruff.

Daisy's eyes flicked around the room, finally coming to rest on Audra, whose eyes were narrowed with... approval?

"I saw that Belinda had started a nice stew. I've been griping to your father about missing my own kitchen— Daisy, why don't you come help me get things ready for supper."

The invitation was more a demand than a question and Daisy reluctantly joined her stepmother in the kitchen.

Audra pulled a loaf of the bread Belinda had baked yesterday from the bread box and put it on the counter. "Get the bowls out, dear?"

Daisy's suspicions rose. Why did Audra want to speak with her now? She got the bowls out of the cabinet anyway.

"We had the most delightful time, and we rode back on the train from the last stop with some friends from Pattonville. They told me about an upcoming after-Christmas social, and I thought you'd want to know."

The bowl slipped from Daisy's hand and *clanked* onto the counter. But Audra didn't even look up from slicing the bread.

"Why?" Daisy asked, hating the tremble in her voice.

"Because I thought you might like to go. You used to attend socials all the time."

Daisy took special care with the next bowl, setting it carefully on the counter. Trying not to show how much this conversation was upsetting her. "That was before."

"You've got to go back out in public eventually. Your father and I talked about you several times while we were gone…"

Audra kept talking, but the ringing in Daisy's head prevented her from hearing.

Audra couldn't *force* her to leave the ranch. Could she?

Daisy was shaking when she set out the last bowl with an audible clatter. "I won't go," she said, voice shaking like the rest of her.

Audra sat the knife down on the table, turning to look at Daisy full-on. Her calm manner was in direct contrast to the emotion boiling up inside Daisy. "Honey, you've got to face your friends eventually. You didn't die in the accident. You lost your arm. It's just like men who come home wounded from war, or—"

"It's not like that at all—"

Audra's firm voice rose over Daisy's wavery one, interrupting her. "You can't hide here on the ranch forever." She paused, hesitated, but finally said, "Your father agrees with me—" Audra didn't see, maybe didn't want to see what just the idea of going out in public did to Daisy.

"No. I can't."

Daisy fled the room.

"What's the matter?"

At the concerned male voice, Daisy whirled, trying to wipe the tears from her face, mostly unsuccessfully.

Ricky. He'd found her huddled on the back porch in the dark.

Her disastrous conversation with Audra had turned into an awkward family supper and she'd had to escape before the dessert course.

But she couldn't bear to go back to her room, not after she'd felt trapped there so much with the twins bugging her while Papa had been gone. Now she shivered in her coat, thankful that the dark would keep Ricky from seeing too much. She hoped.

"I'm fine."

The cowboy stepped up onto the porch, but kept his distance, leaning against the support post. "You don't sound fine."

She shook her head, throat clogging with tears again. She didn't want to be this person, an emotional mess all the time.

But what Audra was asking...it was too much.

"She wants me to be someone I'm not—"

She broke off, because it didn't feel right, telling him.

"'She' who?" he asked.

"Audra—" Again, she stifled the words, though part of her wanted to share with *someone.* "I shouldn't be talking to you about it. It's a family matter."

He didn't argue with her. Just shrugged; she saw the rise and fall of his shoulders in the shadows. "You've got a lot going on. Seems like you need a friend. Why shouldn't it be me?"

Why shouldn't it? She was so confused, and still upset by Audra's demands.

"She wants me to attend a Christmas party," she admitted in a whisper. "And I can't go—I can't face my friends. Acquaintances. Not like this. Audra pushes too hard."

He listened to her ramblings. Just listened. And considered.

"Seems like she's trying to help," he finally said softly.

She started to protest, but he kept going. "Maybe she's going about it the wrong way, but I don't think she's being malicious."

She shook her head. He couldn't know. He hadn't been inside, a part of that conversation. Audra even had Papa agreeing with her!

"You've got to figure out who you are now," he said. "So what if it's different from who you used to be? You're still beautiful. Strong."

She shook her head again. She didn't believe him. Couldn't.

"So maybe you don't go to the party," he said. "Maybe you wait until you're ready and you go have tea with a friend. Sit in her house and make conversation and ease into it."

She couldn't imagine that, either. Hadn't she been the

one to avoid her friends, even running away when they'd come calling? She hadn't been any kind of friend—what if her old friends hated her now?

"I don't know if I'll ever be ready," she whispered.

He didn't argue as Audra had. He just stood, steady and strong. A rock of a cowboy.

She shivered a second time, the cold finally registering. "I should go back in." And hide in her room some more.

She started to move toward the door, but paused when he spoke quietly.

"I ain't the best at comforting, but Beau tells me the Lord directs our paths. If that's true, then I know He'll help you find the way you're supposed to go."

She murmured a good-night and ducked inside the house. The kitchen was empty, dark, quiet. There were muted voices upstairs; the twins on one end of the house and her parents on the other. Probably readying for bed, as they'd been traveling all day.

She stood looking out the kitchen window for a long time. Half afraid of running into Audra on her way upstairs. But also partly thinking on the cowboy's words.

He'd calmed her. She wasn't sure if she could see herself doing what he said—becoming comfortable enough to seek out one of her friends. She didn't know what the future held for herself. If she and Audra couldn't learn to get on, then what?

Where could she go, if she couldn't show herself in public? She had no other family she could turn to for help. Just Papa.

But suppose Audra won over Papa and they both demanded more than Daisy could give?

Parts of her were at war, on the inside. One part

wanted to believe the cowboy's platitude. The other part didn't know if she would ever be brave enough to face the outside world.

Chapter Seven

After several days of Audra's incessant, quiet-but-firm pushing, Daisy reluctantly agreed to attend Sunday worship with the family.

She was shaking as she struggled into the ill-fitting gown she'd worn for Papa's wedding. She sat on the edge of the bed, waiting for Belinda to come and finish buttoning her up and fix her hair where it had fallen out of the braid she'd slept in.

Her mind roiled with the same questions she'd wrestled with since the frank—and hurtful—discussion with Audra.

Was her stepmother right, in some ways? Was she hiding, acting as if she'd died instead of working to overcome the limitations of her injury?

But Audra didn't know what it was like to wake up from a horrible nightmare and find it was reality. To wake up without one's right arm.

How could she ask this of Daisy, when she didn't know?

Panic clawed its way up Daisy's throat as she imagined being in the sleigh with her family, making their way down the drive and to town. Stepping out of the wagon in front of the church building. Greeting neighbors.

Accepting their pitying looks and facing the children's inevitable curiosity.

She couldn't do it.

She jumped from the bed and rushed to the door, just as it began to crack open. She thumped it closed with the weight of her body and twisted the skeleton key that locked it.

"Hey!" Belinda protested. "I thought you were coming with us."

If she went, everyone would see her. Would see her empty sleeve.

Footsteps sounded in the hallway and the sound of the twins' voices came and went, as if they'd passed Belinda to go downstairs.

Remembering the boys' teasing made Daisy's panic worse. Although their behavior had improved slightly since Audra's return, Daisy could imagine several scenarios with them drawing attention to her in the usually crowded church.

She couldn't face the entire congregation today.

She leaned her back against the door, tearfully whispering to Belinda through the portal that she couldn't go. Across the room, her reflection in the mirror showed how pale she'd gone. She even felt light-headed.

Her father came next, asking if she was all right. Her throat was so clogged with tears that she couldn't answer.

She heard his audible sigh, and then his boots clomped away from her door and downstairs.

She listened to the cacophony of voices and activity as they readied to leave. Then the total silence after they'd gone.

Enough.

She dried her tears on a handkerchief and wrestled herself out of the dress. She donned her plain gray working dress with the buttons in front and managed it with only a minor amount of aggravation.

And then what? She was trapped in her room. Alone.

Before she could get herself worked up into a tearful tirade again, there was a firm knock on her door.

For a moment, she thought maybe her father had come back for her, and panic set in.

"Daisy?"

Ricky's voice.

"Go away." She wiped at her face with her wrist. Her cheeks were hot and sticky from her tears. Had he been able to hear the tears in her voice?

There was scuffling from outside her door, as if he'd shifted his feet. "Um...I can't."

What? She couldn't face him, not like this.

"I need your help." His voice was slightly muffled through the door.

With what? What could she possibly do that he couldn't?

But she was already feeling uncertain after the events of the morning and so she softened her voice instead of answering sharply as she wanted to. "What is it?"

"Matilda's having her pups, and I think there's something wrong."

Oh, no. Daisy's heart rose in her throat at the thought of the beloved family pet. The dog might be in danger if something went wrong as she birthed the pups. She knew Papa lost sheep every year during lambing season. But she couldn't countenance the thought of her friend, of Matilda, suddenly being gone.

But...Daisy was a mess. Surely her face was blotchy and nose red from crying. Her hair had come loose from the pins Belinda had put in earlier.

But if Matilda was in distress, did those things really matter? The cowboy would see her, but he already knew about her arm... He could hardly think any less of her.

"I'll be down in a minute," she said through the door.

Moments earlier, Ricky had overheard Audra griping to the boss as they loaded up in the wagon. He'd just finished hitching up the pair and was holding the harness while everyone loaded in, and couldn't help hearing her aggravated whisper, *"She shouldn't be allowed to miss Sunday services because she's pouting."*

And from there, he'd guessed that Daisy hadn't had a good morning. He had the strangest, strongest urge to see her. To make sure she was okay.

That's all it could be. He couldn't allow it to be more.

And Matilda's labor had given him the excuse.

He waited in the half-open barn doorway, the warmth of the barn at his back. The family hadn't been gone long, probably hadn't even made it to town yet, but the wind had turned cold and there was a bite to it as it chapped his face. Probably a storm coming in. Hopefully not until after they got home this afternoon.

He watched Daisy come outside, walk down the porch steps. The wind tugged at her hair, coming loose from the braid hanging down her back. She self-consciously brushed it out of her face.

Her coat was unbuttoned and when she got closer, he saw the tip of her nose was rose pink. She looked peaked, still upset. She cut her eyes away, down to the side. Had she been crying? He couldn't tell, but the thought that maybe she had didn't set well with him, made his gut contract into a tight ball.

"Morning," he greeted her. He hadn't actually *seen* her when he'd stood in the hall outside her room, so he thought the greeting was still appropriate.

She nodded but didn't say anything. She shivered, and so he moved out of her way, allowing her to cross into the barn.

"Temperature's dropping," he said. "Might be a storm coming."

She glanced behind, eyes flicking to him briefly and holding on the slice of slate-gray sky outside, until he closed the door, shutting out the wind and leaving them with the scents of animals and clean, sweet hay.

There was a glass window high above the center aisle, one that must have cost a pretty penny to put in. The shaft of light from the window and the two lanterns he'd pulled close to the stall he'd put Matilda in were the only sources of light.

Daisy hesitated as he drew abreast of her. Maybe she tensed up because of the false intimacy of being alone out here. He didn't know.

If she'd been one of the other women from his past, he might have taken advantage. He might've slid a hand behind her neck and pulled her closer so he could brush a kiss against her forehead. He might've teased her into feeling secure so he could kiss more than that.

But he wasn't the same man he'd been before. And Daisy deserved to be treated better than that.

"She's over here," he said easily, hoping a casual manner would calm her. He led the way to the stall in the back corner of the barn, where he'd put the dog because it was quieter, and he didn't want the animal riled up.

"She was agitated when I checked on her first thing this morning. I put her in here, just like I would one of the dogs at home." He spared a brief thought for Breanna's little white dog. That thing had a habit of following him and his brothers around.

He shook off the thoughts of home.

"At first she was kinda making a nest, but she's been down like that for hours. And nothing's happened." The black dog lay on her side, panting heavily. Lethargic.

He'd seen plenty of animals giving birth and knew how things were supposed to go. He'd even seen a few not make it. And he really didn't want anything to happen to Daisy's dog. Not if there was a chance they could help her.

The horses stamped and settled around them as he explained how he'd washed up and checked the dog's birth canal and thought he could feel a pup stuck up in there.

"My hands are too large to fit and do her any good."

"You want me to…help deliver Matilda's puppy?"

Daisy's voice was slightly incredulous. She half turned and looked as if she might bolt from the barn entirely.

"Yeah. I do."

She shook her head. Her expression was shuttered, and she wouldn't look at him. Isolated. "I can't."

"Why not?"

Before she could say anything, he took her limp wrist and placed her hand, palm down, against his other open hand. The stark contrast of her slender, pale hand against his tanned, rough fingers made his stomach clench in an unexpected way. Her skin was soft, so soft.

He cleared his throat. "Sure seems like your hand is small enough to me."

He'd meant the action to shock her out of her fear. He hadn't realized he would feel the bolt of attraction like lightning down his spine.

She looked up at him with wide, questioning eyes. He tried to keep his gaze steady and reassuring as he gazed down on her.

The dog gave a muffled whine from inside the stall, seeming to reaffirm Ricky's request.

"If you don't help her, there's a chance she might not make it," he said softly.

And that seemed to get through to her. She blinked once. Jerked her hand away.

She knelt next to the dog in the soft hay he'd spread there earlier. For a moment, she rested her hand on the dog's stomach, and just stayed there, quiet. More of her hair had come loose and fallen over her cheek, blocking him from seeing her face, flowing almost all the way to the ground.

She whispered something he couldn't make out to the dog. He liked that she had compassion for the animal. And then she looked up at him.

"All right."

All right.

He nodded. "I'll grab the soap. You'll need to wash up." He knew some about infections from his brother Maxwell, a doctor.

He brought a bucket of fresh, ice-cold water and the lye soap he and the hands kept around for when they needed a good washing.

She was still sitting by the dog, that long hair falling down around her.

She must've sensed him staring at her because she looked back over her shoulder at him. "What?"

"Your hair."

She brushed it back over her shoulder, frowning. "It's all fallen out."

She sighed, and he was afraid she'd use an excuse to leave. She stood up, not quite facing him. "You'll have to help me...I can't do anything with it by myself."

She gave him her back and he stared helplessly at the mass of curls that was still partially pinned to her head. Only some of it had tumbled down.

"Ah..." He hesitated. Was it inappropriate to touch her hair? Did they have a choice? The dog needed her help, and if they didn't tie it back it would be in the way.

"You'll have to take the pins out," she said impatiently.

He swallowed hard, and found his hands were shaking slightly as he put his fingers into the softness of her hair. The pins were small, and tricky, but he had them out in a few moments. He stuffed them into his pockets.

"Can you braid it?" she asked. Was there a tremulous note to her voice?

"Probably."

It had been close to a decade since Breanna had been small and he'd had to help Jonas with her hair. More recently, he'd braided leather together for a tie.

But this was completely different. Separating the thick curtain of her hair, tucking the hanks where they were supposed to go...

It felt too intimate. Like something a husband would do for his wife.

The soft strands hung up on his calloused fingers. Standing so close, the scent of something flowery stuck in his nose and the bottom of his belly fell out.

He fumbled, his fingers tangled in the thick masses.

"Sorry," he mumbled when he'd accidentally yanked her hair one too many times.

Finally he got done. And then realized he didn't have anything to tie it off.

"I'll be right back," he muttered, and lit out of there as if his britches were on fire.

Daisy held on to the end of her braid, face hot. Ricky had flipped the hair over her shoulder before he'd jogged away and ducked into the tack room. At least the barn was dimly lit. Maybe he hadn't seen the blush that had spread up her chest and neck and into her face.

Her heart beat frantically. She wanted to escape— escape the fine tension that had swept through her body at the feel of his hands in her hair, escape the pity she knew he must feel for her. She couldn't even braid her own hair. She had to have help, like a little child.

She wanted to leave, escape the embarrassment. But she couldn't abandon Matilda.

He had been right. She'd seen it when he'd placed her palm against his. Her hand was small and fine-boned. She could help the dog when he couldn't.

Pride lay by the wayside. She wished he hadn't had to help her with her hair, but that didn't matter. Matilda needed assistance. That's all it could be. No matter if he was an attractive cowboy, she was damaged.

He was gone longer than it probably should've taken, but returned with a short length of twine and quickly tied off her hair.

He didn't meet her eyes as he turned away to bend and retrieve the soap and water. She wondered if he'd been uncomfortable, having to help her with such a simple thing.

She firmed her lips. "You'll have to help me wash up," she said quietly. As if he didn't know that already.

He nodded and worked up a lather between his hands, then scrubbed her hand and wrist vigorously.

He kept his head down as he worked the soap into her skin. "My brother's a doctor," he said. "He says washing good will keep infection and such away from humans… seems like the same could be true for animals."

His skin against hers…tingles shot up her arm. And she didn't think they were because of his brisk scrubbing.

Was she attracted to him?

She was. The realization was an uncomfortable pressure beneath her sternum.

He kept talking, face still down as he concentrated on what he was doing. "You ever watch a sheep give birth?"

"Of course." She'd grown up working the ranch with her family. She knew what to expect. Mostly.

Was there a slight pink tinge to his cheekbones? She couldn't see the whole of his face but was he…blushing?

"This'll probably be similar." His blush remained— longer than it should have if he was simply embarrassed about talking about animal husbandry.

Had he somehow sensed that she was attracted to him?

Her discomfort grew as he lifted the bucket and ran the cold water over her hand and wrist. The soap rinsed clean, but her discomfort remained.

His work with the bridle-hanger thing meant he wanted to help her. Did he see her as a charity case? The thought rankled.

Matilda groaned again.

There wasn't time to worry about the cowboy or his motives right now. The animal needed her help.

She knelt in the straw at the dog's hindquarters, accepting Ricky's hand beneath her elbow when she wobbled, saving her from putting her hand down in the dirty straw.

He knelt across from her, behind Matilda's back.

This time, he looked straight at her, as one of his powerful hands stroked down the dog's back. "You can do this," he said firmly. Confidently.

She followed his directions and soon her hand was clamped in a viselike grip.

It didn't let up. And it didn't let up. She began to lose feeling in her fingertips.

"Are you certain about this?" she asked through gritted teeth.

"Mostly," he answered with a cowboy grin, a flash of white teeth against his tanned skin. "I've seen my brother do the same for a cow—"

"A cow!" she gasped. "I can't feel my fingers—"

"You're doing fine," he said, but she wasn't. She couldn't edge her way in any farther, not without leverage. And with her legs tucked up in her skirt, she didn't have anything to lean against.

She needed her other arm. The one she didn't have.

"I can't," she gasped.

She was going to fail Matilda.

Ricky shifted around, his boots bumping her feet once, and his palm met her lower back. It gave her the leverage she needed and she attempted to push against nature.

Then the terrible pressure eased around her hand.

Ricky still had a hand on Matilda's belly and must've felt the contraction ease.

"That's it," he said.

Blood rushed into Daisy's hand, pricking like painful needles. She felt her way forward in the tight space.

And her fingertips brushed against something.

She inhaled deeply through her nose.

"Feel something?" Ricky asked, and for the first time he sounded anxious.

She jerked a nod.

"Can you grasp it?"

She didn't know. Everything was so tight.

She edged forward. And felt the beginnings of another contraction tightening around her hand.

She began to panic.

And pushed forward until she got her first finger and thumb wedged on opposite sides of what felt like… a tiny nose.

If she couldn't get it this time, she probably wouldn't be able to do it again.

"You've got it?"

She nodded, barely, and gripped with all her might.

Ricky's hand cupped her elbow and she pulled and with the contraction bearing down, there was a hesitation and then a rush of movement. She caught the puppy in her palm and let it rest there. It was the largest pup she'd ever seen, black as night. She could feel its heart beating against her palm, and then its chest expanded as it took its first breath.

She was witnessing a miracle.

Matilda gave a huff, almost as if saying, *finally, it's done*. The mama dog grunted and raised her head, turning and shuffling around to the pup. She began vigorously licking it and the pup took another deep inhale and squeaked.

Daisy set the pup down in the hay as gently as possible and let Matilda take over. The dog seemed more active, though she still panted and remained lying down. Were there more puppies to come?

"We did it." She looked up at the cowboy at her side. Her voice emerged tremulous and she realized she was shaking all over. Emotion swirled through her, but not like the chilling fear she'd felt earlier that morning in her bedroom. This was different. Better.

He laid his hand on her shoulder.

"You did it," he said.

Something sparked in the air between them; some intangible connection wavered in the air.

He was closer than she expected—about a foot separated them. With attraction flaring between them...

She was intensely aware of him as a man. Her face flushed. Her heart pounded in her throat and up through her ears.

He leaned slightly toward her, his lips parting on a breath.

And then he cut the connection between them abruptly. He pushed up to his feet and ducked out of the stall. One hand came to grip the back of his neck.

Heart pounding with something unidentifiable, all of the reasons she'd wanted to avoid him came rushing back.

She wiped her hand on a rag he'd left behind and followed him out of the stall.

Chapter Eight

Ricky had to escape. His feelings toward Daisy—the intense *zing* of attraction, his pride that she'd saved the dog, her bravery—all of it threatened to overwhelm his good sense. And he really wanted to do something he knew he would regret later.

Like kiss her.

He needed to get out of here.

But he was the one who'd asked Daisy to help and besides that, the dog might need further assistance. In his experience, most canines had a litter of puppies. Maybe four or five. Maybe more.

They could be here awhile.

Distance. He needed distance.

He moved out of the stall, gripping the back of his neck, back teeth clenched as if he was the one in pain, not the dog.

There wasn't anywhere to go, just across the aisle, and as he whirled back around, he drew up short. Daisy was right there behind him, eyes flashing.

"I want—I want you to leave me alone," she said, voice shaking.

He gripped the back of his neck even harder, pain radiating down his spine. It didn't help.

"I can't." He dropped his arm, hand slapping against his thigh.

"Why not?"

Too many reasons to list. The first, and most important, was that he couldn't leave her like this. Upset. He was supposed to be helping her, not making things worse on her.

Before he could grasp for a response, she advanced on him.

"I don't want your pity, cowboy." Her braid flipped over her shoulder, for a second reminding him of having his hands in her hair. Her hand had moved to her hip naturally and her eyes still flashed at him. His experience with his ma and sisters hinted that he was in trouble with a woman he'd miffed like this. Even if she was beautiful.

"I don't pity you," he argued. It was so much more than that.

"Oh yeah?" Her eyes went over his shoulder.

He turned his head to see the invention for helping her get a bridle on her horse. He shook his head, turning back to her. "I don't pity you," he repeated.

"I don't believe you," she said. "You've been finding ways to *help* me—"

"I'm not—" He shook his head. This was not the time to tell her that he'd caused the accident. She was beginning to trust herself, maybe beginning to heal.

"You feel sorry for me," she accused.

"I don't."

She was getting even more riled. Her hand arced

through the air, gesticulating with the force of her emotions.

Snakeskin, she was cute.

"Just…calm down," he said. But his words had the opposite effect on her. Her cheeks reddened and her mouth opened, probably to blast him again.

She stalked away, and he followed, trying to figure out what to say. He'd never had to work this hard when talking to one of the women in his past—probably because he'd never been emotionally involved with any of them. He thought of Daisy as a friend. And that had never happened before.

This mattered. Daisy mattered.

She pulled open the barn door and a gust of cold wind blew in, punctuated by swirling snowflakes. The icy air hit his hot cheeks. She drew up short, facing out into the sudden storm.

"I want to be your friend," he said quietly.

Her shoulders deflated slightly at his words. Her hand gripped the door as she stared out into the swirling snow.

"I like you," he said, talking to the back of her head. "I genuinely do. Your arm doesn't bother me, and I *don't* feel sorry for you. I do regret that it happened to you." She would never know how much he meant that.

He was a little surprised she wasn't walking off, back up to the house, but she seemed to be listening to him. So he kept talking.

"I've made some mistakes in my past." He swallowed. "Some of them involved women…and broken promises, and…I don't want to do that with you. Friendship is all I've got to offer."

His chest had tightened up as he spoke. He'd never

felt this before—this urge to protect her. Even to protect her from the hurt *he* could inflict.

She turned to face him, standing stock-still in the doorway with snow swirling around her, some sneaking into the barn around her.

She examined him closely, for so long that he grew uncomfortable under her scrutiny.

But finally, she whispered, "I could use a friend."

He nodded, swallowing hard, though he couldn't place the emotion that burned in his throat.

"Do you want me to walk you back up to the house?" he asked.

She looked over her shoulder, out into the blowing snow. "It came on fast, didn't it?"

It was still early afternoon, but he couldn't make out the house through the mass of snow.

"D'you think my family is okay?" she asked, not yet answering his question about whether she wanted to go up to the house.

"I'm sure they made it to town before the storm hit. If not, they probably holed up with a neighbor."

She nodded. Then her brows crinkled as she seemed to come to a decision. "What about Uncle Ned? Is he here?"

She glanced toward the loft stairs.

Ricky shook his head. "Ned and Beau were out in the far pasture—Ned thought he'd seen wolf tracks and he wanted to try and find the predator… They probably took shelter in the line shack."

The small structure, barely better than a lean-to, was shelter from the elements but not much more. If the storm stopped, they'd be back in the morning.

Which meant that Ricky and Daisy were effectively alone, whether in the house or barn.

She smiled tentatively. "Let me check on Matilda again before I go back up to the house."

They walked back to the stall where the dog had been resting and found another round black body had joined the first. Both pups were snuggled up to their mama's belly, maybe nursing. And the poor mama was panting her way through another contraction, although she seemed more animated than she had earlier. Maybe they'd made a difference. He'd like to think so.

"I think I'll stay awhile," Daisy said softly, eyes on the dog.

They found places on opposite sides of the stall door, close enough they could see if the animal got into trouble again, but far enough away to let nature take its course.

Daisy was still intensely aware of Ricky, but…relieved somehow to know that he didn't pity her.

It was still a little awkward for her. Before the accident, and before the loss of her arm, she'd always been able to talk and flirt with the opposite sex. Perhaps Ricky's statement that he wanted to be friends should make her feel more comfortable in his presence, but ultimately she was aware that he was a man and she a woman.

She hated feeling unsure. Hated feeling needy.

She cast about to find something to talk about.

"She seems better, don't you think?" She motioned to the dog.

He smiled. "Yeah. I think you saved her."

The thrill of pride still hadn't worn off. Daisy *had*

done something to help Matilda. Something that Ricky couldn't do on his own.

"Your horse has been taking to the bridle all right. A few more tries, and I think he'll get it."

She looked down the aisle to where Prince's stall was located, but he must've been tucked inside because of the cold weather. She couldn't see the animal's head above the wooden barrier.

"Thank you…for trying, at least."

He shifted, as if he was uncomfortable with her thanks. "I've never told a woman that before."

"That you wanted to be friends?"

He nodded, and this time she was sure he was blushing.

She had to wonder about his past life. She'd had callers before, but there had never been anyone serious for her, not someone she'd considered marrying.

And it sounded as if Ricky had never been serious about anyone, either—but that he'd left some broken hearts behind him. What made a man do that? It should make her wary of him, but instead she found herself curious.

"This is kinda nice," he said, leaning his head back against the stall behind him. "At home it seemed like I always drew the short straw and had to go out looking for mama cows in the cold."

"I can remember being very small and watching Papa and Uncle Ned flipping a coin because neither of them wanted to go out in a snowstorm. Sometimes Uncle Ned would pretend the coin flipped a certain way so Papa could stay in with the family—with Mama." And her mother had laughed and kissed Uncle Ned's cheek and he had blushed…

"Do you still miss your ma? How did she die?"

"She caught a fever, and never recovered. The doctor thought her heart simply gave out." She cleared her throat and the memories away. "Of course, I still miss her. Some times more than others."

Like the other night when Audra had challenged her. Or this morning when Daisy hadn't been able to face going to church.

She blinked the stinging moisture from her eyes and stared across the barn.

"D'you think having your ma here would've eased things…?" With her arm missing. That's what he meant.

She considered a moment. And then a laugh surprised her, bursting from her lips.

"No. My mama didn't appreciate cowardice…" And that's what Daisy had been. Cowardly. Hiding out here.

Until this cowboy had seen her and started her thinking that maybe she was all right.

"She would've pushed more than Audra," Daisy concluded. She shivered, imagining going back to church. Back to social events.

Maybe she could do it slowly. Ease back into a more normal life as her mama would have wanted her to.

Maybe Ricky was someone she could count on to help her.

"My adopted ma is like that," he said quietly, eyes on the rafters above them. "Once she gets something set in her mind, she can be real stubborn."

"Do you ever…miss your real mama?"

"Sure," he said, and his usual easy manner of speaking was missing. He hesitated. "She was a saloon girl."

That statement made Daisy's head turn toward him.

She leaned her cheek against the wood, her face turned toward him but not moving otherwise. "Really?"

His hat lay across his lap, leaving his blond head bare. He tipped his head back against the stall behind him, looking up into the rafters.

The moment hung heavy between them. "Yeah. I was pretty much raised in the back room of a bordello. Until she died."

"You can't help where you were born," she said softly. "Or where you grew up."

Some emotion crossed his face, one she couldn't name.

"I didn't realize why people looked down on her until after she'd died," he said quietly. "And I was put out on my own. Folks painted me with the same brush, didn't want to help little old orphaned me. Thankfully, Jonas got ahold of me."

He smiled when he talked about his pa, even if it was subdued.

"What do you remember the most about your mama?"

He glanced at her from the side, as if he wasn't sure she'd really meant to ask about his saloon-girl mama. He leaned his head back again, and she wasn't sure if his eyes closed or just narrowed to slits. But he said, "She had the fairest, blondest hair I'd ever seen. Always wore a smile, at least for me. She had a kind spirit, even though she did what she did."

"You loved her."

His eyes flicked down and to one side, as if maybe he was ashamed of admitting it. "She was my ma," he said simply.

"I can understand that."

Finally, he turned his head to meet her gaze. His eyes came back up to meet hers, gratefulness in the gray depths. Time seemed to still for the briefest moment.

And she didn't know what to do with the connection opening between them.

"You probably learned lots of ways to sweet-talk a girl, hmm?" she teased, striving for a lighter note to the conversation, which had grown serious.

His brow wrinkled and he looked away again, shifting so one knee stuck up in the air. "I didn't learn until too late that flirting and being charming aren't always good things."

His serious, repentant tone suggested he regretted those things.

Before she could ask, Matilda groaned again and the animal's movements spurred Daisy to turn back toward the stall.

"Four pups," she said in wonder.

"All thanks to you," her companion answered.

She shook her head. She didn't know about that.

The air inside the barn had cooled even more and she found herself shivering.

"Want to head back up to the house?"

She nodded, but at the barn door they found the snow was almost a wall of white between the house and barn.

"My stomach's telling me it's about supper time."

"I didn't stoke the fire," she said aloud, a bit self-consciously.

"We'll get it straightened out."

She'd been in such a rush to get out to the barn, she had only worn her lighter coat and she hadn't brought a glove. Ricky took a look at her and asked her to wait a minute. He disappeared up into the loft and returned moments later with a scarf and lone glove.

"This is all I've got," he said apologetically. His kindness in bringing the scarf and glove was more than she'd expected.

He draped the long, knobby scarf around her neck and drew part of it over her head, bundling everything except her eyes. It was a bit lopsided but it was obvious he cherished it when he said, "My sister made this for me last Christmas."

She was conscious of his closeness, his hands at her neck, the scent of cowboy and leather as she breathed him in.

Then he tucked her hand into a too-large glove, his warm fingers brushing against her wrist. She tried not to feel anything, but a *zing* skated up her arm anyway. Friends. They were going to be friends.

He didn't seem to notice anything amiss as he picked up a coiled rope from beside the door.

"Give me a minute to tie this off…" His voice trailed off as he opened the door and then held the door between his booted feet while he worked to attach one end of a long rope to the outer door handle.

"We aren't that far from the house," she argued softly.

"It's almost a whiteout—" He stuck his head back around the door and she could see his hat was covered in a dusting of snow already, his dark eyelashes matted with white flakes.

"'Sides, your uncle and pa would kill me if I let something happen to you."

She'd lived on this ranch her entire life and never been lost. But when he led her out into the blizzard, she found she was glad of his thoughtfulness. Snow was everywhere around them, swirling and eddying until she had no sense of direction.

She'd buried her hand in her pocket and he gripped her elbow in his gloved hand.

Wind buffeted them and snow was already drifting, making traversing the yard between barn and house feel as if they were climbing a mountain instead of just crossing the yard. Her feet dragged against the drifts. Biting winds drove the stinging snowflakes into her cheeks and forehead.

It was frightening. She hadn't realized how bad the weather had become when she'd tried to correct him in the barn entry.

She was thankful now that he'd been protecting her.

Daisy's collar flapped open on a gust of wind, but she didn't dare take her hand out of her pocket to fix it, afraid she'd lose hold of her cowboy in the mix.

And then he let go of her. For a moment she lost her sense of equilibrium, felt as if she was flying, lost on the wind. Then his arm closed around her shoulders and he drew her into his broad chest, so that she was tucked against him. The connection sheltered her slightly from the bitter wind and allowed her to lean on his strength.

He squeezed once, and she dared tuck her head into the curve of his shoulder. Some of her fear at being out in the elements like this dissipated.

Finally, his boot knocked into something. The back steps.

The snow was so thick that Daisy couldn't make out the house until they were upon it. Without his rope as protection in case they'd lost direction and passed the house—she hated to think of wandering in the snowstorm until they were too frozen to move. It had been too easy to lose their sense of direction entirely.

Ricky ushered Daisy inside the kitchen, shutting the door and closing out the howling wind.

The first thing that hit him was the calm warmth and the scent of stale coffee.

The quiet inside the house seemed eerie after being out in the swirling, screaming wind. The squall outside made it seem dark, not like the bright winter afternoon it should be.

He let out a big huff of air and she jumped. She moved away slowly, unraveling the scarf from her neck and setting it on the table. She pressed her hip against the table and used the pressure to slip the glove off. It worked.

She slowly moved toward the stove and that's when he figured something might be wrong. He knew it was dangerous for a body to get too cold. Was she hypo-thermic?

She was so tenderhearted…if he suggested it, would she get upset at him?

He glanced at the woodbox and had an idea. "Looks like we were all caught off guard by the storm."

He pointed to the woodbox, and she slowly followed his finger to the half-empty box against the wall. Yep. She definitely wasn't her normal, alert self.

"I'm going to run out to the woodpile and bring in another armful. Can you stoke the fire?" It wasn't his favorite task anyway, not with his memories of fire and death.

He waited until she'd nodded. He hadn't taken off his coat or gloves when he'd come inside, so he went back out into the storm, following the side of the house around the porch to where the boss kept a nice stack of firewood. Ricky knew because he'd chopped and stacked a cord or more a few weeks back.

He was chilled again by the time he got inside and out of the storm's fury.

Daisy was squatting in front of the stove with its door open, staring into it.

He let the wood fall into the box; it clattered loudly and she startled with a gasp, looking up at him. Her eyes were vulnerable.

"What's a matter?" He didn't round the counter toward her, just stayed where he was.

"It's out," she murmured, still staring into the ashes inside the cold stove.

She'd stalled, stuck by the problem. She wasn't cold enough to probably be in danger, now that they were indoors in the warmth. But she obviously wasn't back to herself yet.

She hesitated. He could see her almost arguing with herself. Worrying that she couldn't do it. Did she remember that she had helped her family pet deliver pups? Or had she reverted back to her timid, uncertain behavior?

"I'll make you a deal," he said easily. "I'll start supper if you start the fire. I don't know about you, but my stomach is rumbling."

She watched him, eyes narrowing slightly. And then she seemed to come to a decision and nodded.

He found makings for fried ham and potatoes and watched her from the corner of his eye as he peeled and chopped the potatoes. She worked slowly and muttered to herself but soon had the fire going and fed it larger pieces of kindling until she finally put two large chunks of wood in.

"Done," she said quietly as she pushed up from her crouch.

He settled in in front of the stove, his pan clanging against the stovetop, the ham sizzling when he dropped it in after the pan had gotten nice and hot.

When the food was almost ready and the room had warmed around them, he asked, "You mind if I stay in and eat with you before I head back out into that blizzard?"

"Please."

He nodded, inordinately happy that she wanted to spend a little more time with him.

"You want to set the table?"

"All right."

The familiar clink of silverware and plates hitting the table reminded him of home. He missed the big noisy family suppers, his brothers joshing around and jostling for the food, someone always coming or going.

Daisy left for a few minutes to light the hearth fire in the parlor, to warm up the rest of the house. When she came back, he was conscious of her watching him from the doorway.

"You're familiar in the kitchen," she said.

"Yeah. My pa raised us boys without a wife until Penny came along. We all got pretty comfortable in the kitchen.

"What about you? You like to cook?" he asked.

"I used to. Now everything is…difficult. Slower."

"Doesn't mean you can't do it," he said.

She was quiet. Didn't argue with him. He could only

hope she was thinking of the successes she'd had to-night.

Hours later, lying in his bunk in the silence with Ned and Beau still likely out at the line shack, he couldn't stop thinking about what it had felt like when he'd held her close to him as they'd made their way through the blizzard to the house.

It hadn't been pure friendship, that was for sure.

He'd felt like her protector.

The feeling was unfamiliar. Uncomfortable, like wearing boots a size too small.

In his past, he'd destroyed every relationship he'd touched. He wasn't sure he *could* protect her from himself, not if they grew too attached to each other.

What was he going to do?

He wished he could talk to one of his older brothers or his pa. Sure, they were ornery and made trouble when they all got together in a big group, but he trusted their advice.

He didn't want to hurt Daisy any more than he already had by causing the accident that had incapacitated her.

It felt a little like playing with fire, being her friend when she didn't know his part in what had transpired. But if he backed away now, when she was finally starting to build some confidence in herself, would it tear down all the positive things she'd started to experience?

Daisy huddled beneath her bedcovers, her knees tucked up to her chest. She watched the snow fall outside her bedroom window and prayed for her family's safety. Surely they would've stayed in town until the storm passed. Her father would recognize the danger.

She was alone in the house, curled in her quilt, but she wasn't afraid. If she needed help, she could count on the cowboy sleeping out in the barn.

Her braid had slipped over her shoulder, and in the dark the auburn tresses looked near-black against the white of her nightgown. She couldn't resist reaching up and touching the end of the braid. Remembering his hands in her hair.

Being with him in the kitchen had been different than being with Audra. He wasn't combative. His presence eased her.

He'd asked her to do the tasks she could accomplish, like lighting the fire, and he didn't expect more of her.

Something about him settled her.

She had to keep her heart uninvolved. He wanted to be friends. He'd told her as much.

If she came to depend on him too much, she could be hurt if he left the ranch. And she couldn't imagine anything about herself that would keep a man like Ricky interested in her.

But she needed a friend. And he was here.

Chapter Nine

The storm had stopped in the night, leaving behind a crisp, white blanket of snow and the illusion of stillness.

It seemed as if Ricky was the only one up and around, the only one stirring as he shoveled snow between the house and barn. Except for the fragrant smoke from the chimney that made him aware that Daisy was inside. Knowing she was there, close, had him smiling to himself.

His hat shaded his eyes from the worst of it, but he still found himself squinting in the sun's brightness reflecting off all the cover of white.

He'd taken care of the animals first. Now, midmorning, he was almost done with his shoveled pathway when the Richards family came up the drive in the sleigh, the horses' breaths puffing out before them and harnesses jingling.

He was sweating beneath his coat from the back-breaking work, glad to take a break and stable the horses as the family rushed inside to warm up. He'd just finished and gone back to his shoveling when Ned and Beau finally rode in, moving faster than was really safe—there was no way to see what was beneath the snowdrifts and the horse could easily step in a covered hole and get injured.

As they got closer, he saw the pain etched on Beau's face. Ned was a little behind and as he closed in on the barn, Ricky saw that the older man had his teeth gritted.

"What happened?" Ricky asked, moving quickly to lean the shovel against the barn. He met Beau's animal and took the reins, waiting for his friend to dismount.

"Got caught out in it," Beau said. He didn't seem to have full use of his hands, gasping softly as he almost fell off the horse.

Ricky steadied his friend with a hand at his elbow. Beau's jacket *rattled*—it was frozen! Quickly, Ricky looped the reins over the animal's back and slapped its posterior to send it into the barn. It moved slowly, too, just like the man. What had happened?

"We missed the shack by about a hundred yards," Ned grumbled as he drew up. "Spent the night out in the elements."

Ricky did the same for the foreman, holding his horse and sending it into the barn. Worry tensed his shoulders. It had been well below freezing last night, and he vividly remembered the disorienting snow. Beau's lethargic response could mean something was very wrong with his friend.

Both the men's noses were white at the tips. Ned's coat was covered in snow and ice, as well. Beau couldn't use his hands. Could they have frostbite?

Ricky's concern for his friend had him hauling the younger man bodily toward the house. "Let's get you inside."

Ned followed them, and the fact that he didn't brush

off Ricky's help led him to believe the older man was just as bad off—he didn't like to be coddled by his nieces. Ricky had witnessed his determination on several earlier occasions.

In the kitchen, the smell of hot, fresh coffee greeted them. At the counter, Belinda was pulling together lunch onto several plates when the three of them shuffled inside.

"What—"

"These two were out in the cold," Ricky explained before Beau could get all embarrassed or Ned could downplay it. "Likely they've got a case of frostbite. We need to help 'em."

"Oh, my!" Belinda exclaimed.

"What is it?" Audra came into the kitchen from the parlor, pushing her hair back off her face with her wrist. She looked exhausted, a little pale. "The boys are lying down—I'm a little worried."

"What's wrong with the boys?" asked Ned.

"Some stomach bug. They started feeling off about halfway home." Audra tried to smile, then seemed to realize something was wrong with all three cowboys in the kitchen.

"Frostbite," Ricky explained.

She understood without him having to say more. "Come into the parlor. It's warmer in there."

She ushered them in, Ricky still helping Beau. The other man seemed tipsy, off balance, out of it.

"Ma!" a weak cry came from upstairs.

Audra glanced that way. "I'm going to have my hands full with the twins. I'll send Daisy down."

"Good idea," Ricky said.

The older woman met his gaze and held it for a moment before she nodded briefly.

Ricky settled Beau on the sofa. It was far enough from the fireplace that he could get warm but not overheated.

Belinda came rushing in from the kitchen. "Sit down, Uncle Ned," she ordered. She toted two bowls and a pitcher with her.

There was movement on the stairs, in the hallway, and Daisy came around the corner, carrying blankets.

"Let me help," Belinda huffed, abandoning her uncle momentarily. The older man had finally settled into one of the parlor chairs.

After distributing the blankets, Daisy came to Ricky's side. Perfect. She could tend to Beau.

He ignored the pang in his stomach, imagining her soft hand brushing the cowboy's hair off his forehead. He flipped the blanket around Beau's shoulders, focusing on the task at hand.

"This happened to one of my brothers," Ricky said. "Coupla years ago. We don't want their extremities to get too warm, too fast." He used a towel to chafe Beau's hands, hoping to restore some warmth. "We'll need to bathe them in ice water first, then cool water, then warm. Take it in stages, like."

The girls ran to the kitchen, their shoes clattering against the plank floors in their hurry. They returned quickly, Daisy bringing washcloths and Belinda carting two more bowls. She put one at Beau's feet, and Ricky saw it was full of water and a few chunks of ice.

Ricky helped Beau pull his boots and socks off. Beau's fingers and toes were white but not the swollen red or blue that indicated danger. They shouldn't need a doctor, he hoped.

"What happened?" Daisy asked softly as she tended to the cowboy.

Ricky rocked back on his heels, then moved to help Belinda, who was having trouble getting Ned's boots off.

He was still close enough to hear Beau's soft-spoken answer. "Got caught out in it. Missed the line shack and it was snowing so thick we couldn't find it."

Ricky got Ned's boots off and started peeling the old man's socks off, revealing feet that hadn't been cared for well—and toes as white as the other cowboy's.

"Hurt?" Ricky asked.

Ned grunted.

Ricky couldn't help glancing back to see Daisy using a cloth to bathe his friend's nose. The cowboy's cheeks were cherry red.

A knife of pain sliced through his midsection, and he had to remind himself that this was what he wanted— Daisy and Beau getting closer.

"Do you think coffee would help?" Belinda asked, twisting her hands nervously.

Come to notice, she was a little pale, as well. There were footsteps and movement above stairs. How sick were the twins? Could Belinda have caught something, too?

"I'll go pour some," said the younger sister as she loped off toward the kitchen and disappeared.

"I see you lookin' at my niece," Ned said.

"What?" Ricky jerked back to what he was doing, grabbing a rag and dipping it into the icy bowl of water before applying it to Ned's toes.

The older man gasped.

"I seen you looking at Daisy," he said through gritted teeth. Thankfully, not loud enough that Daisy could hear.

Ricky glanced over his shoulder to see her still immersed in caring for Beau.

"You ain't good enough for my niece," the old man growled under his breath.

The muscles in Ricky's shoulders knotted. He knew Ned spoke the truth. With his past, he definitely was beneath her notice. And Ned didn't even know about his part in causing the accident.

But something about Ricky's personality, when someone told him he *couldn't*—couldn't have something, couldn't achieve something—it made him want to prove them wrong.

He tried to remember the feelings he'd had last night, the desire to protect her. That's what he needed to think about. What was best for Daisy. And it sure wasn't him.

"You hear what I said?" Ned rumbled, this time loud enough that Daisy's head came up.

"Yeah," Ricky answered, gritting his own teeth.

As soon as Belinda came back, bearing two hot mugs of coffee, Ricky stood and stormed past her, all the way out of the house.

Daisy felt it when Ricky left. She hadn't been able to hear what he and Uncle Ned were talking about, but he'd seemed angry when he'd rushed past Belinda and out of the house. His face had been flushed, eyes downcast.

What could Uncle Ned have said to make him react

like that? Her uncle was overprotective. Perhaps she should tell her uncle how they'd decided to be friends. Maybe that would ease his mind.

But for now, she had a duty to help the young cowboy. Audra hadn't given her a chance to get out of the duty, even if Daisy had wanted one. Which she hadn't. Uncle Ned was family, and Beau worked for them—the Richards clan took care of their own.

"Any better?" she asked the young man as she put the rag back in the bowl. It had been over a quarter of an hour. Surely it was time to change to slightly warmer water in the bowl. But the cowboy's skin was still cold when she touched the back of his hand.

"A little, miss."

And the lines of pain around his mouth hadn't eased up any.

She shivered, imagining them out in the cold without any shelter. She was grateful Ricky had taken precautions last night to ensure they wouldn't get lost when they'd come in from the barn.

"It came on fast, didn't it?" she said, trying to distract him from the pain, if a little. "Ricky and I had gone out to the barn to check on Matilda—she had four puppies—and a short time later we couldn't see up to the house."

"Four pups?"

"All black, just like their mama."

She decided the water needed changing and stood, then carefully grabbed hold of the bowl with her arm. "I'll be right back."

She passed Belinda in the narrow hallway. Her sister had been peaked since the family had returned home from town. They'd stayed overnight in the church with several other families who had been displaced temporarily by the storm. Daisy was thankful for their safety.

Passing the morning in the ranch house alone had been…different. She'd had no one to help stoke the fires before bed, so she'd had to do it. No one to pour her a glass of water—she only spilled a bit, not the whole glass this time. She'd had to struggle into her nightclothes alone, and had left Ricky's braid in.

She'd managed on her own. Without help.

After the small successes yesterday and being able to help Beau this morning, she was feeling slightly more confident about herself.

It couldn't be because of a certain cowboy…and his smile, could it?

When she'd exchanged her icy water for slightly warmer tepid water and returned to the parlor, she found Belinda had abandoned Uncle Ned for the younger cowboy.

The young man was blushing and stammering, and Belinda was chattering in her charming way. Daisy hid a smile by ducking her chin into her shoulder as she passed them. If she was any judge of character, she'd say the cowboy was smitten with her sister.

But Belinda had been finding her feet with friends from town—male friends—and might just be practicing her flirtation.

Maybe she should talk to her sister. Or…what if Audra overheard and stuck her nose in it, as she'd done trying to push Daisy out of the house? That could cause friction between the sisters… Was it worth it?

* * *

Ricky missed his brothers.

Especially now, just at this moment, when he wanted to pound out his frustration at what Ned had said to him.

The old Ricky would've rushed into town, straight to the saloon. Drowned his upset in a bottle. Maybe gotten into a brawl.

That wasn't a choice for him anymore.

First he cared for the men's horses. Just because he was upset and angry, the animals shouldn't suffer.

Then he climbed into the part of the loft that was left for hay storage and began unstacking and restacking the bales of hay. The mindless, physical activity allowed him to vent his frustration.

He knew what Ned said was true. Daisy deserved way better than him.

He wasn't looking to court her, in any case. Didn't have anything to offer her.

But something inside him rebelled at the thought of Beau having her.

He left off the task and started on the evening chores, making sure the horses were settled for the night, and checked on Matilda and her pups.

Finally, as the sun was setting and streaking the sky with orange and pink, he started up toward the house to check on the other cowboys. The cold air cooled his temper—some.

Daisy met him at the back door, backlit by lamplight, hair haloed in gold.

"Where's everybody?" he asked, surprised to find things so quiet. If not the twins, Belinda or someone was usually around.

"Lying down." Daisy's lips were pinched, and he read the worry in her expression.

He'd intended only to stick his head in the back door and check on the two men, but now came into the kitchen proper, closing the door softly behind him.

"What's going on?" he asked.

Daisy's fist clenched at her side. "They're sick. All of them. My papa, Audra, the boys, Belinda."

Her words were sharp, quick. He could tell she was on her way to a full-blown panic.

"All right," he said. "Why don't you sit down for a second?" He motioned to the nook table behind her.

She glanced over her shoulder, then back at him. She didn't sit. "Uncle Ned and Beau fell asleep in front of the fire and Belinda and I—this was before she took sick—thought it was best to let them rest. She got sick so I sent her upstairs. A few minutes ago, Ned woke complaining of stomach pains and now both he and Beau have…"

She trailed off, suddenly looking unsure. Maybe trying to be polite.

"Vomited?" he asked. And smiled. "Seems like you and I are the only ones around to take care of this. Might as well not dance around the word for the sake of politeness. Besides, we did deliver those pups together…" He raised his brows at her.

And that earned a smile—albeit a small one—from her. "What should we do?"

"Probably let the illness run its course. If they aren't better by morning, we'll come up with another solution."

He helped her sort out pallets for Ned and Beau on the parlor floor—they were still racked with occasional shivers and he had no desire to drag them up to the barn loft, especially if they were going to be sick!

Daisy seemed to calm with him by her side.

Her reaction made him feel protective, as if he was her man.

And that was dangerous. He had to protect her. From himself.

Chapter Ten

The morning dawned with Daisy exhausted. And no one was better. They were all worse—both family and hired help. They'd been unable to keep anything down, though Daisy and Ricky had spooned water into them throughout the night.

Feverish, torn between sweat and chills. So weak they couldn't move from their beds.

Only Daisy and Ricky remained untouched by the illness.

Just after sunup, Daisy put on a pot of coffee. She leaned against the work counter and propped her chin in her hand, her eyelids blinking heavily as the smell of the coffee brewing wafted through the room.

Ricky ducked inside, shutting the back door with a snap, after running out to attend to what needed to be done in the barn. He took off his hat, and turned and smiled at her.

Her companion sported a shadow of whiskers across his jaw, and his hair was endearingly rumpled. He looked rugged, nothing like the exhaustion she felt and was sure was evident in the droop of her entire body.

"You still feeling all right?" he asked.

"Yes, fine. Although cleaning up after them...at certain times I wanted to join them."

He laughed. "It's a thankless job, that's for certain. I'm thinking I should ride to town and fetch the doctor."

A pang of uncertainty shivered through her. If Ricky left, she'd be on her own, caring for seven people. Could she do it?

She was exhausted and unsure. Those small successes of yesterday seemed so far away... And she still vibrantly remembered being out with him in the snow and being unable to put her own mitten on.

He came close, and clasped her hand loosely in his. "Hey."

She couldn't look up at him. If she did, he would see how afraid she was.

He jiggled her hand lightly, until she lifted her chin. He stood close, at an angle to her, her shoulder at his chest.

His eyes were kind, and she thought she read something deeper in their depths, too. Admiration...? Or something else? She didn't know, but his steady presence gave her the strength to take a deep breath.

"I'm sure we'll be all right." She said the words with a further lift of her chin and he responded with warmth filling his eyes and a squeeze of her hand.

Friends. They were friends.

Perhaps she shouldn't depend on him quite so much, but for now...for now, she needed him.

When Ricky arrived in town, the streets were quieter than the usual weekday morning rush.

But there were still folks standing outside the bank

to scowl at him as he walked his horse down the snow-muddied main street. He tried to let their judgment roll off his back, tried to remember the reason he was here in the first place. Daisy and her family.

It helped some, but he still found his teeth were gritted by the time he tied off his horse in front of the doctor's office. The door was locked, and no one answered when he knocked. He'd heard the doctor lived in the small house behind the office, so that's where he went next.

The matronly woman who opened the door for him gave him the same look the folks on the boardwalk had.

"Doc's sick," she said, and started to close the door in his face.

He smacked his palm against the door to keep it from closing. She flinched a little, frowning at his rudeness.

He cleared his throat. "Please." In the face of her judgmental attitude, it was *so* hard to grit the word out, to make it sound polite. "Can you tell the doc that the Richards family is violently ill? Vomiting. They can't keep anything down. They're pretty bad off."

She hesitated and he made himself say, "Please," again.

She shut the door in his face. He heard her footsteps retreat into the house. Hopefully she would really tell the doctor.

Still on the stoop, he took off his hat with one hand and ran his opposite hand through his hair. Well, that hadn't gone well.

In his past, he hadn't cared how people looked at him, what they thought about the choices he'd made carousing, wasting money, getting drunk, womanizing. He always moved on before it mattered.

But now it mattered. He didn't want Daisy tarnished with their judgment—especially when she was just beginning to come out of her self-imposed isolation.

He waited a long time. Maybe the doc's wife thought he was going away, but he intended to get the help that the Richards family needed.

When he was good and chilled, arms crossed and gloved hands stuffed under his armpits, she came back and cracked the door open.

"He ain't up to travelin'," she said. "He's got the same thing. Half the folks in town are sick."

She started to close the door and he stepped up from the bottom step. "What should I be doing for them? To help them get better?"

"I dunno," she said, and closed the door with a decisive snap.

Disappointed at the cold reception and frustrated with inaction, he returned to his horse. What was he supposed to do? Just ride back to the ranch and hope the illness ran its course?

Then a thought struck him—but one that he most definitely did *not* want to act on.

But…it was for Daisy. He'd promised her he would get help.

Still undecided, he wandered down the boardwalk a ways, toward the post office, where the town's only telephone was located.

There was no help here in Pattonville. But there was back home in Bear Creek.

Except he'd left Bear Creek behind. A clean break. No ties.

A bucketload of regrets.

Inside the post office, it was warm enough for him

to take off his gloves. He stood looking at the contraption for several minutes, as if his pa could see through the telephone right to him.

But he couldn't let Daisy down.

A glance over his shoulder showed the postmaster and an older woman standing at the counter, conversing in low tones and shooting glances at him.

He turned his shoulder to them. Swallowed hard and picked up the handset. He had to clear his throat as he recited the direction for Bear Creek.

It rang to the doc's house, Maxwell's father-in-law. But it was his brother's wife, Hattie, who answered, her voice coming through the line clear as a bell.

"Hello?"

Hearing a voice from home, even one he didn't know all that well, was like receiving a punch to the solar plexus. He could barely breathe.

"Hattie? It's…it's Ricky."

There was a beat of silence. Then a hesitant, "Are you all right?"

Heat flared up his spine into his face. Family. She'd asked after him when he deserved so much less.

"Yeah. I need to talk to Maxwell. Is he working at the office today?"

"Yes, he is. I'll walk over. Can you wait a few minutes?"

It was less than a few minutes and Maxwell sounded winded when his voice came through the line. "Rick? You in trouble?"

Had he run all the way from the doctor's office to his residence?

Ricky had to close his eyes against a sharp stinging sensation.

"No. No trouble." Other than what followed him around. He cleared his throat against the emotion. "Listen, I'm up in Pattonville, and we've got a town full of folks knocked off their feet by some sickness."

He explained the symptoms he'd seen to his brother and that even the doc was down with it.

There was murmuring on Maxwell's side of the line, as if Maxwell and Hattie were consulting over what Ricky had said.

"I can't give a true diagnosis without seeing the patients for myself," Maxwell said. Hearing his usual calm, implacable tone reassured Ricky in a way that probably nothing else could've. "It could be a strain of influenza or some kind of stomach virus."

"A virus," Ricky repeated, not really knowing what that meant.

"It sounds like it's pretty contagious. You'll want to wash up real good to make sure you don't catch it. Boil your water, cook your foods."

Ricky remembered similar instructions from when Maxwell and Hattie had treated many folks back in Bear Creek during a cholera outbreak.

"Depending on how long it takes their bodies to fight through the sickness, they're gonna get weak. Try giving them some milk—sometimes it'll sit better on their stomach than plain water and stay down."

Milk. He could do that.

"I'd come, but we've got a situation here at home…"

Ricky coughed again. "I didn't expect you to come. Thanks for your help."

And then he wasn't sure what else to say.

"Will you come home, after you get done nursing… whoever it is you're helping?"

"I don't know."

He'd never planned to go back home. Jonas and Penny knew a little about his past, about his mother and him being out on his own. But not about the fire. Not even Davy knew about the fire.

Don't tell Pa where I am. He thought the words. Almost said them, but something made them catch behind his teeth.

Jonas was busy raising a family and working his ranch. And it was almost Christmas. Ricky was fairly confident his pa wouldn't come searching for him.

He hung up the handset, stomach roiling—but not from sickness. From the contact with his family that he'd left behind. The family that he loved and that helped him out—as Maxwell had—even when he didn't deserve it.

He was crossing the street toward the doc's office, where he'd left his horse, turning up the collar of his coat against the wind's cold bite, when the mercantile owner hailed him from the boardwalk. "Young man! Your mail-order stuff arrived!"

Ricky detoured inside. That same pair of old codgers was sitting at the checkers table and they still glared at him as he took off his gloves and stuffed them in one pocket. As if they wanted to check if he'd snitched something else to stuff in his pocket, too. Ricky tried to ignore it.

The proprietor had been professional when Ricky had been in here before, and today was no different. He delivered Daisy's packages, neatly wrapped in brown paper and tied off with twine, and thanked Ricky for his business.

The professionalism compared to the cold reception made Ricky warm to the other man.

So Ricky told him, "I just talked to my brother, a doctor down in Bear Creek. He said if you've got any loved ones ill to try giving 'em milk instead of water. And to boil all the water before you drink it."

When he turned to leave with the thick paper-wrapped packages, he nodded to the old codgers sitting there. "You're welcome to the advice, too. My brother's a good doctor."

He stowed the packages in his saddlebags and set off for home, and the gal waiting on him.

It was strange to think of her waiting on him… He found himself nudging his horse into a careful gallop over the still-drifted snow. Anticipating seeing her.

That was a dangerous thought, imagining her welcoming smile, that she would be happy to see him.

But it didn't stop him from urging the horse along.

She was asleep, her arm stretched across the nook table and pillowing her head, when he gently pushed open the back door. She must've perched in one of the kitchen chairs and now her head rested on her arm, face slackened and expression peaceful.

He set the packages in the work space beneath the work counter and when he straightened up, couldn't help taking the moment to lean against the surface and look at her.

She was so beautiful.

Strands of her auburn curls clung to her temples. Her cheeks were pink, the slash of her eyelashes against her cheeks dark. Her lips parted slightly, and he remembered being close to her in the barn, wanting that kiss…

He shouldn't be thinking like that. He'd told her he wanted to be friends, and that's all it could be.

He slipped out of the room and went upstairs, making the rounds to check on their patients. They were all asleep, flushed and, he guessed, feverish. Downstairs, Ned was stirring on the pallet they'd made him and grunted when Ricky told him he'd be back in a little while with some milk.

Beau didn't rouse, curled on his own pallet with one arm wrapped around his midsection.

On his way back out, he found Daisy awake when he reached the kitchen.

"You're back," she said with a warm, open, sleepy smile.

He froze, mouth going completely dry. When was the last time someone had looked at him like that—as if he was the only one they wanted to see? As if he was welcome?

An answering emotion rose in him, a desire to reach out for her, to close her in his arms.

She brushed her hair out of her eyes with her hand, looking down self-consciously as she tried to tuck the hair back into the braid. The strands fell over her shoulder again; it was a lost cause. "I didn't mean to fall asleep."

He shrugged, face flaring with heat and the strength of his emotion. He couldn't let her see. He turned his face toward the door.

"Would you help me with my hair again?"

He hesitated, remembering when he'd helped her braid her hair in the barn, remembering his visceral reaction to her then.

She looked down, her hair falling in a curtain and

blocking his view of her face. "It's all right. Maybe I can tie it back myself."

But the slump of her shoulders very clearly showed it was *not all right*.

"Sure, I can help." He affected an easy tone he didn't feel. "Ya got a brush?"

She took one out of her dress pocket, which meant she'd obviously thought about this before she'd asked him.

Again, his fingers tangled in the silky strands as he worked the brush through her hair.

He cleared his throat. "I just checked on everyone, most of 'em are resting. Ned's up."

She shifted in the chair and his grip slipped. He could see the side of her face and there was a soft flush on her cheek, a delicate pink. Had she seen his discomfort with being this close to him?

He struggled to find something else to say. "Half the town is down with the same thing we're dealing with here. Including the doc. He was so bad off his wife wouldn't let me talk to him."

Talking helped distract him from the intense awareness of her as a woman and he rushed on, "I used the telephone in town and called my brother. The doctor."

The lilt in her voice revealed her surprise. "You did?"

"Yes'm. He says we need to give them milk. I was just headed out to visit the cow—didn't get around to milking her before I left this morning with everything going on—she's probably miserable by now."

He finished with her braid and tied it off with shaking hands. He was quick to step away, stuff his hat back on his head. "I'll head out."

She nodded slowly. "All right. Thank you for...this." She flipped up the end of the braid.

He started for the door, but she asked, "Are you hungry? You've been gone all morning." And his feet dragged.

His stomach rumbled in response to her question and he smiled sheepishly. He hadn't eaten before he'd left, in a hurry to get to town and get help.

"I'll take that as a yes. I'll pull something together while you're out."

The intensity with which he wanted to stay in with her staggered him. He forced himself to shrug his coat on. "Sounds fine."

And he rushed out into the cold.

Daisy watched through the kitchen window as Ricky all but ran out to the barn.

Had she said something wrong? She didn't think so.

She leaned to one side, finding a reflection in the window glass. He'd pulled her hair back from her face. She looked tired, a little droopy beneath her eyes.

She was certain she'd felt him pull away after he'd finished her braid.

Had he sensed that her feelings for him were beginning to change? That his closeness affected her?

She'd started to move beyond the pain of losing her arm, the crippling focus on that one fact. Because she'd had no choice. With Belinda and Audra incapacitated by this violent illness, the duty for caring for everyone had fallen to her and Ricky.

Friends. He wanted to be friends.

But as she unwrapped one of the fragrant loaves of bread Belinda had put in the oven—and Ricky had taken out, after everyone had started falling sick—she couldn't help remembering the shadows in his eyes after he'd told her he'd called home.

She anchored the loaf awkwardly against her hip and almost cut herself angling the knife *toward* her body instead of *away*, but it was the only way she could gain enough friction to cut through it.

She did the same with the hunk of cheese from the cold box, looking up when Ricky banged in the back door, bringing a brisk puff of wind before he kicked the door closed behind him. His hands carried two pails of milk.

"What are you doing?" he chided. "You're going to cut yourself…"

"I haven't yet," she answered loftily, cutting another hunk of cheese, trying to hide her embarrassment at the awkward movements. At least she was making do. "I'm afraid it's going to be a simple meal."

He lifted the milk pails onto the counter and came around to her side. "It's not safe to point the blade at yourself like that."

She didn't stop what she was doing, even though he held out his hand as if he wanted the knife from her. "It's the only way I can make it work. If I can't secure what I'm cutting, it sticks to the knife and slides along the work space."

He watched as she finished cutting several more thick wedges of the cheese. "What about a weight?" he mused.

She sensed he was talking to himself more than to her. He reached out and tapped the bread slices she'd already placed on two plates. "But not too heavy…"

Because if it was too heavy, it would smash the bread. Or the tomato. Or whatever she was trying to chop.

This was what she had to face now.

His attention remained on the counter as she plated the cheese and found two late-fall apples to add to the meal. He ran one hand over the surface as if he was measuring it—she could see the wheels turning in his head.

"Have you always had an interest in inventing things…finding new ways to do things?"

He glanced up at her, surprised, shaking himself out of his thoughts. "I'd better check on Ned, bring him something to drink," he said.

"Daisy…" Belinda's wavery voice echoed down the stairs.

"I guess we'll have to grab a bite when we can," he said.

She stuffed a bite of the bread in her mouth, even as she rushed toward the stairs to help her sister.

Later that evening, Daisy found herself back in the kitchen for the umpteenth time. But this time, something was different. It took a moment to see what he'd done.

There was an attachment on one corner of the counter. Two flat pieces of wood had been attached— nailed!—to the counter at right angles to each other. A third piece angled up at the point where the two pieces reached a V. Beneath it, someone—Ricky—had left wedged the remainder of the loaf of bread.

She reached out and ran a fingertip over the wood. It was smooth, the edges softened as if he'd sanded it.

He'd done this, for her? When had he made time for it? Between caring for her family and the chores all afternoon, he must've spent every spare moment he'd had to create this for her.

As if she'd conjured him with her thoughts, Ricky came in the back door, stamping his feet outside the threshold to remove snow clinging to his boots.

His face brightened beneath his hat, and then he was removing it, running a hand through his curls. "You saw it. What d'you think?"

"You can't just…change the kitchen." For her.

He frowned a little. "Maybe I should've asked first, but it's your kitchen, too. Besides, a little modification like this doesn't take up too much room. Belinda and Audra can use the other end of the counter if it's in their way. Try it out," he suggested.

She stared at the contraption, a flash of anger going through her that she needed it. Followed quickly by a flash of thankfulness that the intelligent man watching her now had the capacity to think of something like this and had taken the initiative to install it for her.

She tried it. The knife slid through the bread much easier than when she'd been bracing it against her own body. She didn't mangle it nearly as badly, and imagined that with more practice, she might eventually be able to slice it neatly.

He placed a canvas bag on the counter and a glass. Closer to her, he smelled of the cold and very slightly of sawdust.

He rummaged in the bag and came up with a rectangle, one half of which had been cut away in a half circle. "I had the idea that if I affixed this to the counter, it could steady a bowl you needed for stirring or even keep a glass from falling over while you're pouring."

Pouring had been difficult for her, especially when the pitcher was particularly full.

As her throat was right at this moment.

"Thank you," she said quietly. "For thinking of me."

He looked down on her, eyes holding for a moment. She saw an awareness of their closeness in the depths of his gaze before it cut away. He set the wood on the counter and took a step back. Backing away?

"The horses are all tucked in. Ned and Beau said they spread most of the hay for the sheep days ago, but if the snow holds, I'll need to go check on the flock and spread some more so they don't run out."

She nodded. "The twins haven't vomited in the last several hours. I can't tell if it is because they are on the mend or because there is nothing left inside them. They still have fevers, which concerns me some."

"Not the most enjoyable way to spend Christmas," he said.

Christmas. That's right. Christmas was tomorrow.

"Forgot to tell you, I picked up your gifts in town. Maybe telling the boys they've got presents under the tree will give them incentive to get better."

His steadiness, the camaraderie flowing between them, had eased this whole ordeal.

She smiled slightly. Then had another thought. "We'll have to launder all their bedclothes once the fevers break."

Laundry seemed an impossible task with only one arm. And Ricky was needed to care for the animals. She couldn't ask him to shirk his other duties to help with this one.

"We'll deal with it when the time comes," he said, seeming to follow her thoughts to the hard work ahead.

She sent him a trembling smile. "All right."

He stepped closer. "Why don't you rest for a while? I can watch over everybody for a few hours. You've been on your feet all day—"

"So have you," she countered with a lift of her chin. And he'd ridden to town in the cold, been out to the barn caring for the animals. She didn't expect special treatment for herself—and this was her family.

He shrugged. "We can flip a coin if you like, we'll both take a shift and at least get *some* rest."

So he wasn't insisting on preventing her from working, just that they both get what rest they could.

"All right," she acquiesced. "But I'll pull my share."

"I know you will," he said quietly.

And he was close again, looking down on her again as if he...cared. He was so near, she had to tip her head back slightly to look up into his face.

He leaned slightly down and she thought he might... he might...

Kiss her.

But he quickly pulled away and turned to face the window, though all it offered him was a reflection—he couldn't see outside.

Stung, she swallowed a lump of disappointment.

Of course he didn't see her like that. Friends. They were friends.

She could only hope he didn't see her as helpless as the rest of her family did. Someone to care for, not care about.

"Good night," she whispered.

Chapter Eleven

Ricky had been on the verge of passing out when he'd finally roused Daisy in the middle of the night. He hated to wake her, but Terrance's fever had risen and he thought she'd be upset if he didn't give her a turn to care for her folks.

He'd barely had the energy to drag himself out to the barn loft to his cot before he'd fallen asleep.

He woke later than usual, to find morning light streaming into the barn through the upper window. He rushed through his ablutions, the cold water shocking him fully awake when he splashed it on his face.

The barn was quiet as he worked through the morning chores, as if the animals knew something wasn't quite right with their human caretakers. He missed Beau's cheery whistling and even Ned's grumpy demeanor.

And then, after he'd milked the cow, he couldn't put off going to the house any longer. He traipsed across the yard to the house, hoping Daisy wasn't too put out that he'd overslept. She'd been a real trouper up till now.

In the kitchen, the scent of wood burning in the stove and fresh bread greeted him.

Daisy stood over the sink full of hot, soapy water. She half turned, saw him, and her lips flattened into a white line.

She looked frazzled, brushing strands of her hair away from her face with the back of her wrist, slightly flushed and harried. He felt an immediate rush of aggravation at himself for not waking earlier.

"Sorry I left you to care for everybody," he said quickly.

She shrugged, turning back to the dishwater as he set the two pails of milk on the counter.

"Terrance's fever broke, but Todd seems slightly worse. I can only hope we're coming out the other side of this thing."

She spoke to the basin in front of her. He saw crumbs beneath the wooden holder he'd installed last night. Beside her on the wall counter, there was a towel laid out and an orderly line of clean dishes drying.

His chest puffed with pride on her behalf. Seemed as if his project had worked, if she'd been able to have her breakfast.

He moved toward her, catching sight of the side of her dress. It had dark patches of water as if she'd splashed herself filling up the sink with hot water from the stove.

And then he saw the red mark at her wrist. Everything inside him cinched up tight.

"Did you burn yourself?"

"Not bad." She was still talking to the water and for the first time, he registered that she hadn't smiled at him the same way she had last night.

When he stepped toward her, she turned her shoulder slightly away from him.

Something was wrong. Was she angry that he'd overslept? He had the sudden memory of pulling away last night, when he'd so desperately wanted to kiss her.

Had she sensed his indecision? Was she angry because he'd promised friendship?

"Let me look at it," he said. "I'll help you put some salve on it—"

"It will keep," she said stiffly. "Papa was asking for you—"

"Your pa can wait," he said. "This won't."

When she plunged her hand into the soapy water again, her chin tilted at a stubborn angle. He took it as a dare and gripped her elbow, turning her toward him.

She huffed a breath, but went with him to the table, allowing him to push her into one of the chairs. The house was quiet around them and she didn't speak as he found a cloth and made a cool compress, which he pressed against her wrist.

"What happened?" he asked.

"The pot of hot water slipped," she said stiffly.

He removed the compress and turned her hand palm up in his grip, his thumb resting against the base of her palm. He skated his index finger down from the inside of her elbow until it almost met the red welt where she'd been burned.

Her shoulders stiffened.

"If I hadn't caught it there, the water would have splashed all over me. It could've been much worse."

He frowned down at her arm, not liking the thought of her getting hurt doing an everyday task.

"It's fine," she said, still with a stiffness to her voice

and her manner. She tried to tug her arm out of his grasp.

"At least let me wrap it," he said gruffly.

"Fine," she agreed with bad grace.

He sensed the distance between them. Knew it had to do with that almost-kiss. Wished he hadn't messed things up.

But maybe it was better this way. If she wanted to keep a distance between them, that was probably better. It would lessen his temptation—and lessen his chances of messing up.

He wrapped the wrist quickly and she went back to the dish tub, only throwing, "Papa's upstairs, waiting on you," over her shoulder.

"Daisy—" He didn't know what he'd intended to say, or where the intense urge to *fix this* had come from, but it didn't matter, because she interrupted him.

"I'm almost finished here."

A voice called out from the parlor, and Daisy put the mug she'd been rinsing next to its match on her towel. Her shoulders released some of their tension—as if she was relieved they'd been interrupted. "I'll check on whoever that is."

Her words were a clear dismissal, and he was smarting as he stomped—lightly—up the stairs.

The boss stood at the head of the stairs, white as a sheet.

"What—" Ricky started, and then made a grab for the man when Owen Richards wobbled on his feet.

"Thought I wanted to go down to the office," the older man grunted. "Changed my mind."

Obviously, he wasn't past the worst of it.

When Ricky had helped the man to bed and returned

downstairs, he poked his head into the parlor. Ned was snoring lightly on his pallet, oblivious to what was going on around him.

Beau looked somewhat better. He was sitting up on the floor, legs stretched out in front of him, leaning against the sofa, nursing a cup of milk between his hands.

Beside him, Daisy sat on the floor also, with her legs folded demurely beneath her skirt. Her back was to him and Ricky couldn't see her face, but Beau was as discomfited as ever—but that wasn't stopping him from answering whatever she'd asked as they shared a quiet conversation.

The exchange was spoken in low voices—likely to keep from waking Ned—and Ricky couldn't make out their words.

He didn't have to, to see what was happening. His plan was working. Beau and Daisy were talking, and there must be sparks between them.

Her face turned toward the other man and Ricky saw the profile of her nose, her lips spread in a smile—an open one, unlike the tight pretense of a smile he'd received earlier.

His chest cinched tightly, right beneath his breastbone.

He ducked back into the hall, a floorboard creaking beneath his boot. He put his back to the adjoining wall and tried to breathe through the suffocating pain.

This is what he'd wanted. Daisy and Beau.

He kept telling himself that.

But…

It wasn't really.

The scales had fallen from his eyes. He *didn't* want Daisy with Beau. He wanted her for himself.

She deserved someone like Beau. Someone pure and sweet and without a past hanging over his head as Ricky had. Not to mention that she had no idea he'd been the cause of the accident. If she ever found out the truth, she would probably never speak to him again.

But that didn't stop the awful pain in his gut. He could name it. Jealousy. The confusion prompted by her stiff reaction in the kitchen earlier and now the swift hurt slicing through him made him want to rush into the room and sock one on Beau—a stronger reaction than he'd ever experienced over a woman before.

But he was a new man, and he needed to remember that.

He wanted the best for Daisy, and Beau was it.

Not Ricky.

Midmorning, Daisy found herself at loose ends for the first time since Ricky had woken her in the dark hours of night.

Everyone was sleeping, which must be the best thing for them as their bodies tried to fight off the illness and recover.

Terrance and Todd were much improved and complaining that they were hungry. She thought that was probably a good sign, along with the embarrassment they'd expressed that she'd seen them weak and sick and that she'd cleaned up after them. Maybe their embarrassment would translate to them leaving off the constant teasing and following her around after they'd recovered.

She could hope anyway.

The sounds of pots and pans clanking drew her to the kitchen doorway, where she stopped short. Ricky was pushing a large pan, overflowing with what looked like a goose, into the oven. On the far counter was a large pile of potatoes and a knife, as if he intended to peel them. Carrots and celery were also laid out nearby. The smell of dried herbs tickled her nose.

On the work counter he'd gathered flour, butter, sugar, cinnamon, eggs and baking powder, and as he rose and moved away from the stove, she saw a pot heating there.

"What are you doing?"

He started, as if he hadn't heard her come in. When he turned her way, she saw he had a streak of something white, maybe flour, across his shirt.

He gave her an easy smile that reminded her to take a breath and step back. Ricky was just friendly. He wasn't interested in her as a woman.

His smile faded a little as her lips tightened in reaction. He moved toward the counter, not quite meeting her eyes. "I thought you and I deserved a Christmas supper for all our hard work."

Christmas.

She'd completely forgotten what day it was in the rush of caring for her sick family. It was easy, too easy, to imagine what it would be like to belong together. They made a good team; worked together almost effortlessly as they'd fetched and carried and helped folks out to the outhouse.

But thinking about that wasn't helpful.

"Plus, we can use the bird in a nice stock when the folks start wanting something to eat."

"I think the boys are already there," she murmured.

"What's this?" She motioned to the flour and other things on the counter.

"Going to be doughnuts. I like a nice dessert on Christmas, but I doubt I'll have time to bake a pie..."

He started measuring flour into a mixing bowl.

"You can make a pie?" she asked.

"Sure. If I wanted to and had the time." His voice was relaxed, but there was a tightness around his eyes that belied the easy tone. And he still didn't quite meet her eyes. This wasn't the same easy friendship they'd shared yesterday.

It made her think of how he'd pulled away from her last night, their near-kiss. He wasn't interested in her like that. Maybe he was even uncomfortable knowing she was attracted to him. He'd told her he wasn't an innocent with women. He could probably tell.

"I brought in your Christmas packages. They're under the counter."

She came up with two brown-paper-wrapped packages and brought them to the nook table, thankful for something to focus on, other than the awkwardness between them. The paper crinkled and crackled as she dropped them on the tabletop.

The first one had Belinda's dress fabric. Daisy lifted the top fold, holding it up as best she could, admiring the pattern she knew would make a beautiful gown for her sister. As she lifted it above the table, something fell out of the folds and clattered to the table. Two somethings.

"Slingshots?" she asked, confused as to what they were doing there.

"Oh..."

His voice trailed off and she looked over her shoulder. He was cracking an egg into the mixing bowl, and she tried not to envy his dexterity. His cheeks had pinked. One of them now wore a line of flour, as if he'd swiped at his cheek.

"What?" she asked.

"Well, I… When I saw your list, you wanted books for the boys, and they're not the kind of gifts a boy that age would appreciate."

Already smarting from his withdrawal, now her temper flared. "The boys are rowdy. Learning to sit still and read would be good for them."

"Um, maybe…"

His eyes flicked to her and away. She started to cross her arms, then remembered that wasn't possible, and let her hand rest on her hip instead. "What did you do? Did you choose *these* instead?"

She shuddered to think what her stepbrothers would do with those things. Probably terrorize Matilda.

"Yep," he admitted. "I thought since you were starting out as a new family and all, maybe you'd want to make a good impression on them. Win them to your side or something like that."

His calm demeanor annoyed her.

She shook her head. "With *these*?" She held up one of the slingshots between two fingers, letting it dangle as if it was a dangerous snake or the like.

He smiled tightly, even as he stirred up his doughnut batter in the mixing bowl with a wooden spoon. "You don't have to hold it like that. It's not gonna bite ya. You've got to have ammunition before you can use it."

"I know. I was an ace shot with one of these as a girl."

She'd clearly surprised him, because his eyes came up and met hers. Against her will, she found herself smiling, and he matched her smile, his face going warm and open...

Until he seemed to catch himself, and turned his face back down to what he was doing.

Shutting her out.

She didn't like the distance between them. She wanted things back to the tentative friendship they'd begun. She needed a friend. Temper deflating, she just felt wrung out. Sad.

"I'm—I'm sorry if I made you uncomfortable last night," she blurted before she thought better of it.

His brows came together over his eyes. "Uncomfortable?" He set aside his mixing bowl with a clunk against the counter and wiped his hands on a towel.

"Yes." Now that she'd started, she didn't know how to go on. "When we were...standing close." She motioned to the particular area in the kitchen where it had happened. His head followed her pointing hand before his gaze came back to her. "I thought—I thought..."

He raised his brows, waiting for her to finish. Not making it easy on her. Why had she started this conversation anyway?

"I thought, for a moment, that you might kiss me." She rushed on, a fountain of words babbling out of her. "And I know you didn't want to. I know you said we're to be friends, and I didn't want you to think that I had any expectations, because I don't—"

Three strides brought him to her, but it wasn't until

he took her upper arm in his hand that she went silent. Looking up at him, she could see his face was like a thundercloud, eyes stormy.

"You think I don't want to kiss you?" He grated the words, as if it was hard to speak them.

"I know you don't."

"You don't know anything."

He reached for her, and before she could even think that she should push him away—that she didn't want a *pity kiss* from him—he'd cupped her jaw, his calloused palm sliding along her cheek and sending sparks flying like a summer cowboy campfire. Her palm rested on his shoulder, the muscles hard beneath the fabric of his shirt.

He leaned in close, so close, surrounding her with heat and the contrasting smells of baking and man... but he hesitated a fraction away from her lips, almost as if he was afraid what would happen if he closed the distance between them.

She knew about fear. She'd been living it daily for these past lonely months.

She exhaled, allowing the motion to carry her closer until their lips brushed together.

It was like putting a match to tinder.

Her eyes fluttered closed as his other hand came around her waist in a proprietary hold. Her hand flattened on his chest, and she raised on tiptoes because she wanted to be *closer*.

His lips were gentle, careful against hers.

Until she slid her hand up over his shoulder and buried it in the waves at the back of his head, as she'd wanted to do for so long...

Then his arm around her waist tightened and his lips slanted over hers.

Moments later, he broke the kiss, pressed her head to his chest, and they both panted for air.

"I've wanted to do that since we were in the barn with Matilda," he said.

What had he done?

Ricky's heart raced wildly as he tucked Daisy into his chest. The smell of the roasting duck made him almost nauseous.

He'd seen the hurt buried in Daisy's eyes behind her adorable stammering. The self-doubt that had controlled her since the accident.

Still reeling with jealousy over seeing her with Beau, he hadn't even thought. Not one coherent line of reasoning as to why he shouldn't.

He'd done what he'd always done. Rushed forward on instinct. Took what wasn't his. Kissed her.

And…

Now what?

There was so much Daisy didn't know about him. So much he couldn't undo.

So much he still planned to do to set things right for her.

But a small, violent part of him exulted in the fact that she'd returned his kiss. That she must return his growing feelings for her.

"Shall I help with this Christmas meal you're determined to prepare?" she asked, mouth moving against his shoulder through his shirt. Her hot breath through the fabric set his heart to pounding all over again.

Relief zinged through him that she didn't ask what this meant for them, how a shared kiss changed things.

He didn't have an answer for her.

He *liked* her. Oh, how he admired her strength, her quick wit and determination.

But he didn't know if he could be the man she needed, even if he was a new person.

"You can help by sitting and resting a bit. You've been going since the middle of the night."

He forced himself to release her, when what he wanted most was to keep her close. Why did he feel the loss of her warmth so acutely?

"I can chop the vegetables," she argued.

"You could. But we've got plenty of time and who knows when someone is going to wake up and need something?"

He crossed behind the work counter, pointing a finger at her when she attempted to follow him. "Over there," he said, pointing to the opposite side of the counter. "You're dangerous when you get too close."

She didn't look offended at his teasing words. She looked pleased.

How easily the charming, flirting Ricky returned.

His stomach coiled into a tight fist of apprehension, but he showed none of his internal misgivings.

She acquiesced with a small, almost secretive smile and turned one of the chairs at the nook table to face him.

He floured the surface of the counter and rolled out the dough quickly. Doughnuts were a treat he rarely got to enjoy, and one that would make this day seem more like the holiday it was supposed to be.

He hadn't been able to find a doughnut cutter, so he

used an upended glass to cut the larger circle shapes, then a knife to cut rounds out of the middle. He tested the heat of the fat he'd set to warming on the stove by flicking several drops of water into it first. When it sizzled satisfyingly, he dropped in the first of the doughnuts.

The hot oil bubbled up around the dough, sizzling, and he stepped back, sweeping his palms against each other to lose some of the flour. He was warm from being near the hot stove, but maybe even more so from the awareness that Daisy had been watching him this whole time. The smell of frying dough wafted through the room.

"You seem so comfortable in the kitchen. I know you told me about your papa and brothers, but it amazes me," she said from the table.

"We've had some memorable times—a coupla pranks pulled in the kitchen. My brother Edgar once baked a crow inside a pie after he'd proved another brother—Oscar—wrong. Couldn't get Oscar to eat the thing, though."

She laughed, and he found himself smiling in response.

"They sound like the twins."

"I guess we can get a little ornery like that," he admitted.

"Maybe once all of this is over, you can help me figure out how to deal with the twins." Her soft-spoken words were the question he'd been expecting after their kiss.

Was he staying around?
Did he want to be a part of her life, of her family?
And the answers weren't easy.

"Sure," he said easily, but he was still full of turmoil. Full to the brim.

He grabbed a spoon and began fishing out the first round of doughnuts, using the slender end to scoop through the holes instead of trying to dip them out.

He put the last of the doughnut dough in and then the cutouts from the holes, as well. The smaller pieces were his sister Breanna's favorite.

Returning to the work counter, he used a sieve to drop powdered sugar over the doughnuts, watching it mushroom above them as it rained down like miniature snow flurries.

He could keep his hands busy, but he couldn't stop his mind from playing over the problem of that kiss over and over again. He tried to distract himself. "If everyone is a little better by tonight, I'll need to go out tomorrow and make sure the sheep have feed."

"Will you be able to do it yourself?" There was a hint of concern in her voice.

"It would go faster with two riders, but I'll be able to handle it."

From the corner of his eye, he caught movement out the kitchen window. He approached the window, using a cloth to wipe off the flour and powdered sugar from his hands.

A lone rider trotted into the yard. From this distance, Ricky couldn't identify him. He wore a long slicker and a Stetson. He could be anyone.

"Someone's riding up," he told Daisy.

"On Christmas? Who would be coming here?" She joined him at the window, her elbow brushing his biceps, comfortable at the nearness.

He wasn't.

The rider dismounted and took off his hat and Ricky got a look at his face.

His stomach dropped out.

"It's my pa."

Chapter Twelve

Ricky's papa had arrived?

Ricky ducked out the back door, not even donning his coat. He left the door cracked, almost as if he expected her to follow him. Bright afternoon sunlight slanted in.

She paused in the shadows just inside the door, the cold air washing over her. But it wasn't the cold that caused gooseflesh to rise all up and down her spine.

Except for the preacher the day of Papa's wedding, she hadn't faced anyone outside the ranch since the accident had taken her arm. And although she'd made progress working inside the house—mostly because she hadn't had a choice but to help her family—she was still afraid of what others would think of how she looked.

But this was Ricky's father.

And Ricky was becoming important to her.

The unexpected kiss had changed everything. She *liked* Ricky. And it seemed apparent that he felt the same way.

She didn't know whether a relationship between them could work, but she couldn't imagine a man like him desiring to be with someone who was as good as a hermit.

She breathed in deeply, lungs burning.

The door fell open easily under her hand, with only the squeak of a hinge, but it was anything but easy to make her feet move and cross the threshold. Fear gripped her.

"What are you doing here?" Ricky was asking his father as she stepped out onto the veranda, down a step.

The man who met him in the yard was much younger than Daisy had thought he would be—thirty-five at the most. As Ricky had described his large, unusual family to her, she'd expected someone older. This man must've been barely an adult when he'd begun adopting Ricky's brothers. He held the reins loosely in one hand, the horse behind him following placidly, blowing once and sending a puff of white steam into the air.

"Maxwell told me you'd telephoned and were in a bind." The older man's brown eyes flicked up to her and he nodded, doffing his hat to her.

Ricky turned and caught sight of her. His eyes widened. Maybe in surprise. She couldn't read the emotions crossing his face.

She smiled, even if it was tremulous. "Hello."

Ricky stepped up two stairs, his boots thudding against the wood planks. He reached for her with one hand. She met him, allowed him to clasp her hand. He was warm, even though it was cold out and neither of them had put on a coat. He stood on the step beneath her, the difference in height putting them at the same level.

"My pa, Jonas White."

She nodded.

"This is Daisy Richards. Her pa owns this place. I work for him."

She was conscious of Ricky's words, how he described their relationship—but more conscious of his papa's eyes on their connected hands.

She swallowed hard. Would he say something about her arm? He had to have noticed…

"Nice to meet you, Miss Richards. It's a pretty place." His eyes went to his son, and he said, "Maxwell said it sounded like you could use some help."

She waited—again—for a flick of his eyes to her arm, for him to say it must be true if she was Ricky's only relief.

But none of that happened.

"There's seven of them down with a real bad stomach virus," Ricky said. "Lot of folks in town affected, too. The two youngest, twin boys, seem to be coming out of it all right."

Ricky seemed stiff and uncomfortable. Which surprised her, because every time he'd spoken to her of his family, it was with evident warmth and affection.

"Won't you come inside? Have you been traveling long?" She put the questions out without really thinking about it, because Ricky hadn't asked.

"On the train a couple of hours. Do you mind if I put the horse in the barn? Took me some finagling to get the liveryman out of his house today."

"Of course."

She'd almost expected Ricky to go with his father out to the barn, but he followed her into the house.

He dropped her hand to hold the door open for her and allowed her in first. Inside, he ran one hand through his hair, looking lost.

She started to ask him what was between the two of them, why had he left home, but there was the sound of movement from one of the upstairs rooms and her eyes lifted to the ceiling.

"I'll go check…" She waited, gave him ample time to dissuade her from leaving the room, but he didn't.

When she returned downstairs, coming after a fresh glass of milk for Belinda, she could hear two distinct male voices in the kitchen. She slowed, her footsteps quiet in the hallway.

"I'm a little surprised you came, after the way I left." That was Ricky's voice.

So he hadn't left home under the best of circumstances. At least, that's what it sounded like. What had happened?

Jonas's response came quietly. "Of course I came. Maxwell thought you needed some help, but he's got… another situation brewing at home."

"Something with Hattie?"

"Something else."

She was almost to the kitchen now, hesitant to interrupt their conversation. The smell of coffee was stronger the closer she got.

"I can't believe you left the little ones on Christmas," Ricky said.

At the threshold, she could see Jonas and Ricky standing at the counter. Jonas had a mug in front of him, so at least Ricky must've extended the basic courtesy of a cup of coffee. He was watching Ricky, while Ricky stood in profile to him, eyes on his hands where he'd begun peeling the potatoes.

"You're my son, too," Jonas said.

Ricky shook his head. Then he looked up and his

eyes met hers and some of the tightness of his expression leached away.

She crossed into the kitchen, smiling for both of the men. "Belinda woke, she's asking for a fresh glass of milk. Says she feels a little hungry."

"That's good," Ricky said. "I'll have the soup on a little later."

He didn't leave off peeling the potatoes to help her.

She was a little nervous with Jonas watching her as she wedged the glass against the curved piece of wood Ricky had attached to the counter. As long as she angled the pitcher slowly and didn't overfill the glass, she should do all right.

"That's a pretty slick way to make sure the milk doesn't spill," Jonas said after she'd finished pouring.

She looked up at him, almost afraid to see censure or to see him staring at her injured arm, but she saw neither, only an acceptance that warmed her.

"Ricky made it for me," she said softly.

"He's always had lots of ideas," Jonas said. "Most of them geared toward playing pranks on his brothers."

Ricky shook his head, a flush spreading across his cheeks. "I did rig a lock for the gate when Oscar had that horse that kept opening the standard one."

Jonas chuckled. "I remember."

Ricky popped a broken piece of doughnut into his mouth, still shaking his head.

His papa watched closely and Daisy got the idea that the older man remembered a lot, but Ricky's tight expression revealed that maybe he didn't want to remember some of those same things.

The question was, why?

* * *

"Are you ready?"

At Daisy's question, Ricky looked up from the kitchen counter, where he'd been staring at the plates he'd filled moments ago.

She poked her head into the kitchen, fine eyebrows raised in question. She and Jonas had spent the past half hour settling her family in the parlor for a quiet Christmas afternoon meal.

That hopefully they would keep down. He'd made the soup as mild-flavored as he could.

For himself, Daisy and his pa, he'd plated the roasted goose and vegetables, along with thick slices of bread. He was proud of the meal, proud to have pulled it together for her.

But was he ready to break bread with his pa and Daisy's family?

The knot in his stomach belied the smile that he gave her. He picked up two of the plates and let her take the third. He followed her into the parlor, where his pa sat near the boss and Ned, both pale but talking ranching in low voices.

Audra had elected to remain upstairs, still not feeling up to a gathering, family or not. Both boys lounged on the sofa. Beau and Belinda sat on the floor, both wrapped in blankets but upright.

Daisy joined them on the floor, and that left Ricky to sit next to her or to take the chair in one corner of the room. He took the chair. It was slightly closer to his pa.

"The food's good, son," Jonas said.

Ricky tensed at the sobriquet. How could Jonas still call him *son* when he'd abandoned the family?

"It's impressive that a young man can cook a meal like this," Owen said.

"Roll's good," one of the twins echoed through a stuffed mouth.

Growing uncomfortable with the praise, especially with Ned's narrowed-eyed gaze focused on him, Ricky shifted in his seat. "Any of my brothers could do the same."

"All your sons can cook like this?" Belinda asked Jonas curiously.

Relieved that the conversational focus had turned to his pa, Ricky shoveled food into his mouth.

His gaze met and clashed with Daisy's. Her eyes were warm, and there was a depth of emotion behind them. She might not know what had gone on between him and his family, but somehow she understood that he wasn't entirely comfortable with his pa here.

He loved Jonas. His pa was one of a kind, honest, generous, compassionate to a fault.

He just didn't think Jonas would feel the same way about him if he knew the truth about Ricky's past, and what he'd done. But a holiday wasn't the time to bring something like that up. If there ever was a time.

"Doesn't seem like Christmas without presents," one of the twins said under his breath.

One corner of Daisy's mouth twitched. He only saw it because he was watching so closely.

It was probably the quietest Christmas he'd spent. His boisterous family was probably crowded around the long dining table at home, jockeying for the last scoop of potatoes or tossing the last roll about.

He missed them with an intensity he hadn't expected

when he'd left home. Having Jonas here somehow made the emotions more real.

But when Daisy's lips spread in a small, real smile, he couldn't regret being away from his family.

She'd changed so much, improved in her attitude and her abilities. She was so courageous.

And he couldn't imagine leaving the ranch, not yet.

Daisy was thankful for her family's improvement over the course of the afternoon. She couldn't ask for a better Christmas gift.

Getting to know Ricky's papa had been a surprise blessing.

Jonas had helped all afternoon, more like a hand than a guest. He'd carted firewood, mucked out stalls, served bowls of the hearty soup Ricky had cooked and swapped ranching stories with Papa and Ned.

The only thing that didn't fit quite right was how quiet Ricky had remained in one corner of the parlor. He'd barely spoken at all, only focusing on his food.

She hadn't been able to tell if he'd been avoiding her, or his father, or both.

The kiss they'd shared had been unexpected for them both. She knew that. If he intended to court her, she would expect him to talk to her papa about it first, and that hadn't happened because of the sickness. And with Jonas's arrival, his attention *should* shift to his family.

Of course it was logical that he acted as if nothing had changed between them.

But there was a part of her that worried. Still.

The unsure part, the part filled with doubts about her

desirability to the opposite sex, whispered that maybe he was regretting that he'd kissed her at all.

She tried to act as if nothing was wrong as the subdued festivities concluded and everyone went to bed. Even the twins were still weak and not themselves, as they'd acquiesced to receiving their gifts on the morrow.

As Daisy banked the fire, Papa offered Jonas a room, but she overheard him say he would bunk with Ricky out in the barn loft. The two hale men helped Ned and Beau outside.

Daisy trailed them as far as the kitchen as her papa followed the twins and Belinda upstairs. She banked the fire in the stove as well, slowly. Dawdling.

Wondering if Ricky would return to say good-night. With her family a bit improved, maybe he expected her to take care of things inside the ranch house.

Maybe she was the only one anticipating repeating their kiss.

But as she shut the stove door with a clang, the back door closed. She looked up to see Ricky take off his snow-dusted hat. Judging by the few flakes, it must not be coming down very quickly.

"You get everybody settled in here?" he asked.

She nodded, chest still tight from her earlier thoughts. Unsure.

He shifted his feet. "I guess my pa and I are going to ride out first thing in the morning and check the sheep and the watchdogs, feed 'em if they need it. With the two of us, we should be back by lunchtime."

He didn't seem entirely happy about it, even though having Jonas here would lessen his workload.

"Your papa seems like good people," she said softly.

"He is." Ricky didn't seem to question his quick,

truthful answer at all. But the shadows behind his eyes remained and that made her wonder what put them there.

But it was late. They'd both been up in the night and had a long day of caring for the others. Now wasn't the time to ask about it.

"I'm glad we got to...spend some time together today," she said softly.

He remained across the room.

She was afraid to ask what was coming next for them. If he intended to speak to her papa or what he wanted...

She wasn't even entirely sure what she wanted, but she had *hope*.

"You sure you'll be all right in the morning?" he asked, working his hat between his hands.

She nodded again, swallowing hard.

He hesitated, still. And then he tossed his hat onto the clean counter and crossed to her, his strides sure.

He pulled her into his arms, but didn't tip her chin up. He squeezed her close to his chest and brushed a kiss against her temple. "I'll see you at lunch," he said firmly.

Then he strode back to the door, stuffing his hat onto his head and going out without a glance back at her.

Which was probably a good thing, because she was certain she wore a completely ridiculous smile.

He *did* feel something.

She hugged her arm around her waist, biting back the happy squeal that wanted to break free. Everyone was already resting upstairs, and she didn't want to disturb them.

And she wanted to savor the warmth enveloping her for just a bit. It was all her own. Hers and Ricky's, and no one else's.

The next morning, it was still dark when Ricky and Jonas rode out of the farmyard, with just a sliver of pale light showing at the horizon. They were tucked into their coats, with scarves and gloves protecting them from the wind as much as possible.

Ricky had put his pa driving the wagon while he rode ahead, scouting for the herd. He needed the distance. He still didn't know why his pa had come.

They found the flock near the back of Richards's property, and with snow covering most of the ground, it was good they'd loaded up with hay.

Jonas forked out the hay while Ricky rode the perimeter, counting heads.

"Three missing," he told Jonas when he'd returned to the wagon.

"All right."

Jonas untied his horse from where he'd had it attached to the back of the wagon and slid into the saddle easily.

"There's some scrub brush out this way. They've been hiding there some. Let's check there first."

Jonas nodded and set out at a leisurely pace, until they were riding about a hundred yards apart, each scanning the brush and landscape for those missing sheep. Jonas's steady, unhurried presence was just the same as it would've been at his own homestead. Ricky's pa had always known who he was, even before he'd fallen in love with Penny and their family had grown.

Ricky had always envied his pa's steadfast spirit. For

someone with a past like Ricky's, the guilt had eaten him alive. He could never be like Jonas. He wasn't good like that.

Now with Beau's teachings in mind, Ricky knew that he was forgiven. But his past didn't just disappear, either. He'd done so many things he wasn't proud of…

He didn't know what to say to his pa.

They found the three missing sheep holed up near a stream in some marshy grasses and drove them toward the main flock so they could get some hay.

Jonas and Ricky returned to the wagon and they both dismounted, Jonas tying off his horse to the back of the cart and Ricky picking up the pitchfork to toss it into the back. On the other side of the wagon, the animals milled around, occasionally bleating their appreciation for the meal.

"Thanks for…coming out," Ricky said awkwardly. "I guess now you can go home, back to the family."

Jonas knotted the reins and moved toward Ricky, laying one hand on the back of the wagon. "If you've got something to say to me, I'd rather you just said it, instead of dancing around the issue like the two-step you've been doing since yesterday."

Ricky shrugged, squinting off into the blinding morning sun. His face was cold. Even more, he was cold on the inside, frozen to the bone. "I just don't understand why you came up here."

"I came because you needed help."

"Yeah, but…I walked out on the family. I left after Edgar got those cattle to Cheyenne." Jonas and Penny had taken fifteen-year-old Breanna on a trip across the country to Boston. His brother Edgar had been left in charge and they'd clashed. It had been the last straw for Ricky, who'd let his selfishness blind him.

"I figured you'd come back when you were good and ready. You ready yet?"

Ricky glanced at his father. Jonas watched him with those unwavering brown eyes. Not pushing. Just watching.

"I'm not done here yet."

"That's about what I thought. Your ma will like Daisy."

Ricky shook his head. "I'm not..." *Good enough for her.* "There's a lot she don't know about me." There was a wide chasm between them—the accident.

Jonas shrugged. "So tell her."

Ricky winced. He knew he was going to have to tell her about his part in the accident that had cost her her arm. He didn't know if she'd be able to forgive him. "It ain't that easy."

"I thought the same about winning Penny, until the lot of you boys set me straight."

Ricky rounded on his pa. "It ain't like that. I'm not the same as you were—"

Jonas didn't react to Ricky's heated words. "You're a fine catch."

But Jonas didn't know about the woman he'd killed. Bile rose to choke Ricky. "I'm not. You want to know why I really left home?"

"If you want to tell me."

His pa's implacable answer just fueled Ricky's ire. "I left because none of y'all know who I really am— and if you did, you wouldn't think the same of me." His brothers, his ma and pa wouldn't care about him anymore if they found out the truth about him. He knew it.

"You think I don't know who you are?" Jonas asked. He seemed confused.

"You don't," Ricky said firmly. He was sure of it.

"I know you're my son. That's all that matters."

The matter-of-fact words released a flood of emotion in Ricky. He turned away, raising one hand to mash his hat onto his head.

"All that…bad behavior, the carousing and fighting back in Bear Creek, that was the least of it," he muttered.

And that's when he felt a hand on his shoulder.

Holding back the emotion, the truth about his past was too much under Jonas's steady, fatherly love.

Tears rose, blinding Ricky. He raised a hand to swipe at them but didn't get the chance. Jonas spun him around with a shove to his shoulder.

Ricky was used to fighting, used to wrestling, but he couldn't fight against it when Jonas slung an arm around his neck and hauled him into a hug.

Every barrier holding back Ricky's emotion crashed down and he found himself bawling like a baby, spilling the whole story in gulps and bursts to his pa, mumbling into the man's shoulder.

How his ma had died in that dingy bordello and left him homeless; how he'd tried to survive and started a campfire that had turned into a wildfire and killed a woman; running away. The choking, overpowering fear.

And then, how years later he'd found himself in a saloon in Pattonville, drunk and looking for a release from the frustration and guilt that filled him to boiling. How he'd found a fistfight, how their brawl had spilled out into the street and scared the horses tethered to Daisy's wagon, ultimately causing the conveyance to overturn with her inside it.

How the guilt still crippled him. How he wanted to fix things for her.

And when he was done, when he'd spilled it all, Jonas didn't pull away as he'd expected.

"That's what you've been keeping to yourself all these years?"

Ricky was the one to pull away, wiping a sleeve across his eyes. He looked across the wagon to the sheep, afraid to meet Jonas's gaze and see what was there.

But Jonas didn't let him run away. He stepped next to Ricky so they were shoulder to shoulder. "You were a kid. You didn't mean it to happen. Besides, you ran away. How can you be sure she died?"

Ricky shook his head. He'd known.

"Beau told me I'm a new man—God's man. But how can He forgive me for all that I've done?"

"Probably because He loves you. Even more than I do."

Jonas's words gave Ricky the courage to look up. His father didn't turn away, didn't try to hide what was in his eyes.

And nothing had changed.

Warmth infused Ricky. Warmth, and hope.

If Jonas knew about his past and it didn't change the way he felt about Ricky, maybe there was a chance for a relationship with Daisy.

Ricky had never had a *real* relationship before. He wasn't entirely sure he could maintain one.

And Daisy didn't know the biggest barrier between them. That he'd been a part of her accident.

What would she do when she found out?

Chapter Thirteen

"What are you two doing?"

Midmorning, Daisy came up behind Todd and Terrance in the hall outside the kitchen, where they crouched outside the doorway, obviously up to something. It seemed as if the household was getting back to normal.

They both jumped, and Todd looked vaguely guilty as he looked over his shoulder at her. "Jest listening," he mumbled.

"Spying?"

Terrance scoffed, but his face had gone red.

This morning, the family had exchanged gifts over the breakfast table. She hadn't been sure how the twins would react to the substitute gifts Ricky had chosen for them, but she needn't have worried. They'd been elated to receive the slingshots and both had looked at her as if they didn't quite know what to think about her gifts. Or her.

They'd mumbled subdued thank-yous, but she'd caught Terrance looking at her several times throughout the meal, almost an…indecision written on his face.

Now Todd said, "Belinda and Beau are in there, cooin' like lovebirds."

Curiosity overtook her for a moment, before she laid her hand on top of Terrance's head, the same way she would've done if it had been Belinda caught spying.

"You two need to leave them alone." Both boys had already turned to peek through the doorway again. Todd was apparently not listening to her, but Terrance glanced over his shoulder. Did she have a chance to win over at least one of them?

"Besides, I need your help," she said, with as much cheer as she could muster.

"What?"

"Why?"

Their twin complaints made her laugh a little. "Someone's got to launder all those sheets the lot of you soiled when you were sick. And we three are it."

They groaned. And the embarrassed looks they'd worn when she'd witnessed them being sick returned.

"But we still don't feel well," Todd whined.

Terrance looked as if he might protest, too, but she prevented it by saying, "If you're well enough to spy, then you're well enough to help me. Or I can ask your mama if she's got another job in mind for you."

She lifted her eyebrows, daring them to challenge the threat.

They didn't.

"Start hauling some buckets of water from the well. I'll stoke the fire and put some pots out and we'll fill the tub together."

The twins slunk through the kitchen toward the back door. She followed them into the room, noticing Beau leaning one hip casually against the counter, Belinda leaning on her elbow.

Both of them started in surprise when the three entered the room. Beau started stammering and grabbed for his hat. Belinda watched him with a bemused smile on her face. Bright morning sunlight streamed through the window, warming the room and making the dreary events of the past few days seem far removed.

The boys slammed out the back door while Daisy fetched the laundry washtub and began dragging it from its spot behind the stove.

"Let me help ya," Beau said, but she looked over her shoulder and shook her head, declining with what she hoped was a polite smile.

"I've got it. But thank you."

"Well, thanks for the coffee, Miss Belinda," the young man mumbled. "I'd best get back out to the barn—"

"In the future, you might want to check that the boys aren't around," Daisy suggested, unable to contain a smile. "Else your private conversations might not be so private."

Beau flushed an even darker pink and stuffed his hat onto his head before making a run toward to the door.

Daisy shook her head. That young man was so *shy*.

The twins clattered in with full pails and set them on top of the stove to warm.

"We'll need more than that," Daisy said. "One more load."

They groaned but traipsed back outside without voicing complaints.

"You've got them toeing the line today."

Daisy could only hope their compliance would last.

She started down the hall and up the stairs to begin stripping the beds.

Belinda followed her, lagging a little behind.

Daisy took her sister's presence as assent to ask the question her curiosity couldn't contain. "Do you fancy him?"

"Beau?"

Daisy looked over her shoulder at the top of the stairs and saw the blush high on Belinda's cheeks. But her sister's eyes skipped away.

"He's sweet."

"Awful shy," Daisy commented.

"I was thinking of asking him to take me to the after-Christmas social."

"*You* were thinking of asking *him*?"

Belinda's shocking statement had Daisy skating over the mention of the event Audra had previously been pushing Daisy to attend. She ducked into her sister's room, hiding a wince at the messy space. Shoes were strewn across the floor, books piled haphazardly in one corner, ribbons in a tangled mess on top of the writing desk. Two dresses lay across the foot of the bed rather than hanging neatly on their hooks.

Daisy bent over one side of the bed and began stripping the sheets, while Belinda did the same on the opposite side. The task was difficult with only the use of one arm, but not impossible.

"I want to go to the social." Belinda continued their conversation. "And Gerald Mains told me he was taking Adelaide."

It sounded like a recipe for disaster. "You aren't using Beau to make Jerry jealous, are you?"

Belinda didn't answer. She picked up the armful of sheets and quilt and brushed past Daisy.

"Belinda—"

"That would be a shallow thing to do," she tossed over her shoulder.

It wasn't a complete answer. Before the accident, Daisy had witnessed her sister's flirtatious manner at social events and in town, but her sister had never behaved in a malicious manner. But Daisy sensed that Beau wasn't the kind of man to take flirtation lightly.

She put off the sense of unease. The event wasn't for several days. She would make time to talk to her sister before then.

She crossed the hall and began stripping the sheets from the twins' beds. She had her arm full of sheets, pressing them against her midsection, when she nearly ran into Audra in the hall.

"Washing sheets, dear?" The question could be answered easily as Audra looked at her bundle.

But Daisy smiled. She was happy, hopeful, today. "I'm going to give it a shot."

She didn't even know if she'd be able to wield the heavy paddle to stir the soiled laundry, but she was going to try.

"Is this about that cowboy...?"

Audra's question sent both a thrill of anticipation and momentary concern through Daisy. "What do you mean?"

"I've seen the way you light up when he comes in the room. You've spent some time together these last few days, caring for all of us..." Audra let the sentence hang. Maybe she was hoping for Daisy to offer up a tidbit of information on how she felt about Ricky.

But Audra wasn't her mother. They were still feeling out their relationship. And Audra had pushed her before, that first night home after the wedding trip.

"He was a big help, wasn't he?" She met her stepmother's eyes with a steady glance.

Her feelings for Ricky—that *kiss*!—were so new. Daisy didn't want to share them with anyone.

Five days later, Ricky rode into the farmyard as the sun was setting. He was cold, dirty, tired to the bone.

He'd been out all day, first looking for a few stray sheep that had wandered away from the flock. He'd found two, but the third had been taken by a predator. He guessed a coyote, judging by the tracks. He hated losing animals, even if they weren't his own.

He just wanted his bedroll.

All right, he really wanted a glimpse of Daisy, maybe a smile…maybe a stolen kiss.

After his talk with Jonas, he didn't feel healed exactly. But hopeful. That if his pa could forgive the past, maybe Daisy could, too.

Jonas had gone home after that first day, and Ricky had barely seen Daisy since. Maybe Ned had gotten an inkling of his feelings for Daisy, he didn't know, but it seemed as if the foreman had kept him busy working far away from the farm buildings.

And he found he missed her. Prickly as she could be sometimes…warm as she could be at others.

He genuinely liked her.

He still thought Beau might be the better man for her, but at this point he didn't think he could stomach throwing them together anymore.

He dismounted outside the closed barn doors—it was

dreadfully cold today—and pushed open the portal, the sharp smell of animals assaulting him after he'd been out in the fresh air all day. His horse nickered, as if it was happy to be out of the elements, too.

Ricky was surprised to find the object of his thoughts in the back of the barn.

She looked over her shoulder at the disruption, losing her one-handed hold on her horse's head.

"Afternoon," he said, with a tip of his hat, hoping his face wasn't showing just how happy he was to see her.

Was she…? She was attempting to get her horse bridled, using the contraption Ricky had rigged but hadn't had time to keep working with, not with everything that had happened since the family's illness.

A spark of pride for her roared through him, lighting him up, almost as much as when he and Jonas had ridden back into the farmyard to see what must've been all the sheets in the house hanging on the clotheslines like flags declaring her independence.

"Hi," she said, almost shyly.

"Don't mind us," he told her. "This guy needs a good brushing after being out all day…"

Their eyes connected. She smiled at him before she nodded and turned back to what she was doing.

And suddenly all was right in his world.

He shucked his gloves, thankful for the warmer barn air against his cold-chapped skin. He still fumbled with the buckles but eventually got the saddle off and hauled it to the tack room, along with the saddle blanket. The familiar tasks suddenly made him self-conscious, knowing she was there, nearby.

When he returned with a towel and curry comb, she was murmuring to her horse, standing beside its head with her arm wrapped under and her fingers rubbing along the bridge of Prince's nose.

Ricky began rubbing down his animal. He couldn't help watching over its back as she got the horse to step forward, but it balked as she tried to guide its head down into the bridle.

She spoke to it quietly. Clicked her tongue. Didn't give up. Glanced once over her shoulder at him.

Ricky had to turn his back to her as he rubbed down his animal's opposite side, but still heard her encouraging the horse firmly. Bridling a horse was fairly simple with two hands, but Daisy was asking the animal to do more by slipping its nose down into the bridle, because she only had one arm to work with. Most horses took to the bridle without a problem. It was a matter of training. But maybe Ricky's idea had been wrong because this animal was older, set in its ways.

But it didn't sound as if Daisy was giving up.

He finished with his mount and tucked it into its stall, making sure it had plenty of oats. That brought him closer to Daisy, who had backed up Prince farther into the main aisle.

"Want an assistant?" he asked as he closed the bar over his horse's stall.

She looked back at him and shadows played in her eyes. "Do you think it would help?"

"Couldn't hurt. I haven't had much time to work with him since I installed the straps to hold the bridle."

She nodded, her previous smile turning a little brittle.

Ricky moved beside the horse's head on the opposite side, and Daisy clucked to get it to move forward.

The horse did what it should. They approached the bridle suspended in the air, all three of them together.

But Ricky could sense the tension in Daisy. He could see the stiff set of her spine beneath the horse's neck. If he could sense it, so could the horse.

"How long you been out here?" he asked, hoping that maybe conversation would take her mind off whatever was bugging her.

"Not long. I needed a break from the kitchen—Belinda and I have been baking bread all day."

She said the words lightly, but the tension in her remained. They were so close now, there was nothing to be done for it.

"All right, old fella," Ricky said quietly, hoping that if he projected confidence, the horse would pick up on it.

Daisy continued to guide the horse forward with her arm wrapped beneath its jaw and hand splayed across its nose. Ricky used his right hand to help spread the bridle, though it really didn't need it. His hooks from the leather straps hanging from the crossbar were near perfect.

"That's right," Ricky encouraged them both.

But at the last moment, the horse balked, rearing its head back and shaking off Daisy's hold. It neighed, shaking its head in agitation and backing up farther.

Without the animal between them, Ricky saw Daisy's expression fall.

"It's all right," he said softly. He went for the horse, got its halter back on and put it back in its stall.

When he got back to Daisy, she was staring at the bridle suspended in midair, her arm wrapped around her middle.

"I think it might be a little too high up—maybe that's why he was balking," Ricky offered. "I'll adjust it for you."

She nodded, eyes still far away.

* * *

Daisy's confidence had crashed around her in pieces as Prince had rejected the bridle.

She felt Ricky sidle up beside her, but she couldn't meet his eyes, not yet. Hot prickles of embarrassment crawled up her spine.

She'd been doing so well. Tackling some of the housework. Even her handwriting was improving slowly. She'd thought to come out here to the barn and bridle Prince and be waiting as Ricky returned from his long day of outdoor work. She'd wanted to show him the accomplishment like a child showing a school assignment to their parents.

And she'd hoped that he would ask her to the social tomorrow night. Belinda had convinced Beau to accompany her. Over the past few days, Daisy had come to peace—mostly—with the idea of attending. She had held out hope that the two cowboys had discussed it and that Ricky would be prompted to ask her.

They'd barely had a chance to talk since everyone had recovered from the stomach sickness, so she'd manufactured the time tonight.

Except it hadn't worked out as she'd thought it would.

"Want to see Matilda and the pups?" he asked softly from slightly behind her. Still steady. Still himself.

Matilda. There was something that Daisy hadn't messed up. She'd told Ricky about baking bread with Belinda, but she hadn't mentioned the eggshells she'd had to pick from the batter as she'd crushed several eggs trying to crack them open with only one hand. Or the loaf she'd dropped while taking it out of the oven that had fallen apart on the floor and been hopelessly ruined.

Everything was more difficult than before. Even learning, relearning how to do things all over again.

"All right," she said, trying to smile.

He led her to the stall where Matilda had birthed the puppies. It had obviously been cleaned, probably daily. In one corner, there was fresh hay that had been scattered throughout the large area. Someone had put a wooden plank across the doorway, blocking the puppies from getting out but allowing Matilda to come and go as she pleased.

The huge black dog looked up from where she lay next to a pile of nursing, squeaking pups, her tail beating rhythmically against the floor, lips stretched wide in a doggy smile.

"She's a good mama," Ricky said. "Doesn't get too fed up with them when they're making so many demands of her."

"She usually does fine." This hadn't been the dog's first litter. "Likely there'll be several of my papa's friends interested in having one of the pups."

She didn't know what to say, how to go about bringing up the social in natural conversation. Had Belinda really just *asked* Beau to go with her?

The cowboy beside her shifted, and she glanced over as he propped one shoulder against the stall, tucking his thumbs through his front belt loops. "You want to tell me what's bugging you?"

A hot flush stole up her face. She looked down on the dog to avoid his gaze. "Nothing."

He scooted his boot forward on the floor and knocked his toe against the toe of her boot. She glanced up at him, still hot. And bothered.

"I've got enough sisters and sisters-in-law to know when *nothing* means *something*. What's going on?"

She hiked her chin, intending to tell him *nothing* again, but instead found herself saying, "I—I want to go to the social tomorrow night."

If she'd hoped he would understand that she wanted him to ask her to go, he didn't. A look of confusion passed over his face, followed by shadows passing through his eyes.

But he smiled widely. "Good for you. I'll bet your friends will be happy to see you."

He didn't get it.

"I'd like it if you would go with me," she blurted.

And then squeezed her eyes closed, humiliation washing over her in a hot wave.

Did he think her incredibly forward, after asking that question? He'd kissed her before, but maybe he was really only interested in being her friend... What did he think of her now?

She couldn't even look at him.

There was a momentary silence, when all she could hear was the rushing in her ears, punctuated by the grunts and rustling of the puppies.

Then, he said, "I'll have to check with Ned, make sure he's all right with me taking the evening off."

She allowed her eyes to open slightly and watched him. He stood in the same casual pose, but she thought his shoulders had tightened up.

"You'll go? With me?" she asked over the lump in her throat.

He stepped forward, surprising her into opening her eyes fully. He cupped her cheek, his warm palm sliding against her jaw.

This close, he smelled of the outdoors, cold, horse and the cowboy that he was.

"I'd be glad to have the prettiest girl in town on my arm."

She started to lower her eyes, shake her head, because she wasn't that girl, not anymore, but with his hand firm against her jaw, he didn't let her move.

"Real glad," he said, and there was no doubting the sincerity in his eyes.

He brushed a kiss across her cheek and then ushered her back to the house before saying good-night.

As she readied for bed, part of her was elated, but the other, larger, part was terrified. What had she gotten herself into?

Chapter Fourteen

Ricky helped Daisy down from the wagon's bench seat and moved to tie off the horses in front of the little Pattonville café, among the other wagons and some saddled horses that had been tied, as well. The other businesses were dark, obviously closed for the end of the day, but the café was bustling with activity, the front windows lit up and shadows of people moving about inside. Muted voices carried through the night.

Daisy had been quiet on the ride to town. So had Beau, which had left Belinda and Ricky to carry the conversation between the four of them.

And he hadn't particularly wanted to carry it. He was too worried about what was going to happen tonight.

There was a reason he'd stayed pretty sequestered out on the Richardses' ranch. His reputation from before he'd accepted Christ into his life. If someone talked about him, if Daisy found out what had happened that night...chances were, whatever she found admirable about him would go up in smoke.

But he was done trying to hide his past. Coming clean to Jonas had been freeing, somehow. As soon as he could find a way, Ricky was going to confess to Daisy.

If they could make it through this night.

He finished tying the horses and turned, only to see Daisy standing frozen beside the wagon. She huddled in a patch of shadows between two squares of light, as if she was afraid to even move out into the open.

He made his way to her side.

"I can't do this," she whispered, and he saw that she was trembling. "What was I thinking, even contemplating it?"

But Beau and Belinda had already disappeared into the café. Even though Ricky might want to, they couldn't turn tail and leave the other two stranded.

He rested his palm against the small of her back. "What are you afraid of?"

She swallowed, the sound audible in the stillness around them. "That—" she began whispering, then broke off.

Ricky glanced around. The most important thing to him was keeping Daisy's reputation intact. But there was no one around.

And he couldn't resist taking her in his arms, not when she was this upset.

He tucked her close to his chest, rested his chin on the crown of her head, his arms around her back.

She wasn't crying, but she continued to shake, violent trembles racking her entire body. Her breath puffed hot against his sternum as she panted through the fear.

"That they'll see your arm is gone," he whispered into her hair.

She nodded jerkily, her chin brushing his collarbone with each movement of her head.

He squeezed her once.

"That they'll stare at you," he whispered again.

Again, she nodded.

He lowered his head, his jaw brushing her temple as he brought his mouth close to her ear.

Tucked up against him, her shivers had started to lessen.

"Do you know what I see when I look at you?" He was barely speaking, voice low and hoarse and right in her ear.

This time she barely moved, shaking her head, the motion rubbing against his cheek, they were so close.

"I see a beautiful woman strong enough to survive a wreck that could've killed her."

He shivered as the thought struck him, and he had to close his eyes. She'd almost died.

And it was his fault. The words pressed against the inside of his chest, but now wasn't the time to tell her, not when she was already upset.

"I see a woman who might be scared, but isn't willing to let the loss of her arm dictate how she's going to live her life."

He put his hands to her shoulders and pressed her slightly away from him, until he could look down into her face. A few rays of light from one of the windows shone down on her so he could read her.

"I see you. A survivor. Beautiful. Daisy."

Her eyes were luminous, and she blinked once slowly.

He wanted nothing more than to kiss her and keep kissing her until she believed what he'd said. But he heard the jingle of a harness and the soft clop of hooves in the dirt-packed road. Someone was coming.

He let her go, and cold rushed in against his chest where she'd been.

She looked up at him and he moved beside her, in front of the boardwalk stairs. He let his hand rest on her lower back, this time a casual touch.

She took a deep breath and stepped up the first step. The second. The boardwalk.

She hesitated slightly at the door. She looked back at him over her shoulder and smiled a trembling smile. He nodded.

And she went inside, leaving him to follow.

Daisy stepped over the threshold, and the noise of multiple conversations instantly muted.

She felt the sharp prickle of eyes on her. Just as she'd thought.

But also the warmth of Ricky's presence behind her.

She could do this. Because he was here with her.

Smells of hot coffee and sugary-sweet punch and baked goods threatened to upset her stomach. Her eyes flitted to the left, to the right. Landing only briefly on the curious gazes of people she'd known all her life and some she didn't know at all.

"Daisy Richards!"

Her head lifted to meet the familiar voice, her friend Ethel. The brunette had her arms full of a blanket-wrapped bundle. Her baby girl, the one Daisy hadn't even seen yet.

She was followed closely by Mary. All three girls had been as close as sisters since their school days.

Daisy hesitated, afraid of what they would say. She'd been avoiding them at all costs, even the day they'd come out to the ranch to see her. She hadn't been a good friend at all.

But they didn't hesitate before enfolding her in a three-way hug, the baby tucked in Ethel's arms and right in there with them.

Tears rushed to the surface, filling Daisy's throat and eyes. She blinked them away.

Ethel pushed back, exclaiming, "Look at you! You look so *good*!"

Daisy was glad she'd allowed Belinda to talk her into borrowing one of her sister's newer gowns with its sleeve pinned up. The cut was more fashionable, and the color favored her. The other women's dresses were stylish, new to Daisy, who had been isolated on the ranch for months.

"I'd like you both to meet Ricky White." She moved aside so that Ricky was more visible to the girls from where he'd been standing behind her. "He's one of my father's hands. And a…friend."

She had looked from Ricky back to her friends in time to see a warm smile appear on Ethel's face, but Mary's frown was a surprise.

"Evening. I don't suppose we've got you to thank for getting Daisy to attend the event tonight," Ethel said.

Ricky's eyes came to Daisy and held. "No, ma'am. That was all Daisy."

Warmth infused her. Maybe it hadn't been too forward of her to invite him. And maybe it had been her idea. But she would never have made it in the door without his steady presence.

Just remembering his whispered words from outside sent shivers down her spine. *I see you. Beautiful.*

She wasn't beautiful, not anymore, but that he had said so meant so much to her.

"Come sit with us," Ethel invited, and to Ricky, "My husband is over there..."

Daisy allowed herself to be pulled through the crowded restaurant. After the initial surprise of her entrance, now everyone had gone back to their own conversations.

For the most part.

She was conscious of a whisper as they passed one of the tables. She couldn't help the turn of her head. An acquaintance, not someone she knew well. The girl's eyes cut away, and Daisy couldn't help the flush that spread up her cheeks.

Ethel's husband, Harry, rose from his chair as they approached, offering a warm smile to Daisy. They'd only been married for about a year, and he was from a neighboring town, so Daisy didn't know him terribly well, but she liked him well enough.

But Harry's smile didn't extend to Ricky, in the same way Mary's hadn't. She was momentarily confused, but pushed it away as she settled at the table with her friends.

There was something she needed to say immediately. "I'm sorry I didn't see you when you came out to the ranch a few weeks ago."

Ethel's eyes lowered, but it was Mary who reached across the table to touch the back of her hand. "We understood. We didn't like it, but we understood."

"How have you been?" Ethel asked. "You look in good health, but how have you really been?"

"Better," Daisy said with a glance and half smile at

Ricky. "My body has healed, but some of the tasks I am having to relearn are…difficult."

Compassion flitted across her friends' faces. But she didn't want to dwell on her challenges. Not tonight.

"I haven't gotten to see the new baby. Audra told me you named her Ruth."

She leaned forward as Ethel tucked the blanket down lower beneath the baby's chin so Daisy could see her face. The little one slept peacefully, even in the midst of the noisy atmosphere, her lashes a dark slash across her cheeks and the tiny bow of her lips suckling in her sleep.

There was a slight hesitation before Ethel asked, "Do you want to hold her?"

She did. But the baby was so new, and she wasn't sure she'd be able to do it correctly with only one arm. "Perhaps later."

She probably imagined Ethel's small sigh of relief.

"I'm going to grab some punch. Be right back."

Ricky excused himself and stood, weaving through the tables toward where a punch bowl and light refreshments had been set up at the back of the room. Harry also excused himself.

Daisy couldn't help following her cowboy with her gaze, feeling somewhat empty without him next to her.

She saw two girls she didn't know approach him and say something, saw his feet shift as if he was uncomfortable.

Across the room, Belinda chatted with a group of friends. Where was Beau?

"You seem quite attached to your cowboy," Mary said, bringing Daisy's attention back to the table and her friends. Her expression was closed, hard to read, which was unusual for Daisy's usually expressive friend.

"We're not... He hasn't asked if he could come courting," Daisy said. "We're friends."

Ethel shook her head, her dark curls bouncing around her face. A new hairdo? "You don't look at him as if he's just a friend. It's more than that."

"What do you really know about him?" Mary asked quietly, tracing a pattern on the table with one fingertip. "He's not from around here, is he?"

"His family is from Bear Creek. I met his father over Christmas, when everyone was ill."

"Yes, but...what about him? The cowboy? Who is he? What's he doing in town—" Mary's words cut off.

Daisy saw Ethel shift as if she'd kicked her friend below the table. "I think it's delightful that you've found a friend."

But Mary wasn't smiling. What was wrong? Did her friend know something about Ricky that Daisy didn't know? How could she?

"I can only guess that he's encouraged you to get out of the house," Ethel said with a sly smile.

Daisy blushed. It had been rather the opposite. "He's certainly helped me see how I could accomplish tasks around the house. I've spilled so many things and made so many messes—I feel like a little child again. You have no idea..."

Ethel's attention was diverted. Daisy looked over her shoulder to see Harry motioning to his wife.

"Oh, he's talking to Delilah—I've got to go over there." But Ethel didn't sound thrilled about it.

Daisy knew the other girl had fancied Harry when he'd first come to town but Ethel's quick upset reaction made her wonder what she'd missed.

But Daisy wasn't ready to stand up and become the

center of attention, especially if there was an altercation brewing.

"I'll go with you," Mary offered. Both women bustled to their feet.

"Thank you." Ethel sounded genuinely thankful. "Daisy, would you *please* take the baby?"

Before she could get a word of protest past her lips, Ethel had settled the sleeping baby against her breast and brushed past.

Daisy clutched Ruth, her own breath coming in pants and gasps. What if she dropped the baby?

But the slumbering cherub only cooed in her sleep, settling her cheek against Daisy's shoulder.

The noise all around seemed to dim as she looked down on the baby.

Wasn't this what she'd wanted all along? A husband and baby and life on the ranch, their own flocks and their own *place*.

As her eyes slid to half-mast and her imagination soared, it was *Ricky* beside her on the front porch.

And then the man was there, sliding into the chair at her elbow. "Did they abandon you?"

He sounded offended on her behalf, and thunked a mug of what looked like cider down on the table in front of her. Not that she could do anything with it since she was holding the baby, but she smiled at the gesture anyway.

"They'll be back. Ethel left this little one…"

His eyes took in the baby and his entire expression softened, the tension around his mouth easing and a deep warmth entering his eyes.

He didn't say anything, but their connection seemed

to expand, filling the space between them until she was buoyed by the hope and anticipation swirling through her.

And she had to look down on the baby again, to keep from bursting out in song.

Then the baby coughed. Her tiny head wobbled and Daisy adjusted to try and steady her, but the baby coughed again, her face scrunching and turning an alarming shade of red. Baby Ruth threw her head back, the movement wild and unexpected.

Daisy clutched the baby, trying to stabilize her. The infant coughed again, face going blotchy and then she let out a squall that silenced the conversations around them.

Panicked, Daisy jerked her head to the side, looking for Ethel, but she couldn't see her friend.

Her frantic movement upset the baby even more, and it squirmed.

Half afraid she would drop Ruth, she cried out, "Take her!"

And Ricky was there, his wide hands scooping up the baby. He tucked her against his chest, patting her back and jiggling her. She quieted some but then let out a piercing scream.

The conversations around them had gone from frozen silence to murmurs and whispers.

Daisy's face flamed. Were they all talking about her? How she couldn't do the simplest things, like hold a baby?

"Is she all right?" she asked, breathless and hot. Upset.

"She's fine." He said the words without looking up at her, his focus on the baby.

Hot prickles went up her spine. People were watching her. Judging her. She knew it.

She wanted to escape.

"What happened?"

There was Ethel, rushing in with Harry just behind. Ethel took the baby from Ricky with shaking hands.

"Just a little cough," Ricky said, in that same calm manner that Daisy recognized.

Harry had somehow got a shoulder between Ethel and Ricky. He said something to Ricky, but with the surrounding conversations buzzing louder and louder— or was that only in Daisy's head?—she couldn't hear what it was.

Ricky's expression tightened.

She couldn't think, couldn't breathe. She needed to get out of here, now.

She stood up, her chair scraping loudly against the wooden floor.

Ricky glanced over Harry's shoulder, and he seemed to see her distress, because he edged past the other man and met her with a hand at her waist. On her bad side.

She closed her eyes briefly, trying to stem the emotion threatening to swamp her. When she reopened them, nothing was better.

Several people nearby were looking at her with open curiosity. Voices buzzed around her; she was so upset she couldn't make out the words.

"You want to get some air?" he asked.

She couldn't answer him, but she managed a nod.

Chest tight, she allowed him to usher her through the snarl of tables and booted feet and long skirts in the way.

They closed in on the door and she pulled ahead of him, almost running in her haste to escape.

Finally, she burst out into the cold night air. Her shoes clicked against the boardwalk. Alone.

The quiet was a welcome relief, and she sucked in breath after breath of the biting air.

The door opened behind her, sending a shaft of bright yellow light and a louder murmuring of voices inside.

Were they all talking about her?

The door closed behind Ricky, cutting off the light and putting him into darkness. He stepped toward Daisy, bootsteps muffled against the boardwalk.

"You didn't even grab your coat," he chided gently.

She glanced at him very briefly over her shoulder but allowed him to help her into the garment. He saw her trembling and wanted to clasp a hand on her shoulder or *something*, but a glance to the side revealed several curious onlookers just inside the café window.

He didn't want his reputation to tarnish hers. So he shoved his arms into his coat and shrugged into it, then came beside her at the railing. They stood shoulder to shoulder, overlooking the darkened street, the clapboard buildings and the sleepy horses tethered to several wagons. Down at the very end of the street, piano music wafted out into the darkness from the town's saloon.

"That was *awful*," she whispered.

"Was not." He hadn't thought it had been that bad. She'd lit up when she'd seen her friends, and they'd clearly been happy to see her.

Her friend Mary and the other gal's husband had been tight-lipped when they'd greeted him. Likely they knew of his reputation.

Then when the baby had been crying and he'd tried to help, the friend's husband had crowded into Ricky's space.

Frustration and anger still coursed through him at the intrusion, but he tried to shove it down deep inside. Daisy clearly needed a friend.

She shook her head, a strangled sound coming from her throat. In the darkness, he couldn't tell if she was crying, but she hadn't sniffled.

He really wanted to clasp her hand in his, offer her what comfort he could.

But he didn't.

He had to protect her.

"Want me to round up Belinda and Beau?" Inside, he'd seen Belinda chatting with a group of men and women, with Beau hanging slightly back from the conversation. Ricky hadn't really talked with the other cowboy in a few days and didn't know if he had gone to the social with Belinda as a friend or a potential suitor. If it was the latter, Ricky feared the boy was in for a rude surprise.

"No. No, not yet."

"Do you want to go back inside? You didn't get to talk to your friends very long—"

"No!" Her quick exclamation came on a harsh breath and then she took a deep inhale. "No. I'll—I'll catch up with them later."

"It's cold," he said quietly. "You can't just stay out here."

It wasn't as bitterly cold as it had been during the recent storms, but with night having fallen, it wasn't warm, either.

"I can bundle up in the wagon, with the blankets."

She still didn't look at him. "If you want to go back inside and visit—" Now he was sure he heard the threat of tears in her voice. She inhaled sharply. "I know there are plenty of others in there you might want to talk to—other girls—"

He didn't know if she really thought he might be interested in someone else or was just saying that because she'd been embarrassed.

He didn't really care.

"I'm right where I wanna be," he said firmly.

Then she did sniffle. She reached up and touched her face as she might've brushed away a tear and he could just imagine the tremble of her full lips.

He couldn't resist.

He slid his hand against her lower back and turned her a little into his chest. It wasn't a full embrace. He made sure it was completely innocent.

Because when she figured out that she was just as good as all those other girls, even without her arm, and decided she wanted to be around someone better than him, he didn't want there to be any questions on her morals.

He started guiding her down the steps. Still tucked a little against his chest, but if they were moving, they couldn't be doing anything untoward.

He boosted her up into the wagon. It creaked as he helped settled the blankets around her, tucked up behind the bench seat, where she'd get a little bit of a windbreak.

It would be warmer if he was snuggled up there with her, but he kept his boots on the ground and leaned his elbows on the side of the wagon instead. Kept it all innocent, in case any of those voices chattering inside decided to come outside and check on her. Right now, they were alone, the only two crazy enough to be out here in the cold.

She sniffled again, and he racked his brain trying to think of something to get her mind off what had happened inside.

Before he could distract her, boisterous male voices called out from close—too close.

"Ace, that you?"

"Lookey-look, it *is* Ace."

He recognized the two loudmouthed cowboys vaguely from when he'd visited the saloon those first days in Pattonville. And being around them was the last thing he wanted, especially with Daisy in the wagon. They were walking down the middle of the street and she was somewhat behind him, tucked inside the wagon box. Maybe they wouldn't even see her there.

"My name's Ricky," he said quietly. "Maybe you've got the wrong cowboy."

"Nooo…you're definitely Ace," one of them said. His words were slightly slurred.

Great. They'd obviously been to the saloon and were deep in their cups.

And it sounded as if they'd been there the night of Daisy's accident. Another cowboy had accused Ricky of cheating at cards, and since Ricky had been full of alcohol and hubris, it hadn't been hard to rile him into losing his temper.

"This the guy that Duke thought was cheating?"

He really didn't want to talk about that night. He'd promised himself he was going to tell Daisy the next time he had the opportunity, but he didn't want to do it now, when she was already upset.

"For the record, I wasn't cheating then and I'm not interested in any card game tonight," he said. Or ever again.

Two against one wasn't a fair fight and he prayed they'd just keep walking, go on their way. But then one of them crossed close, and someone opened the front door to the café, letting light spill out, right onto Ricky.

One of the drunken cowboys wobbled closer to Ricky, now only a few feet away. Ricky could smell the liquor on him, even from here.

"Wait a minute," he slurred. "This's the man that was kissing Judy when you was on the range that weekend coupla months ago."

He didn't know who Judy was, but he'd kissed a couple of gals in Pattonville before he'd reformed.

The other cowboy bristled and Ricky got the sense that maybe Judy was *his girl*.

"I don't know any Judy," Ricky said.

He held both hands up in front of himself. And then the worst thing that could happen, happened.

"Why don't you leave us alone?" Daisy demanded.

He felt as if he'd been punched in the gut.

He looked over his shoulder to see she'd risen up on her knees in the wagon box. It put her up higher than the three of them, but now it made her a target.

"Whoohee," the closer, louder cowboy said. "Ace's got hisself a gal out here."

His friend didn't comment, but that didn't mean he wasn't spoiling for a fight, not after the nearer one's comment about *Judy*, whoever she was.

"Hop out the other side, and go inside," he told Daisy, hoping against hope she would listen.

"I won't."

Woman! He experienced a moment of intense fear. He wanted to swear, but he bit back the word. He didn't do that anymore. Didn't mean he wasn't angry that she was putting herself in danger.

"Whatchu been doing out here in the dark?" the obnoxious cowboy asked.

"I'll ask you kindly to move along," Ricky said.

"Aw, don't be like that," the loud cowboy said.

And then Ricky realized the other cowboy had sidled up behind him. He wasn't ready for the punch when it came, not in the dark and from an unexpected direction.

The hit rang his bell, clocking him in the cheek and sending him spinning, knocking his shoulder hard against the front of the wagon. The horses shifted in their traces, agitated by the movement from behind them.

Daisy screamed, the shrill sound making his head feel as if it was cracking open. His cheek ached, and something warm trickled down the corner of his eye. He wasn't crying, so it must be blood.

Ricky heard the obnoxious cowboy's voice cajoling, "C'mon, missy, we're just having a little fun—"

"Get away from her," he growled, pushing away from the wagon and trying to spin at the same time.

The silent cowboy met him with an uppercut to the gut that raised Ricky's feet off the ground by at least an inch and doubled him over in excruciating pain.

Light spilled out of the café. Voices rose, questioning.

He barely held on to the coffee he'd drunk at the social minutes ago. Nausea swirled, or was that his head?

"Judy is *mine*," the quiet cowboy said, voice low and deadly.

I don't even know a Judy. He tried, but the words wouldn't come out.

Then the cowboy was gone as the crowd from inside spilled out into the street. Daisy was there at his elbow, asking him if he was okay and if she should get the sheriff.

"No," he managed in a hoarse groan. He couldn't risk the sheriff disclosing his identity. The man had been there the night of Daisy's accident, and although it had been ruled an accident, Ricky had taken the blame on himself. Assigned his own punishment.

Ricky tried to stand up straight, but his insides protested and he wrapped one arm around his midsection.

Beau came running up, panting and shoving his arms into his coat. "What happened?"

The whole night had been ruined. For both Daisy and Ricky.

That's what.

Chapter Fifteen

The next morning, Ricky stood just inside the door of the boss's office, facing Owen and Ned. The boss sat behind the desk with his hands steepled in front of him.

Ned stood behind the corner of the desk, glowering at Ricky. He'd taken one look at Ricky's mug in the morning light and told him to meet up in the boss's office after morning chores. Ricky wore a visible shiner and a scrape on his cheek. Both stung.

And his ribs ached from the punch to the gut he'd taken.

Right now, he wished he was anywhere but here.

Ricky still simmered with temper even after spending a restless night in his bunk. He and Beau had delivered Daisy and Belinda to their doorstep after a silent, cold ride home where the men had shared the wagon seat and the women had curled up beneath blankets in the back.

He'd only said a cursory good-night to her. No explanations, though she had to be bursting with curiosity. He needed to talk to her.

But now this.

The fire crackled in the hearth. It should've been homey, welcoming, but the two men glowering across the desk at Ricky made it anything but.

"Wanna explain what happened last night?" Owen asked. "Why you're so banged up?"

"Daisy and I were outside, when a coupla cowboys came walking down from the saloon and picked a fight."

"What were you doing outside?" The outright suspicion in Ned's voice was like flint on steel to Ricky's bruised temper today.

"Daisy got upset about being inside with all those people." It had been more than that. Something had happened while she'd been holding the baby. He'd seen enough to know that. But that was her business. If she wanted to talk to her pa, she would.

The boss's eyes narrowed on him, and Ricky felt like squirming, felt as if he'd been called up in front of the teacher. He didn't. He stood stock-still, his hat held loosely against his thigh.

"I was a little surprised she said she wanted to go with her sister," Daisy's father said. He looked at Ricky as if maybe Ricky had had something to do with that.

Ricky didn't say anything about how she'd invited him to the social. He didn't answer at all.

He wasn't entirely sure why he was staying in this office anyway. Times past, he'd have walked off the job the moment they questioned him. He didn't do well with authority. But this was Daisy's pa. And for some reason he wanted to make a good impression on the man.

As if that was happening with his bruised face. He stiffened his shoulders as the thought crossed his mind.

"I'd like to know what your intentions are toward my

daughter," Owen said. The man should play poker. He wasn't revealing anything with his expression.

Ricky hesitated. It was true he'd never faced a woman's pa before—never even thought about it. It had never mattered before. But his feelings for Daisy were too strong to deny. "I care about her."

A glance passed between the two brothers. Ricky had been able to do the same with Davy before he'd left home, share a message without needing words.

"You ain't good enough to lick the dust off her boots," Ned said gruffly.

He knew that. He did. But it stung, coming from the man who had seen him working long hours at hard labor for the ranch these past months. He didn't know if Ned held his reputation against him, or if the dislike that had grown stronger lately was simply a clash of two similar personalities.

"I didn't ask those drunk cowpokes to come talk to me."

"Naw, but yer reputation around these parts sure did," Ned growled.

It was true, but... "I don't do those things anymore. Don't visit the saloons, don't sweet-talk women. I'm not the same person I was before—" *Before Daisy's accident.*

Ricky saw the recognition of what he didn't say in Owen's face.

"A few months don't prove nuthin'," Ned said, crossing his arms over his chest. "Man could decide he was having more fun the way things was before and go right back to that kind of life" Ned turned to his brother. "That the kind of man you want for your daughter?"

"Ned." The boss's quiet word was also a command, and Ned went silent.

But Ricky stood panting, riled, ready to slug Ned for the hurtful words. Maybe more hurtful because they were true, and Ricky knew it.

"You didn't really answer my question earlier. What are your intentions toward Daisy?" Owen repeated.

Ricky faced off with the man who had the power to change his future.

"I'd like permission to court her."

His face flamed at the admission. He'd *never* asked permission to come courting, for anyone. He'd never respected or cared about a woman enough to do it.

He swallowed hard, holding more words back with his back teeth clamped together. Words to try and explain just how strongly he felt about Daisy, how much he admired her strength and spirit. Promises about how he'd treat her and how he'd never go back to that way of life.

"I don't like that you got mixed up in a fight last night," Owen said. "I don't want my daughter around that kind of riffraff."

"I didn't fight back," Ricky said, a little desperately. It was true, he hadn't fought back, but he would've if those two hooligans had threatened Daisy any more than they had, or if the rest of the crowd hadn't spilled outside.

The boss stared at him, and Ricky had never felt more judged in his life. How had it come to this? Wanting this one man's approval more than just about anything?

He felt nauseous, knowing he didn't deserve approval. His past might not shackle him anymore, he was free to be the man God had created him to be.

But that didn't mean that others could see past who he *had* been.

And Daisy didn't even know all of it. She might not want him when she did. There was a good chance of it.

He met Owen's gaze, trying to show the new man he was when his temper still simmered and he stood here under their judgment.

Finally, Owen shook his head.

Ricky's heart plummeted down to his toes.

"I'm sorry, son."

His chest cinched tight as Owen looked straight at him.

"I'm just not sure that's the best thing for Daisy. She's…sensitive."

Because of her arm. He knew.

"And I don't want her to get hurt."

Numb, Ricky nodded. He wanted to argue, wanted to plead his case, but Owen knew about his part in Daisy's accident. He'd allowed Ricky to work on the ranch with intentions of making reparations, if possible. And look what Ricky had done. On their first trip to town together, he'd gotten into a scrape.

Maybe the boss was right.

He wasn't good enough for Daisy.

He let himself out of the office and she was there, in the hall. Had she overheard what he'd said? What her father had said to him?

The back of his neck burned like an inferno. He couldn't face her, not now.

"'Scuse me, miss."

He nodded, stuffed his hat onto his head and scooted past her, almost running for the barn.

Beau was out checking the flock. Even if he'd been here, Ricky didn't know if he could talk to the other man. Although Beau had been his sounding board before, Ricky just really wanted to punch something, or someone. The aggression, the anger, wasn't new to him.

But trying to tame it was.

This was the hardest thing he'd had to face since he'd accepted Christ those months ago.

Getting hit by those drunken cowboys hadn't been anything.

This was painful. Wanting Daisy and not being able to have her.

The woodpile. Maybe he could work out some of his pent-up frustration there.

He hurried outside, grabbing the ax and going after several chunks of wood. The ax made a satisfying *thunk* every time he sliced through a log, and the physical exertion loosened his shoulders a little.

But it wasn't helping, not really. The cold air against his heated skin did little to cool him off.

Because nothing could help him.

He grabbed two chunks this time, balanced them on the stump. Hit harder.

Wiped his forehead with his sleeve.

Harder.

Not good enough.

He'd deserved that punch. Deserved more.

Harder.

He would never deserve *her.*

Daisy watched out the window where she'd stopped as Ricky had slammed out of the house.

Behind her, she could hear her father's and Ned's raised voices in Papa's office, though neither had emerged yet.

On her way upstairs after breakfast, Belinda had

whispered that Ricky was inside talking to Papa, and Daisy hadn't been able to contain the leap of joy her heart had taken.

Was he asking permission to court? After what had happened last night?

She could hardly believe it.

Everyone in the café had witnessed her ineptitude at holding baby Ruth, even for a few minutes.

If she couldn't even hold an infant successfully, how was she to feed it? Diaper it? Give it a bath?

She closed her eyes against the panorama of the empty barnyard, closed her eyes against the hurt.

How could she be a mother, if she couldn't do the simplest things for her baby?

And everyone knew that courting could lead to marriage, which led to children.

How could Ricky be asking such a thing after how she'd embarrassed herself, and the realization it had led to?

He'd been upset when he'd stalked past her and gone outside. He'd called her *miss*, not *Daisy*. She'd watched from the kitchen window as he had disappeared into the barn.

Maybe he hadn't gone in to talk to Papa about courting her. Maybe it was something else, something to do with the cowboys he'd run into. Her humiliation on one hand and curiosity on the other had kept her from falling asleep for far too long last night.

She opened her eyes and saw Ricky emerging from the barn. Her heart leaped in anticipation, expectation. Maybe he'd just gone inside to clean up or retrieve something.

But he didn't come back up to the house, only went

to the woodpile and began chopping, heaving the ax with such emotion, such disregard for his own safety. She was a little afraid he was going to miss the block and chop his leg off.

Something was wrong.

And she expected she knew what it was.

She wanted to go upstairs and hide in her room, but hadn't she been learning that she couldn't curl up and die because of her limitations? If she still intended to take over the ranch—and she did—and if Ricky still worked here, then they would see each other around.

She should face him now and prove that she could do it.

He was still chopping viciously as she stepped out onto the back porch, though he stopped as she descended the stairs. The bright morning sun mocked her.

His back was to her, and he must not have seen her. Wood chips littered the ground around him, evidence of the fury he'd attacked the job with.

He wiped his brow with his shirtsleeve and the slump of his shoulders told her what she needed to know. This wasn't easy for him, either.

"Ricky?" she asked.

He whirled so fast, it was a good thing the ax was still in the stump or she might've been hurt.

He glanced over her shoulder to the house. "Help you with something, Miss Daisy?"

She bit her lip against the proper name. He'd called her Daisy for weeks before this. His cheek beneath his eye was purple and swollen, and she wanted to ask about his injuries but didn't dare.

She steeled herself as much as she could, propping

her hand on her hip and raising her chin. "I'd like to talk for a minute."

He eyed the house behind her again and she turned, thinking to see someone standing on the porch or at the window, but there was nothing.

She turned back to him. "Did you ask my father if you could come courting?"

Her face flamed. She hadn't meant to blurt it out like that. But then, she was who she was. No hiding, not now.

"Yes," he said flatly. "He said *no*."

Everything around her went white, as if her eyesight had gone crazy. Her extremities tingled.

She inhaled sharply, and all the colors rushed back, almost painfully.

"Did you—" Her voice trembled and she worked to steady it. "Did you press your case?"

"No." Again, his voice was flat, dead. Like a slap to her face.

It jarred her out of her stillness. "I see."

After last night, she should've known. She'd embarrassed herself, embarrassed them both. She could've injured Ethel's baby.

But still, she'd wanted things to be different.

Her chin trembled, but she refused to cry in front of him. "Perhaps it's for the best," she said stiffly. She was ready to flee back to the house, but not until she said, "I'd hate for us to be saddled together if you'd later come to think of me as a burden." And how could she think of herself as anything *but*?

She whirled and took a step toward the house.

He said something low under his breath; she couldn't make it out.

"This isn't about your arm," he called after her.

She didn't look fully back at him, just answered over her shoulder, softly, "I don't see how it could be about anything else."

Then his footsteps crunched in the gravel behind her, and he grabbed her shoulders, spinning her to face him.

"It isn't about *you*," he said, and he was livid. His entire face had flushed red and a muscle in his jaw jumped. His black eye made him look sinister, but she knew without a shadow of a doubt that he wouldn't hurt her. Even now, so upset, his hold on her shoulders was gentle. "It's because of *me*."

She was on the verge of tears, unable to do anything but shrug, raising his clamped hands along with her shoulders. What did he mean?

He heaved a great sigh and let her go. Another glance at the house. Again, she followed his gaze there but didn't see anyone moving around.

"Let's take a walk," he said. "You bundled up enough?"

She'd put her coat on before she came outside. She nodded and put her hand in her pocket, following him out of the barnyard and across the field that would eventually lead down to the nearby creek.

He was silent for a long moment.

"Didn't you hear those cowboys last night?" he demanded softly.

Everything had been a muddle. Ricky had been comforting her, tucking her into the wagon, and she'd been a mess, upset by what had happened inside the café.

"Part of it," she said truthfully. "They knew you from playing cards?"

"Not...not really."

He wasn't looking at her, was looking down at the ground as he walked, as if he didn't particularly want to talk about this at all.

"When you're in the saloon, you don't really *know* anybody," he explained. "Not like I know my brothers, or how Beau and I have become friends."

He stuffed his hands into his pockets. Her heart was in her throat as he spoke. He'd never really opened up to her like this before.

"So, no…I didn't know those two, not really. But the old me—the person I was before, I was a lot like them."

She remembered what the one had accused him of. "Did you… Did you kiss the cowboy's sweetheart?"

He laughed, a harsh, ugly sound. No mirth in it. "I don't know. Some nights, I got so drunk, I couldn't tell you who I kissed…but it was a lot of girls."

His neck had gone red and the blush spread up his jaw and into his face. "I'm not proud of it."

They'd wandered down the gentle slope and now they'd reached the privacy of the wooded creek. The earthy, wet smell of decaying leaves rose around them.

They stopped walking, but Ricky wouldn't really look at her. He put his palm up against the trunk of a scrub oak and leaned into it, nudging the toe of his boot through the dirt at his feet.

"My past is why your pa doesn't think I'm good enough for you." He said the words quietly, matter-of-factly, but she sensed the deeper hurt beneath them.

Her heart was fluttering in her throat like a trapped hummingbird. *He did want to court her.* He wanted to be with her. "But—you haven't done any of those things since I've known you."

He put a hand to the back of his neck, a sign of stress she'd seen him make before. "That's not all of it. It's worse than that."

Tell her.

Ricky kicked at the exposed tree root, pulse pounding in his ears. The bark of the oak bit into his hand.

He needed to tell Daisy about the part he'd played in the night of her accident.

He wasn't even looking at her, but in his mind's eye, he could still see the tears in her beautiful eyes from a moment ago. His heart pounded, and his mouth went dry.

He couldn't see a way forward. If her pa refused to let him come courting—well, he wasn't going to ask her to go against her family.

Not for the likes of him.

But she deserved the truth. So she could know, and he hoped, forgive. Find peace. She deserved it.

With or without him in her life.

But when he turned to her to find her shivering in the cold breeze howling through the scrub trees, her eyes luminous and hopeful, he couldn't force the words out.

Instead he blurted, "I killed a lady. When I was young."

She gasped softly. But she didn't draw away as he expected. Instead, she closed the small space between them and reached out and touched his forearm.

He didn't know what to do with her closeness, not when he was telling something that only one other person, his pa, knew about. He looked down at her hand because he didn't seem to be able to look anywhere else.

"My ma had died and I'd been thrown out of the place

we were living. The bordello. I had nowhere to go and ended up on the edge of town, close to this little creek. There was a cabin nearby. I knew, because I'd spied on it earlier. I was cold and hungry and could barely think through my grief. I started a fire, got warm, fell asleep. I woke up in the night and the fire had spread. I couldn't stomp it out, it was too big."

He could still smell the sulfur, could still feel his lungs burning with the intense smoke.

He stared at her hand, trying to remember he was here, in the present, but his memories still felt real even after all these years.

"I ran back toward the cabin, but I couldn't outrun the fire. I don't remember it being a particularly dry summer, but it must've been. Everything caught fire so fast—the grass, the underbrush, even the small trees." *Wildfire.*

All because he'd been careless and left his fire untended when he'd fallen asleep.

"When I got to the cabin it was on fire. I shouted, but I couldn't get through the front door. I went around, but the entire building was engulfed."

He swallowed, closing his eyes against the painful memories.

"Then I heard her screaming."

The eerie shrieks were scalded into his memory, just like the scar on the back of his wrist from when he'd tried to rescue Daisy.

They never went away.

He was jerked forcibly from his memories as she stepped closer, slid her arm around his neck and held him close.

Without his consent, his arms came around her back

and he buried his face in her hair, holding on to the comfort she offered freely.

He'd never expected this. Never thought that Jonas would accept his past. And now Daisy.

He didn't deserve their understanding, their forgiveness.

But he couldn't turn away from it, either.

Ricky was shaking.

The tall, powerful cowboy was trembling violently in her embrace.

She pressed her face against his shoulder as she held him, as they held each other.

She couldn't imagine what he must've gone through, losing his mother and then this tragedy.

"How old were you?" she whispered, her mouth pressing against his shoulder.

His voice was rough when he answered. "Old enough to know you don't leave a fire untended."

"How old?" she pushed.

"Nearly nine."

So young. Too young to be carrying this burden around.

"I ran away." His breath was hot against the crown of her head as he spoke, but it didn't seem either could move away. "I should've gone back and faced what I did, but I was afraid... I met up with my brother Davy in Cheyenne. He was alone, too. We sort of banded together and went on our own, up until my pa found us camping in the woods and took us in."

"I'm glad he found you."

"So was I, until I started thinking how all the other brothers were *good* and I wasn't. None of them knew, not even Davy…and it just got to be too painful, *pretending* to be someone I wasn't."

"Oh, Ricky." She just held on to him tighter.

"And then…" He swallowed audibly. Hesitated. "And then Beau told me the truth. We're all ugly, all sinners unless we accept Jesus into our lives. Your pa and your uncle…they're not sure I've left all that behind."

He shook his head, and she felt strands of her hair hang up on the fine whiskers on his jaw.

She lifted her chin, met his gaze for a long second and then moved her hand to his nape and pulled his head down. She pressed her lips into his, uncaring that she didn't know what she was doing, only knowing that she wanted to *show* him that she knew.

He kissed her back, his lips moving against hers, one of his hands flat against her upper back.

She broke away, afraid of going too fast, a little afraid of the passion sparking between them. Looking up at him, she told him what was in her heart.

"I don't care what anyone else thinks or says about you. I know the man you are now."

Chapter Sixteen

I know the man you are now.

Daisy's words from two days ago had stuck with Ricky and haunted him even now as he and Beau rode out in the predawn gray to check the sheep.

He'd barely seen her in the past forty-eight hours. She'd come out to check on Matilda's pups once, and he'd loitered in the barn, breathing her in and just chatting. Half afraid to get too close.

That kiss…

The only other time he'd seen her, she'd been hanging clean laundry on the lines, on a blustery cold day. He'd quit chopping the wood he'd been working on—much less violently this time—to help her, and they'd laughed and shivered as the wind had tangled them in the wet fabric.

Every time he saw her, his gut panged. He should have told her about the night of the accident.

He'd tried. And failed, although he'd shared about the fire from his childhood. He didn't know how they could go on with this huge thing between them. He wanted it cleared up, but he was also afraid.

Because he was falling in love with her.

He'd never felt this way before, about anybody.

Surprisingly, the sheep were all bunched up and easily accounted for. Ricky and Beau started back for the house, chins tucked into their slickers against the biting wind.

Until Beau sidled closer than they usually rode. "Can I ask ya somethin'?"

"'Course." Ricky reined in his horse until they were riding at a talking pace.

"Do you— I need to know—" The other cowboy stammered, obviously agitated.

Once again, Ricky was reminded of his brother Maxwell, and his heart ached. He missed home. After Jonas had left, Ricky had told himself he would get things resolved with Daisy and go back, but now he was falling for her. But how could they have a future when she didn't know the truth about why he'd come into her life?

"There's a girl, someone I fancy. A lot."

For a moment, Ricky's gut tightened. All he could hear was the creak of the saddle beneath him. All he could feel was the shifting of the horse.

He was the one who had encouraged Beau to woo Daisy in the first place. He'd thought there were sparks between Belinda and the cowboy but now suffered a moment of stomach-curdling worry. What if Beau fancied Daisy, not Belinda?

"Belinda?" he was able to ask quietly, without revealing the jealousy eating him alive.

"Belinda," the other cowboy confirmed morosely.

Relief raced through him. "What happened the other night?"

The other cowboy's shoulders slumped. "I thought

she wanted to go to the social with me, but then when we got there, she spent all her time with her friends and making eyes at this other fella."

That was about what Ricky had thought had happened. He'd mostly been paying attention to Daisy but had noticed Beau hanging back from Belinda's close-knit group of friends.

"Have you talked to her about it?" Ricky asked.

Beau shook his head. "After the dustup the other night, she and her sister ran in the house and I didn't get a chance. I've been watching for her, but she's barely come out of the house. And I... And I don't got the guts to go knock on the back door and ask to talk to her."

Poor guy. "I don't know if I would either, after she'd treated me like that."

"What should I do?"

Ricky looked over at his friend, the man who'd showed him the way to faith in God and helped him more than anyone else.

Ricky exhaled loudly. "What do you want to do? If you want to fight for her, you've got to show her why she should be with you. You're a hard worker. You'll support her if y'all two get to the point of being married. You're steady and conscientious—"

"And *boring*," Beau concluded.

Ricky laughed. He couldn't help it as his friend shot him a dirty look. "I'm sorry. You're not *boring*. You're one of the smartest guys I know... You're just a little shy talking to women."

"I wish I knew if she genuinely liked me..." the other cowboy mumbled.

"It would make things a lot easier on men like us if

they could just pin a note to their aprons or something, wouldn't it?"

Beau shook his head. "You ain't got a problem with that. It's clear to everybody who's got eyes that Daisy and you are a match."

His spirits fell. "Yeah, well, her pa ain't too keen on me. And I don't wanna make trouble for her with her family."

The other cowboy looked over at Ricky. "Hard to believe *you're* gonna give up."

Beau was right. Ricky hadn't given up when it had been hard to get Daisy to open up. Not when he'd had to face his painful past.

He resolved to do the right thing. He'd tell Daisy about the night of the accident and then he'd do everything he could to prove his heart.

"But how do I get close to her?"

He hadn't meant to say the words aloud, but Beau's head turned in his direction and he explained, "Her pa don't want her in my company."

And Beau grinned. "He can't fault you for going to church, can he?"

The idea caught hold of Ricky. Tomorrow was Sunday. Richards always gave the cowboys the option to go to town and attend worship. Up until now, Ricky had been laying low, trying to stay outta town.

But if Daisy was going—and after she'd faced her fears of going to town the other night, he had to imagine she would be—he could go, too.

Sunday morning, Daisy fidgeted in the pew next to Audra. Belinda had run off to sit with a friend the moment they'd entered the sanctuary with its rows of simple wooden pews. On Audra's other side, the twins whispered together. She didn't even want to know what they were up to. And on their other side, her father sat at the end of the family pew. The entire church was crowded, folks filling up almost every seat. But she couldn't focus on the whispered voices, not as she would've the other night.

After Ricky's confessions and their kiss down by the creek several days ago, Ricky still had shadows in his eyes. She didn't know if they were because of his past, or something else, or because her father still didn't approve of him.

She'd gone to her father several hours after her poignant conversation with Ricky. Papa had been unusually taciturn and hadn't given her a straight answer about why he wouldn't allow Ricky to come courting. But he hadn't outright forbid her from talking to the cowboy.

She missed Ricky. Missed the closeness they'd shared while they'd had to tend to her family over Christmas. Missed how he'd taken care of her the night of the social.

She just missed him.

And she'd held out hope that he was coming to worship this morning. She ignored the swirling self-consciousness as she looked around the room once again. No Ricky.

She'd forgotten the smell of wood polish, soap that mamas had scrubbed their children with, too much rose water and powder from some of the older women. The overlapping smells gave her an inappropriate urge to giggle. She stifled it and nodded to Ethel, across the way, who sat with her baby and husband. Her friend looked surprised and happy to see her, and Daisy hoped there were no hard feelings about what had happened with the baby. Little Ruth looked fine from here.

The rear door opened once more with a rush of cold air, and then there he was. Ricky met her eyes and gave a solemn nod. He was hatless, hair mussed slightly but slicked down for church. His white shirt wasn't new but was clean and pressed.

Her heart rose in her throat as he walked down the aisle, then she realized that there wasn't room for the cowboy in the family pew—and anyway, she was stuck in the middle next to Audra's aunt Pearl, who lived in town.

Ricky took a seat on a near-empty row two back and across the aisle. She looked back at him again, and again their eyes connected. He lifted his chin, a slow, intentional acknowledgment of her.

"Daisy!" Audra hissed from next to her.

Looking forward, she saw the preacher approaching the pulpit.

Someone whispered behind her, and she couldn't make out the words but felt hot all over, same as she had the other night at the social.

But…

He'd made the effort to come this morning. To face censure from the people in town—maybe even from her father.

It meant something. To him, to her.

And she wasn't going to let him sit alone. Even if it meant embarrassing herself to get over there.

She stood up, over Audra's whispered protest, and scooted past her new stepmother, past the boys. She thought her father would stop her or forbid her from going, but he only watched with narrowed eyes as she stepped over his boots and out into the aisle.

She didn't see the crowd around her or the eyes watching her as she took that second step across. She did register Ricky's surprise and delight from the upward tip of his lips and the way his eyes warmed.

He quickly made room for her, and she settled in beside him. And she only felt a little twinge that her injured arm faced the aisle, out there for everyone to see.

Seconds later, everyone stood, the congregational singing focusing everyone on what they'd come to do— worship.

She was intensely aware of Ricky's presence next to her. He couldn't carry a tune. When she couldn't suppress the twitch of her lips, interrupting her own singing of the verse, he looked down at her, his own eyes shining with mirth. He shrugged.

The preacher asked them all to sit for his sermon. Though they were at a respectable distance, several inches separating them, she dearly wanted to reach across and take Ricky's hand.

She didn't dare. She didn't want to cause any kind of scandal in Sunday services.

She hoped that her presence next to him was enough.

She'd made her choice. She would always stand beside him, this man she was coming to...love?

The thought hit her in the solar plexus, a silent cannonball exploding. How had this happened? After the accident that had taken her arm, she'd thought she would never find anyone who would accept her as she was.

But then the cowboy beside her had barged into her life and turned everything upside down. He'd made her see herself differently. Made her believe in herself again.

Showed her the man he was, that he wasn't afraid to fight for what he believed in. And he believed in her.

She must've made some kind of noise, or maybe her breathing changed pace, because he looked down at her, his blond head bending, eyes silently asking if she was all right.

She could only nod, the force of the realization leaving her breathless.

After the service concluded, Daisy remained at Ricky's side. She saw Papa's frown directed at her, but Audra spoke to him and neither came after her.

She wasn't a child anymore. She could make her own decisions. And Papa hadn't forbidden her from being Ricky's friend.

She greeted some folks she'd known since childhood, introducing the cowboy as one of her papa's hands and a friend.

And they all knew. That she was sweet on him, belonged with him. Maybe Papa would be angry, but that was a problem for later.

Having him beside her eased her when the inevitable questions and pitying looks came. Folks asking about her arm and how she was faring. Well-intentioned, but it was still hard to talk about.

Ricky's casual hand on her lower back was the support she needed, silent but present. She felt a little silly that she'd waited so long to come back. This wasn't so bad, after all.

When the crowd had trickled down to stragglers as everyone went home for their Sunday suppers, Ricky was distracted by Audra's twins and Daisy made her way to Ethel and Harry, in a nearby quieter corner, near the open back doors.

Ethel embraced her while Harry held the swaddled baby.

"I'm glad to see you out," Ethel said, releasing Daisy but holding on to her shoulders. "I thought, after the social, that you might become a hermit again."

Daisy laughed, feeling freer than she had in a long time. "As if Audra would let me. Once I stepped foot out of the house, I thought she might bar the door to keep me out."

Ethel raised her brows. "How are things going with your new stepmother?"

"Fine. She's fine."

Daisy sent a glance over her shoulder to where Ricky stood, still in conversation with the boys.

"And I don't have to ask how things are going with your cowboy. I can see it on your face."

"Oh, Ethel," Daisy breathed, unable to contain the emotion oozing from every pore. "He's…"

She couldn't go on, but a happy, high-pitched noise escaped her throat and Ethel was laughing and clasping her hand.

"I'm happy for you. After all that's happened, I'm glad that you can find a way past what he did. You deserve to be happy, and if it's with him, then I'll be pleased for you."

Daisy hadn't heard anything past *what he did.* "What do you mean?" she demanded softly of her friend.

Harry and Ethel exchanged a loaded glance before Ethel whispered, "You know. The accident. Your arm."

Daisy went still, her lungs seizing tight. She shook

her head, trying to convey to her friend that she didn't understand what was meant.

Ethel's face creased in concern and she glanced at Harry again briefly before going on. "Harry saw him that night. Your cowboy."

Daisy's breath caught painfully. She remembered the terror of that night. The screams of the horses, her own panic as the wagon had flipped and the blinding pain…

She hated to think that Ricky had seen her like that. Weak and hurt and probably screaming.

"I knew he was there," she whispered. She'd seen the scar on the back of his wrist.

"He caused it." Harry's simple, plain-spoken statement left no room for doubt.

Daisy went hot and then cold. The walls around her seemed to swell in from their moorings until she felt constricted, unable to catch her breath.

No.

It couldn't be true.

She had to know—from him.

She half turned and he was there, frozen only a few feet away. His face was guilt-stricken, eyes pleading with her for understanding or forgiveness or she didn't even know what.

He must've heard the whole thing.

And she knew.

It was true.

Thankfully, Audra swept in before Daisy could make a fool of herself in front of the folks remaining in the sanctuary. "Daisy, it's time to go."

She would never know if Audra had overheard their conversation or just recognized that Daisy was incapable of even moving, but she took Daisy's arm and swept her up the aisle and out of the country church, leaving behind the man Daisy had thought would be her future.

Ricky followed Daisy's family out of the church, unable to stop himself from watching as she allowed herself to be boosted into the wagon box and settled between Belinda and the twins. His heart thundered in his head, and he desperately wanted to call out after her, but didn't dare.

She didn't look back at him once.

His entire world was crashing down around him. The elation he'd felt when she'd stood up out of her family's church pew and joined him had had no equal. He'd been thinking that surely there was some way to win over her pa, some way to prove he could be worthy of Daisy.

Now it was too late.

This was all his fault. He should've told her sooner.

Part of him wanted to hop on his horse and chase after her and demand she listen to him.

But the hurt that had filled her eyes unmanned him, made him unsure what was the right course of action.

He loved her. He knew it like the sky was blue.

He had to make this right. Somehow.

Chapter Seventeen

Numb, Daisy sat in the parlor, watching the fire in the hearth while Audra and her father conversed in low tones across the room. The flickering fire didn't warm her, not at all. She felt frozen inside.

They'd only been home a few minutes, and Belinda had ushered the twins away quickly to *help prepare lunch*.

Ha.

Audra hadn't wasted time, but quickly filled Papa in on the tail end of the conversation she'd overheard in the church. Daisy was grateful—so grateful—Audra hadn't overheard the beginning. She didn't know the depths of Daisy's feelings for the cowhand.

Papa shook his head, face grave. "This is exactly why I didn't want him around her. I didn't want Daisy getting hurt."

"How could you hire him on?"

"He claimed he'd reformed, that he wanted to make restitution. And she deserved help after missing her arm—"

It took a moment for her papa's words to register,

and Audra was in the middle of saying something when Daisy interrupted. "Wait—"

Her break from the silence she'd held on the wagon ride home brought both of their gazes to her.

Her voice trembled as she asked, "You knew that his brawling caused the accident?"

The guilt on her papa's face was enough proof to guess the truth.

"How could you keep it from me?" she gasped. He'd had the perfect opportunity to tell her, when she'd confronted him about why he wouldn't allow Ricky to come courting.

Her papa's betrayal was almost worse than Ricky's. Almost.

And then there was a knock on the back door.

Audra shot a look at Daisy's papa, and he nodded once, grimly.

From her perch on the parlor sofa, Daisy could see through the hall and part of the doorway into the kitchen and watched as her stepmother answered the door and Ricky followed her through both until he'd joined them in the parlor.

He held his hat between his hands, clearly nervous. He glanced at her papa once, but other than that his eyes remained on Daisy.

She couldn't hold his gaze, couldn't bear it. She looked away, into the fire again.

"I'd like to talk to Daisy for a minute. Alone."

"I don't think so, young man," Papa said.

"Please." She heard clearly the emotion in the roughness of his voice.

"That's not necessary." She was surprised she could get the words out, surprised by the cool tone in her voice when she wished she was upstairs and could vent her sorrows into her pillow. It helped that she didn't look at him. "We've nothing left to say to each other."

His boot scraped on the plank floor and she sensed him take a step closer to her.

"I have some things to say." His voice was low and rough, he sounded as upset as he'd been the other day down at the creek. "I'll say them in front of your pa, if you want, but I aim to get them out."

She didn't know what was worse—Ricky's demand to talk to her or having her papa and Audra overhear it.

She sent a panicked look in her parents' direction. Surprisingly, it was Audra who said, "We'll give you a few minutes. No more."

Her heart pounded in her ears as they vacated the room and left her with Ricky.

Her eyes flicked to him of their own accord, then away, back to the fire. His shoulders were slumped, as if he knew she'd already decided against him.

"I'm sorry," he said. "You have no idea how sorry. That night, I was drunk—"

She shook her head against the distorted images of the accident. She remembered sitting in the wagon. The feeling of falling, the crushing weight of the wagon pinning her to the ground—

"I don't want to talk about that night," she blurted.

He moved. She saw the movement from the corner of her eye and couldn't resist a slight turn of her head. He ran a hand anxiously through his hair.

"If I could take it back, I would—that whole night… my whole life." He laughed, but there was no humor in it.

In her mind's eye, she saw again the dark shadows

of two men stumbling in the street, smashing punches into each other—one shouting—the horses had jumped in their traces—

She stood up, more to escape the memories than anything else, but she put distance between them and went to the window, looking out over the pasture.

"I should've told you sooner. I wanted to. I've been trying to—"

Yes. Then she wouldn't have fallen in love with him. How could she have fallen in love with the man who had caused the loss of her arm?

"I was afraid if you knew, it would change things between us," he said softly.

Because…

She whirled to face him. "You pitied me! The entire time. I thought—"

He flinched. From her words or her tone, she didn't know.

She'd thought he'd honestly cared about her. Had wanted to be her friend.

"All this time while you were *helping* me—finding ways to make my life easier…it was all out of guilt, wasn't it?"

"No." He cleared his throat. "No, it wasn't."

She wanted to believe his sincerity, the depth of the pain on his features, but she couldn't, not now. How could she trust him?

"It was all lies, wasn't it?" she demanded.

"No. My feelings for you—"

She couldn't bear for him to finish. "Stop." She held up her hand in front of herself, trying to protect herself from the damage his words would do.

* * *

Ricky wanted to reach for her.

He ached to reach for her.

Of its own accord, one of his hands moved, twitching away from gripping his hat. He stopped the motion, knowing how useless it was. He swallowed hard.

She wasn't interested in his apology. Didn't want to hear it or even hear him out.

But he had to know...

"The other day, you said that you saw more than my past. *That night* was in my past," he explained. "It happened so fast, I couldn't stop it."

He'd had blood on his hands, her blood. He'd raced against the fire, working with several other men to lift the wagon off her, but it had been too late to save her arm, just as it had been too late to save the woman from his childhood.

Her face went completely white at his words, as if all the blood had drained to her feet.

"Get out." At first she just mouthed the words, but then stronger, louder, "Get out."

"Daisy, please—"

She shook her head, eyes filling with tears. He wanted to go to her, hold her—

He wanted for none of this to happen. How could he have messed up so badly?

"I think you'd better go." The soft statement from behind him preceded Audra's entrance through the hallway. She went to her stepdaughter.

Ricky turned, unsure if he should stay or go. Deeper in the hallway, he could see the boss standing in the shadows. Daisy had been angry with her pa, too, for keeping Ricky's identity from her.

Who would comfort her now? He knew she didn't always see eye to eye with her stepmother, and that sister of hers could be flighty.

He looked over his shoulder once as he exited the parlor and trudged through the kitchen. Audra had put her arms around Daisy, who was still white-faced and tearful.

He didn't want to leave. He wanted her forgiveness.

But he knew he didn't deserve it.

God had forgiven him. Beau had told him that much, and he'd read it himself in the Good Book. But he didn't feel forgiven, not with the hurt his actions still carried for Daisy.

Chapter Eighteen

It was after dark when Ricky returned from a bracing ride in the cold air. He walked his horse up to the barn, noting the dim light from a single lantern left on a hook. Beau must've left it lit for him.

He had played hooky from his afternoon chores. He'd spent some time sitting on his bunk, head in his hands, mind running over and over the events of the afternoon. What could he have done, what could he have said to convince Daisy that he cared about her?

Sure, his guilt had been the driving force behind his actions initially, but he'd gotten to know her, found that he liked her. That was all real.

He couldn't forget the abject terror on her face, the harsh lines of her pain, the tears in her eyes. He'd done that to her.

He'd just as good as taken her arm. His brawling had spooked the horses attached to her wagon. They'd bolted, and without anyone controlling them, the wagon had overturned. A lantern had been tied to it, and smashed, the fuel splashing across the overturned conveyance and lighting the entire thing on fire.

In the melee, the wagon tongue had snapped and the horses ran loose.

Somehow, he and two other men had lifted it enough to drag Daisy free. She hadn't died, not like the unknown woman from his childhood that Ricky hadn't been able to save.

But she was still lost to him.

He'd gone for a ride as evening had fallen, wanting to avoid Ned and Beau and hoping to clear his head.

What would Jonas do? His pa was like Beau, had a kind and compassionate heart.

Ricky couldn't help thinking that it would be better to leave. He hated the thought of causing Daisy more pain. She'd started to heal. She'd learned she could still do the things she had before. She would learn to do the rest. Her family was there to support her.

She could even find someone to fall in love with, if she opened her heart.

That thought was an arrow straight to his heart as he brushed down his horse and settled the animal into its stall. He carried the lantern with him as he climbed to the loft, using his hat to shield as much of its light as he could to find his way to his bunk.

He banged his knee hard against a corner of the bunk. He bit back a cry at the sharp pain, but it was nothing compared to the deeper anguish reverberating through him since the afternoon.

Ned sawed logs in the corner, always an early-to-bed, early-to-rise man. But Beau shifted in his cot.

"You all right?" the other cowboy whispered.

No. No, he wasn't all right. And he never would be, not without Daisy in his life.

"Go back to sleep," he whispered back.

He took off his boots and sat down on his cot, resting his elbows on his knees and running both hands into his hair, gripping the back of his head painfully.

How had he let this happen? He'd never fallen in love before. Never gotten close enough to a woman to even think about it.

Because he'd been afraid of *this*. That his past would come between them. Of course it had. He'd done so many unforgivable things.

She would be better off without him. He knew it.

He reached beneath his bunk, past his boots and the extra pair of clothes he kept folded there. All the way to the back, to his satchel. He stuffed the extra clothes in, felt around at the foot of his bunk for the extra blanket folded there. He couldn't see in the dark.

"What're you doing?" Beau whispered.

"Packing," came Ricky's terse reply.

Ned grunted. His blanket rustled, but the old man slept on after resettling.

Ricky heard the strike of a match, and there was a flare of light. He squinted against the brightness in the dark room. Beau held a different lantern, shielded it with his blanket so only the other cowboy's face and shoulders were visible, and Ned's bunk remained in darkness.

With the aid of the light, Ricky spotted the worn *Aesop's Fables* that he'd kept in his saddlebags, a gift from Breanna when he'd been a teen. He stuffed it in his pack.

"Don't leave." Beau's blanket rustled, and the other cowboy sat up, planting his sock feet on the plank floor.

"I have to," Ricky mumbled. "It'll be better for her. Easier."

"You sure it won't be easier for *you*?" the other cowboy challenged.

"You think this is easy?" Ricky demanded in a whisper. "I'm in love with her."

Admitting it out loud was like the punch he'd received the other night. He wasn't expecting the crushing blow and he sat back in his bunk under the weight of the admission.

He was. He was in love with her.

"You told me the other day to fight if I liked the girl—if you're in love with Daisy, *don't leave*."

He'd learned to listen when the quiet cowboy spoke. But how could he trust Beau's advice when Beau had no experience with the opposite sex?

But how could he not?

The very idea of walking away from Daisy was like a knife to his innards. Felt as if it could suffocate him.

"At least think on it tonight, wait until the morning."

He didn't answer Beau, just flopped back in his bunk, bringing one arm to cover his eyes.

He'd been running for so long…from what he'd done in his childhood, from the man he'd become.

Was leaving the right thing now? Or just a habit ingrained in him so strong it felt like part of his marrow?

Ricky didn't have an answer when the sun came up the next morning. He'd spent the sleepless night praying, begging God for a clear answer. He didn't know if he should stay and try to win over Daisy. Or go and rip his heart out but allow her to heal.

He had no idea what path he was supposed to take. Even as he saddled up his horse, he was unsure if he was supposed to climb back up in the loft and grab his pack and ride out of there. Or stay.

Owen met him in the barnyard in the predawn light. Ricky had been watching smoke curl up from the chimney, imagining Daisy inside the house. Wondering what she was doing. If she was still crying.

"How is she?" Ricky asked, because he couldn't help himself.

The other man considered him. Ricky hated standing under the scrutiny, feeling a hundred times more exposed than he had been the other day in the boss's office. But he withstood it.

"Upset," the man finally answered.

Ricky nodded. She had a right to be upset. He'd held something back from her, his presence, how he'd caused the event that had changed her life.

"This was the reason I didn't want you two courting," Owen said. "I didn't want her hurt."

Ricky nodded. "My pa is just as protective of his daughters. For the record, I never wanted to hurt her."

"*Wantin'* ain't got nuthin' to do with *doin'*."

He knew that. Oh, how he knew that after everything he'd been responsible for.

"You leavin'?"

Ricky shifted his feet. Now was the time. He had to make a decision. Stay? Or go?

"You askin' me to?" he asked.

Owen's eyes narrowed. "I should."

The *but I won't* went unspoken.

And there wasn't really a decision for Ricky, either. His gut wrenched, but he said, "I'd like to stay. Prove to her that I ain't the kind of man who walks away."

Owen's jaw shifted. "You hurt her again, you're off

my property." He looked away, eyes on the lightening horizon. "I figure a man deserves a chance to prove himself."

It was a warning.

But it was more than Ricky had hoped for. His heart rose to his throat. "Thank you. Sir."

Their eyes met and they nodded the acknowledgment of what had passed between them.

"I'd like to ride out with you and Ned and Beau today. I want to bring the sheep up to the closer pasture—that coyote has been sneaking around again."

Ricky nodded. It would be a cold, hard day.

But he wasn't afraid of hard work.

The question was, could he work hard enough to prove himself to Daisy again?

Daisy let her curtain flick back in place. From her upstairs bedroom window, she'd been watching Papa talking to Ricky in the barnyard for several minutes.

"Maybe Papa will fire him," Belinda said from her perch on Daisy's bed.

I don't want him to be fired. But she didn't voice the thought aloud.

She didn't want to talk about him but had made the mistake of answering when Belinda had asked what she was watching out in the yard.

She went to the bureau and mirror, feeling a bit like a caged bird. The room that had been her solace for so long now made her feel trapped. But she was afraid to leave it, for fear of running into Ricky.

His betrayal still cut to the bone.

How could Ricky have not told her that he'd been there that night, that he'd been one of the men brawling in the street? How could Papa have not told her about Ricky's part in it?

If not for the cowboy, she would still have her arm. She would still be beautiful. Able to run the ranch when her papa retired. Able to hold a baby without worrying she'd drop it.

The familiar excuses didn't burden her as much as they had previously. With Ricky's inventions in the kitchen, she could still cook and bake, chop things and pour out of a pitcher without spilling liquid all over the place.

She was learning to make do.

And who was to say that if Ricky hadn't been present, someone else wouldn't have gotten into a drunken brawl in the street?

It had been an *accident*. Unforeseen. She'd thought she was perfectly safe, waiting in the wagon for her papa. How could she have known the horses would spook?

It was a blessing she was alive, and she refused to take that for granted.

But she still couldn't forgive him for not telling her. If she'd known from the beginning that he simply felt sorry for her and was trying to make reparations, she would've protected her heart better. She never would have fallen for the charming cowboy.

Daisy lifted her hand and attempted to pinch some color into her cheeks, but her eyes remained dull and lifeless.

Belinda got up from the bed, throwing down the book she'd been fiddling with. In the mirror, Daisy watched her sister cross to the window and push aside the curtain, where Daisy had been only moments ago.

"He should tell that cowboy to leave," Belinda said again.

Daisy remained silent, though she was impatient with Belinda's behavior. Her sister had treated Beau callously, inviting him to the social and then ignoring him. For a moment, she wished she and Belinda had a closer relationship.

Her sister would never know how much Ricky had really come to mean to Daisy.

Ricky would leave soon enough. Hadn't he told her that it was his habit to move on? He'd warned her about his past relationships with other women, even cautioning her not to get involved with him.

His regretful, repentant spirit over the past had touched her heart, especially that day down at the creek when he'd mourned for the woman in the burning cabin.

Remembering that day, the kisses they'd shared, was painful.

Had he felt sorry for her even then, been close to her out of some mangled sense of guilt over what had happened?

She couldn't trust his motivations, not after she'd found out that nothing between them had been real.

She'd begun to feel alive again. He made her feel beautiful again.

And it had all been based on a lie.

She allowed her eyes to travel her form in the mirror, as she had so many times after the accident, though not recently.

She'd seen the looks she'd received from women and men alike, both the night of the social and at the church service yesterday. She was different. An anomaly.

Daisy reached up and touched the stump of her arm that remained after the rest had been lost.

Ugly.

Unattractive to the opposite sex.

Ricky had been the only one interested in her, and she'd hoped for more.

And now to find out that he'd lied—

Her hopes for a future were shattered at her feet.

There was no suitor for her. No marriage in her future.

Who could want to be with a woman like her, one who wasn't whole?

No one.

Daisy had been dreading the talk she would receive from Audra all morning. The woman *pushed* and *pushed*, always challenging Daisy.

The expected attack came as Daisy was washing the dishes after the quiet lunch the three women had shared. Papa had ordered the twins to ride out with him and Ned and the two cowboys to work with the herd, and Audra had allowed it.

Now, up to her elbow in hot, sudsy water, Daisy scrubbed at the corner of a bread pan where a crust had burnt on, attempting to ignore Audra's silent-yet-loud presence behind her.

No such luck. Audra joined her at the washtub. "Let's switch. Why don't you dry, dear?"

She shrugged and moved to the counter, where earlier she'd placed two towels out to catch the clean dishes.

"What are you going to do about your cowboy?" Audra asked.

Daisy wasn't surprised at her blunt question, not anymore.

"He's *not* my cowboy," she mumbled as she took the clean pan from her stepmother and began patting it dry.

For once, Audra didn't argue or push, just waited.

As the silence swelled between them, Daisy finally burst out, "I suppose I'll keep working at getting back to normal. Some tasks are coming easier to me now. I'm sure with more practice I'll relearn others."

She'd thought that the answer would be enough for Audra, proof that she was improving, at least thinking of moving on with her life.

"Hmm. Like bridling your horse?" Audra handed her a plate.

The soft question reminded her of the unfinished task. And Ricky's help. How he'd calmed her that last time.

She didn't want to think about him. She rubbed the plate dry with more force than was strictly necessary, the action a reflection of her agitation.

"Maybe. Maybe tacking up the livestock is like sewing, something I'll have to give up on." She couldn't imagine a way to sew with only one hand. How would she hold the fabric? Better to concentrate on the tasks that were doable.

"Or perhaps you shouldn't give up so easily," Audra said quietly.

Daisy jerked, setting the plate on the counter with a too-loud *clunk*. She couldn't believe Audra would dare say that.

"Are you talking about the task or the man?" she demanded, facing Audra directly.

Her stepmother calmly turned away from the washtub, drying her hands on the apron she wore over her day dress. Calm, in contrast to the emotional upheaval Daisy felt.

"Regardless of what you might think, I'm not your enemy, young lady."

Daisy's shoulders tensed. But Audra wasn't done yet.

"I love your father, and that means I love his family. I love you. I want the best for you. That's why I didn't want you hiding out on this ranch, afraid to go out in public."

Well, that was…nice.

It had been a long time since Daisy had had the comfort of a mother. And she and Audra were still getting to know each other. "Thank you," she said stiffly.

"I know that cowboy hurt you by not telling you the truth up front. What he did was wrong. We both know that. But I think you're gonna regret it if you just let him walk out of your life."

Daisy shook her head, turning away and looking out the window. "How could I ever trust him again? Knowing what he's kept from me?"

"I'm not saying you should marry the man," Audra said. "I'm saying that maybe you should think on it. Give it a few days to sink in, remember the things that have passed between you two. Find out if you can forgive him, so you can move on. With or without him."

Forgive.

"I don't know if I can," she said stiffly. It was impossible to fathom, knowing that he was the one, that he'd been right here all along.

That he'd made her feel like a woman again, and it had all been based on his guilty conscience.

"Perhaps that's what you need to find out."

Daisy was relieved when Audra insisted on finishing the dishes herself. Her stepmother's calm, reasonable manner rubbed the wrong way, like a blister in a boot, against Daisy's emotional upheaval.

She still didn't know what to do.

Without that task to do, Daisy felt unmoored, at loose ends.

She stood by the back door for a long time, staring at nothing, before she finally donned her coat and made her way out to the barn. The men would likely be gone all day, so there was no danger of running into Ricky out here, not today.

It was time to resolve at least one thing. For herself, and no one else.

Out in the barn, the familiar smells were comforting. Prince was happy to see her, whickering in welcome when she approached his stall.

"What do you think, old friend?" she asked. "Do you want to go riding with me today?"

He accepted her affectionate scratch of his nose, met her forehead to forehead. He'd always been a friend. And it was more than time for this.

She led him out of the stall and they plodded together to the back of the barn where Ricky had hung his bridle contraption. The bridle was still rigged to it from her previous failed attempt.

She met the horse's eye steadily before taking off his halter and sidling up shoulder to head with him. She wrapped her arm beneath his chin and rested her fingertips on his nose.

She clucked softly and he stepped forward in time with her, stuck his nose into the suspended bridle.

He was doing it! Hope and confidence grew, like a

shoot tentatively sticking its head up for the first time in the spring.

His nostrils quivered.

"Easy, Prince," she encouraged him. "C'mon now."

She removed her hand from his nose, bringing it down to the bit, gently guiding the bit between his lips, between his teeth.

He stood still as she unhooked the bridle from its suspension, one clasp at a time, then slid the last leather strap behind his ears.

Then finally, buckled it against his cheek.

"We did it," she whispered, scratching beneath his forelock.

Joy thrilled through her, but she kept her calm, not wanting to spook the animal with the loud shout of elation that begged to escape.

She'd bridled Prince! And he'd been so calm, she knew she could do it again.

She led the horse over to the nearest stall. He sidled close under her direction, and she was able to use the post to get a leg up, and then she was up on the horse, bareback.

She rode him through the open barn door, out into the yard, and then kicked him into a gallop as they left the yard behind and flew into the pasture.

With the cold wind in her face, the animal moving beneath her and her hair flying loose behind her, she felt free.

The wind in her face brought tears, or maybe she was crying, she didn't know.

For the first time since she'd woken after the accident, she felt that she could survive. She might not be able to do a great many things, but she could *ride*.

And it was all because of Ricky and his inventions.

More than that, because of his confidence in her. He had given her the confidence, but she owned it.

He'd believed that she could slice a loaf of bread. Pushed her into caring for her family when there was no one else to do it.

Provided support when she'd been scared to face her friends.

He'd been there all along.

Because he was that kind of man. He might've been a drunk, a carouser, someone who ran away from his problems before.

But he wasn't that man anymore. He'd proved it over and over.

No one had made him stay in the beginning. He'd worked for her father for months before they'd even been introduced.

And couldn't he have left with his father? She'd been well on her way to discovering that there were still tasks she could perform even with her limitations.

But he hadn't.

It was true, he hadn't told her about his part in the accident. But every action he'd taken since then had been proving he was a man she could trust.

But could she forgive him?

Chapter Nineteen

Late that night, Ricky was out with the flock. Ned had insisted on a night watch as they worried over the predator stalking the sheep. Though Ricky had the boss's okay to stay on as a hired hand, it was abundantly clear Ned didn't like Ricky.

Sitting in the saddle, he'd bundled up in his slicker and wrapped himself in a blanket and was still cold.

He just hoped the morning came soon.

Everything was quiet and still, and he couldn't keep his thoughts from going to Daisy.

He didn't know if she would ever be able to forgive him. But he intended to make himself indispensable until she told him to leave.

She was worth it. She was special.

He sang a little to his horse and to keep himself awake. The flock was quiet, only the occasional movement or bleating sheep.

He let his horse wander a bit. No doubt the animal was cold, too.

He found himself facing the house and barn, though

he was far enough out that he couldn't see them over the horizon.

But as he watched, an orange glow lit the night sky. From far away. From the farmhouse?

Fear leaped into his throat and he kicked his horse, shouting, "Hiyah!"

A glow that bright could mean only one thing. Fire.

Fear for Daisy and her family had him spurring the horse for more speed. The icy air pelted his cheeks, and he found himself praying that he was imagining it.

He wasn't.

The orange glow grew brighter the closer he got.

He closed in on the barnyard and faced his worst nightmare. The barn was ablaze, flames shooting from the roof and out the now-broken loft window. Sparks swirled into the night sky and showered down from the gaping maw of the barn door. Acrid smoke billowed from the structure at every orifice, so thick Ricky choked on it even as he rode into the barnyard.

Ned and Beau must've gotten out, must've woken the family, because Owen and the twins had formed a bucket brigade from the well to the burning building. Audra drew up bucket after bucket while Belinda watched from the porch.

Even as he splashed through the muddy river where water had been splashed out of their buckets, Ricky could see it was hopeless.

The barn was too far gone. With the dry hay in the loft and the aged wood going up too fast, their weak efforts would never stop it.

The orange light reflected on the twins' faces as they hauled buckets to the men. They were fighting an enemy they couldn't possibly win against.

"What about the horses?" Ricky shouted, grabbing a bucket and plunging it and his hands into the icy water trough. He hesitated, but forced his feet to move toward the barn when he wanted to run the other direction.

"Got 'em out!" Ned answered as he passed by.

That was a relief. Daisy would have Prince, even if they had to rebuild the barn.

Then his heart stopped beating completely. Daisy.

"Where's Daisy?" he asked Audra as he returned to the pump for another bucket.

"On the porch!"

But the flickering firelight revealed only Belinda. He strained his eyes, trying to see into the shadows around the sides of the house. Or maybe she'd ducked inside for a pot or another bucket for the men.

"Belinda. Where's Daisy?" he shouted, abandoning the water line and running toward the porch.

Belinda was glassy-eyed, seemingly unable to look away from the disaster unfolding in front of them. Finally, she tore her eyes away and met Ricky's gaze. "What?"

"Daisy. Where is she?"

But Belinda looked around, confused, as if she didn't realize her sister had disappeared.

And he remembered the puppies, trapped in their stall. Would Matilda have abandoned them? Would Daisy have tried to go after them?

How could she have gone into the barn without anyone noticing?

He ran toward the inferno, yelling her name. "Daisy! Are you in there?"

The men didn't seem to hear him, shouting orders

at each other. A beam crashed somewhere in the back of the barn.

It was his worst nightmare, revisited.

His memories overlapped the present. He could see the small cabin, engulfed in flames, hear again the woman's screams from inside.

"Daisy!" Ricky shouted, coming so close that his face burned from the heat of the raging fire.

If she was in there, was there any chance she was still alive?

Then he thought he heard a return shout.

There was no choice, no conscious thought. His feet simply took him toward the woman he loved.

Inside the burning barn.

Voices yelled behind him as he ran through the fire-surrounded doors.

But he didn't heed them. He had to get to Daisy. She couldn't die, not if he could do something about it.

Daisy had remembered the puppies as Papa and Ned had ushered the last of the horses from the barn. She'd ducked back inside, coughing as the smoke had filled her lungs. She held her elbow over her mouth and nose as she raced toward the back stall where Ricky had kept the pups confined.

Smoke swirled above her head, curling between and around the rafters separating the loft from the first level.

The darkness made it hard to see, and her eyes burned from the noxious odor.

Something large crashed above her head, jarring the entire building.

Daisy cried out.

She finally reached the stall, and Matilda was there,

curled around her four pups. The dog whined, tail flapping lightly against the floor. Happy that someone had come to rescue her.

Daisy dragged back the barrier. "C'mon, girl."

But the dog didn't move. She nudged one of the pups with her snout, as if trying to tell Daisy to get the pups first.

This was the part Daisy hadn't thought through very well. If she'd had two arms, she would have gathered the four pups together and grabbed them up.

With only one arm, how could she manage?

There was another crash, and Daisy whirled to find that a large beam had dropped, partly blocking her way out. One end of it was visibly burning, fire racing along its length.

Someone shouted her name from outside the barn. She wasn't stupid.

"Help!" she yelled. And then doubled over coughing because the smoke was stealing all the oxygen.

She couldn't wait for someone to assist her—and what if she'd imagined the voice anyway? She knelt to the ground, scooting forward on her knees to the pups.

She scooped one of the pups into the fold of her skirt and prayed that this worked. Another pup joined the first, then the last two, quickly. She gathered the skirt as best she could, containing the squirming, whining pups, and held the fold of fabric tightly, folding it up into a bundle of sorts.

"C'mon, Matilda!" she ordered, leaving no room in her tone for the dog to do anything but comply.

And Matilda seemed happy to oblige, racing through the stall doorway, bumping against Daisy's thigh.

The smoke had grown thicker, flames licked the roof overhead. There was another crash.

The whole building creaked, and Daisy tried to run, but she couldn't breathe. Her head felt stuffed with cotton.

She attempted to skirt the fallen beam, but fire licked at her back and she couldn't make the gap that the black dog had just jumped through.

"Matilda!" a familiar shout, filled with relief, brought her head up.

Across the beam, she met Ricky's beloved face. She saw the stark fear in his expression and knew what it must've cost him to come into the barn, especially knowing his past.

Daisy. She saw his mouth move, but couldn't hear anything over the roar of the fire surrounding them.

How were they going to get out of here?

The beam remained in her way, the gap between the flames licking up the beam and the flames crawling up the wall becoming smaller every second.

She couldn't breathe.

"Help me," she tried to say, but her throat was so dry, and would he hear her anyway?

But he knew. He took off his coat and tossed it onto the beam, momentarily smothering the flames in just a small area.

"C'mere!" he shouted.

She leaned toward him and he met her, clasping her shoulders in his wide, capable hands, and towing her over the beam.

She still clutched the pups in her skirt, as they ran together toward the barn doors.

There was another loud crack and an ominous shifting of the building all around them.

"Go!" Ricky shouted, pushing her through the doorway and out into the cold, fresh air.

Someone grabbed her and she cried out, stumbling as she was dragged away from the heat and chaos. The puppies wiggled in her skirt, their whines muffled through the fabric.

The barn groaned and there was a great crash as part of it collapsed.

"Ricky!" she cried.

She fought the hands containing her, and Belinda was there, taking the puppies out of the tangle of her skirt.

She strained her neck to try and see him—and there he was, bent over coughing and hacking, safely away from the fire.

They'd made it out alive.

Ricky couldn't take his eyes off Daisy. She couldn't stop coughing as Audra dragged her to the porch and forced her to sit on the steps. Belinda was there, sobbing even as she forced a dipper of water into Daisy's hand.

Still Daisy coughed.

His lungs felt singed from the inside out, and he hadn't been in the burning barn nearly as long as she had. He had grit between his teeth. His eyes watered.

Her cheeks were smudged with soot, black marks staining her hair and dress.

How had she survived? Was she in danger from inhaling the smoke?

She was alive. That was all that mattered.

Another section of the barn wall collapsed, sending

a shower of sparks into the air like drunken fireflies, tizzying up into the sky.

He'd done it. This time, he'd saved the woman. Daisy hadn't died.

And she'd saved the puppies. She'd done it on her own. She hadn't been scared, had just done what needed doing.

Who was he kidding? She didn't need him.

But he loved her.

When he could finally get his weak knees to support him, he made his way over to Owen and Ned, who stared at the almost completely incinerated building. The ground between the house and barn had been soaked from water sloshing out of their buckets and maybe on purpose while he'd been inside the barn.

"Should I ride to town and fetch the doc for Daisy?" he asked.

But it was she who answered. "I'll be all right." Even those four words cost her, and she collapsed in another fit of coughing.

He figured if she was talking to him that meant he had the right to sidle up to her and he sat down on his rump in the grass beside the steps.

"You sure?" he asked. He looked to Audra, who nodded. Daisy was really okay.

He couldn't stop the tears that filled his eyes. He pretended they were from the soot and smoke and turned his face away as he tried to blink them out.

"I couldn't leave them in there to die," she whispered.

He nodded. He still couldn't look at her because of how things had been left between them and the emotion swelling up in his chest right this moment, but his chest was busting with pride for what she'd done.

She hadn't let her arm hold her back. She'd just done what was needed. Gone in and saved those pups.

He watched Matilda licking the pups and Belinda trying to keep them all cornered up on the porch out of danger of being stepped on.

Beau approached and Ricky forced his still-shaky legs to support him, with a little help from the railing.

"Boss wants us to round up the loose horses, if you're up to it. Put 'em in the closed pasture."

He was still more scared than anything else. Adrenaline pulsed through him, and he kept seeing visions of Daisy screaming in the barn as it collapsed on top of her. God had kept that from happening this time, but he imagined he'd be having nightmares for some time to come.

"The barn is gone," Beau went on.

Daisy gasped softly behind him. They all knew what it meant. The destruction of all that hay, the expensive tack, the cost of rebuilding the barn. It was a painful loss for the family.

"I'm all right." He'd lost his hat somewhere in the melee and ran a hand through his hair. He looked back at Daisy to find her eyes on him. "You good?"

"Yes. Thanks to you."

He nodded slowly and held her gaze. He didn't know if she was just talking to him because of what they'd just been through together or if it meant she was on the fence about forgiving him.

Audra bustled out of the kitchen door, sending a shaft of light over the two of them and breaking the connection.

"You young men are sopping wet. Here." She shoved

a pile of quilts in Ricky's direction, and he didn't have a choice but to take them.

"They'll at least keep you a little warm while you round up the horses. Come back to the house when you're done."

It was a nice gesture, especially since he'd lost his coat.

But he could've lost so much more.

"I'll be back," he told Daisy. He wanted to talk, wanted to resolve things between them.

She nodded, eyes wide and vulnerable on him.

And he went back to work, riding out into the night.

Chapter Twenty

Ricky woke in a rush, came aware suddenly that he was facedown on the Richardses' parlor rug, where he'd all but collapsed after he and Beau had finished rounding up the horses in the middle of the night. After the fire.

What was that smell? It only took a moment to realize it was him. Not only had he been soaked and sooty, his fear and sweat had left behind a stench that his ma would've been appalled at.

He ached all over, probably the remains of the adrenaline that had crashed through him when he'd had to go into that barn, and riding out half wet without a coat in the cold January night. He figured he'd shivered his muscles sore.

He was plenty warm now, under the blanket and not too far from the hearth fire.

He pulled one arm up beneath his body, groaning low at the motion, and pushed himself up.

What was he supposed to do now? His worldly possessions hadn't amounted to much. An extra shirt and pair of trousers and a book his sister had given him, but his pack had contained all the cash he'd earned this fall, working for the Richardses. This was the first time he hadn't gambled or drunk away his earnings, and he'd started to get a nice chunk of cash saved up. Been thinking he might be able to make a start for himself. Or a new family, if Daisy would have him...

And now it had gone up in flames. Literally.

"Oh! You're awake." Daisy's soft exclamation had his head turning toward the hall, where she peeked in from the doorway.

She looked as pretty as he'd ever seen her, fresh-faced, her hair pulled back, eyes shining.

"Mornin'." His voice was rough, as rough as the rest of him. He worked himself to sitting up and found that his clothes had dried as stiff as the rest of him. Looking down, he could see they were caked with mud and soot, but he hadn't had the presence of mind to get out of them last night when he'd come in.

Besides, what would he change into?

He smelled like a side of beef come out of a smoke-house and wrinkled his nose.

Daisy smiled, then attempted to cover it with her hand. "I'll draw you a bath in the twins' room. Papa put a change of clothes in there for you."

"It'd be quicker to just dunk me in the creek." Quicker, but much colder.

"It won't take long."

He stood up, biting back the groan this time since she was watching. "I can do it."

"So can I." There was something more behind her words, a sureness that had settled deep in her eyes. As if she'd come to peace with herself.

"All right."

He waited until she and Belinda had toted the warm water in for him before he gave himself a good scrubbing in the twins' room and donned some of the boss's clothes. The shirt was too big around the chest and he had to cinch the pants around his waist with his fist as he padded barefoot back toward the living areas.

Daisy was in the kitchen, with a tub of steaming water and a scrub board, washing clothes. On second look, the water in the tub had turned gray, probably from all the soot and ashes.

She looked up when he entered, smiling crookedly at the sight of him in her pa's britches. She pursed her lips and blew a hank of hair out of her face, her cheeks pink, eyes bright.

"Sit down, I'll get your breakfast."

Judging by the slant of the light coming in the windows, he'd slept much later than usual.

She hung the wet linen over the side of the tub, so most of it stayed inside and wouldn't drip on the floor.

The very normalcy of the action was in direct contrast to how they'd spent last night. And the empty space outside the window where the barn had stood before.

It was quiet inside. Everyone else must've gone out, or was resting.

Exhaustion still weighed heavy on him, and he found himself content to just watch her lean down and open the stove, use a towel to take out the plate warming inside. He met her at the table.

His stomach felt glued to his backbone and the food smelled so good that his saliva glands started working overtime, but he still caught her hand before she walked away.

"Forgive me if I'm taking liberties, but last night...

Knowing you had run into the barn—" Thinking about it again, remembering the gut-wrenching fear he'd felt, brought the terror of last night back and he had to swallow hard before he could keep speaking. "I don't want to go another day—another hour without settling things between us."

Her cheeks went pink, but she didn't pull away. That gave him the courage to keep going.

"I'm sorry for keeping things from you. And I'm sorry—" He choked up again, had to clear his throat again. "Sorry for what happened months ago. I wish I could take it back."

He squeezed his eyes shut, head down. He knew he didn't deserve her forgiveness. But he had to know...

"Is there any way you can forgive me?"

Daisy's heart went out to the man she'd come to love as she looked at the top of his bowed, blond head.

Last night, when he'd come for her in that burning barn, facing his deepest fear, she was reminded of the man he was. How could she withhold forgiveness from someone who'd seen the error of his ways and changed?

She wanted to reach out and touch him, but he had ahold of her hand. She squeezed.

"I forgive you," she whispered.

He looked up at her and the desperate relief in his eyes caught her breath in her chest.

"That's good," he said, voice rough. "Real good. 'Cause I'm in love with you."

His simple, heartfelt statement and the gentle tug of his hand against hers sent her into his arms. He let her hand go to wrap both arms around her waist and she rested her cheek and hand against his chest.

"I'm in love with you, too," she whispered.

He exhaled deeply through his nose and gathered her even closer, squeezed her even tighter.

She tipped her chin up and he met her in a fiery kiss. Sparks flew behind her eyes to rival those that had flown up into the sky last night.

Then he was tucking her back beneath his chin, still clasping her tightly. "I was so scared last night, when I couldn't find you... I can't believe you ran back into that barn."

"I had to get the puppies out," she murmured.

"And you did." He didn't sound angry. He almost sounded...proud.

"You weren't afraid of coming in after me." She ran her thumb along the line of his shoulder, just enjoying being close to him.

"Yes, I was. But I had to get to you." He squeezed her waist lightly. "Don't ever do that to me again."

He set her away from him, his expression changing from teasing to serious. "Sit down with me a minute?"

They sat down and he continued to ignore the food on his plate in favor of holding her hand across the table. She wouldn't complain.

"I want— I'd really like to be able to ask your pa for your hand in marriage..."

Her heart, already pounding, galloped even faster. "But..."

"But there's several things standing in my way."

She swallowed. "Such as?" For one fleeting moment, she imagined he might say that her missing arm was a hindrance; the thought passed so quickly it almost didn't stick.

"Such as the fact that your pa don't approve of me. He didn't even want me courting you."

Yes, there was that.

"I think he's softened a little toward me now that you know the truth. But I don't—" He shook his head. "Family is important. I found that out when I left mine behind. And I don't want to cause any kind of rift between the two of you."

"But…" Her voice warbled and she inhaled sharply to keep from protesting too loudly.

He squeezed her hand. "I think, if I keep working and proving to him that I'm not gonna spend time in saloons, not gonna even look at any woman but you, that he'll come around. I hope."

And surely if she made a case to Papa as well, he'd listen. She would start right away, making sure Papa remembered that Ricky had saved her life in the barn last night. "All right."

"Second," he said softly, "is that I've lost all the cash I'd built up to make a start for us. Before this summer, I'd drunk it or gambled it all away. I hadn't seen the need for putting anything up in a bank. It was all in my pack, up in the barn loft last night."

And gone now. Except…

"Wait," she said, and rushed to the back porch. There was his leather pack, among the few other things that had been able to be salvaged. She picked it up and lugged it inside. It was waterlogged, had probably been tripped over and spilled on in the chaos of last night, but it was whole.

His face lit when he saw it. He took it from her hands and began rifling through its contents, revealing soggy and muddy clothes, and a few other things tucked into the bottom. "How—"

"Beau was up in the loft when Uncle Ned dropped the lantern. From what Uncle Ned says, the fuel that spilled spread too quickly and the fire right along with it. He couldn't stomp it out or muffle it. When Beau realized what was happening, that the barn was on fire, he threw what he could out of the loft window."

"And my pack was out on my bed," he concluded softly.

His face had brightened somewhat.

"And the last thing?" she asked, because surely there couldn't be that many things keeping them apart.

His expression darkened. "I've got to go back to Clarkston. I might've been just a kid, but I *did* kill that woman with my carelessness. I've got to make it right. Whether that means I'll spend time in jail or have to make other restitution, I don't know. But I won't feel right about shackling myself to you when I don't even know what the future holds for me."

Tears rose in the back of her throat. Her honorable cowboy, trying to set things right, yet again.

"That's not gonna work for me," she said softly.

His head came up from where he'd been looking down at the satchel, focused on something in the flap. His expression turned wary.

"I don't want to wait for folks to know I'm proud to be your wife—even with your past. If you have to pass time in prison, I'll wait for you."

"Daisy, no—"

She shook her head sharply. "It's not up for discussion. This is my answer. Yes, I'll marry you. I'll talk to Papa this morning."

She laid her palm over his forearm. "I love you, and I want everyone to know it."

He pulled her forward into a passionate embrace, clutching her tightly to his chest, with her head tucked beneath his chin.

How she loved this tenderhearted cowboy.

Epilogue

Two weeks after the fire, Ricky rode into the small town of Clarkston, Wyoming, with Daisy and her mount at his side.

His wife. He still couldn't fathom it. That she loved him back. That she accepted him, scars and horrible past and all.

And somehow she'd got her pa to accept him, too. She'd disappeared into Owen's office that first afternoon after the fire and a good half an hour later, they'd invited him to join them. Owen hadn't taken it easy on him, had demanded to know how Ricky would support his daughter. He'd made Ricky promise that his days of visiting saloons and playing cards were over. It was the easiest promise he'd ever made.

The promises they'd exchanged on their wedding day four days ago had been harder. Ricky had barely been able to choke out the words as he'd vowed to love, honor and protect Daisy. He'd had to blink tears from his eyes when she'd repeated the vows back to him.

But now…now all this newfound happiness—happiness he didn't quite trust—threatened to disappear. But he had to do this. Had to settle the past.

Daisy reached out and touched his sleeve. "Are you ready?"

He wasn't. He was afraid that he would be sent to jail, even though he hadn't meant to set that fire years ago, and surely hadn't meant to kill anyone.

But Daisy was shivering in the cold. He'd wanted to take the train, but she'd demanded they ride together, make the trip in three days instead of one.

She loved being on horseback. And he couldn't deny her anything, not when this might be their last few days together for a very long time.

Everything inside him was cinched tight as he urged his horse into a walk. She followed. They rode into town, pulling up in front of the sheriff's office. He figured that was the place to start, at least.

He helped Daisy dismount, then stood for a moment with his hands resting at her waist, just looking down on her. Thinking that this might be the last time he did so as a free man.

"I have faith that this will turn out all right," she whispered. But her eyes were luminous, large in her face, and she was biting her lip as if she was as nervous as he was.

He brushed a kiss against her cheek and they turned toward the sheriff's office together.

As they stepped up onto the boardwalk, the door opened. But it wasn't the sheriff who emerged, it was—

"Pa?" Ricky's incredulous surprise manifested in the squeak of his voice. "What're you doing here?"

His pa grinned, and some of the tension Ricky felt eased.

"Probably the same thing as you," Jonas said.

"Who is that?" a familiar voice called out from behind Jonas. To Ricky's amazement, his younger brothers Matty and Seb followed behind Jonas.

They were quick to offer handshakes and slaps on the back, and of course, quick to notice Daisy and the simple silver band on her fourth finger. Their eyes appraised her only long enough for him to bristle—he knew exactly how beautiful she was—before they were hugging her, too.

"You got *married*?" Seb asked.

"Without the family?" Matty added on. "Ma is gonna be so mad!"

"Not as mad as Davy," Seb came back. It was probably true. Davy had been Ricky's closest friend since their childhoods had brought them together. Hopefully he could make it up to his brother.

"Davy has his own surprise," Matty mumbled aside to Seb, the comment rousing Ricky's curiosity.

But he didn't really have time to catch up with his brothers right now, no matter how much he wanted to.

He looked to his pa. Jonas didn't seem surprised to see Daisy at Ricky's side. His pa's eyes held a quiet pride that had Ricky standing a little straighter.

Jonas clapped a hand on Ricky's shoulder. "I had a feeling you would end up here. After all that talk of being an honorable man, I knew you'd want to make things right. Your father-in-law sent a wire." And the unspoken part was that Jonas must have come to be with him through whatever happened.

Ricky nodded, throat too full to speak. Until he had to clear it, so he could force the words out. "Will you... make sure she's taken care of? If I can't?"

He trusted his pa to get Daisy home if Ricky had to serve time. His brothers had distracted her, questioning her about Ricky's job working for her pa, and Ricky was thankful for a chance to watch her with them. She sparkled, answering their questions and firing back some of her own.

No nervousness, no self-consciousness about her arm. She'd grown into the beautiful woman God had intended her to be.

He was going to miss her.

"You don't have to worry about that," Jonas said, and Ricky had to take a moment to track back to their conversation.

"What d'you mean?"

"I've already talked to the sheriff, to several people who are well-respected in this area. I wanted to clear your name, if I could, or at least find out what you were facing."

Ricky swallowed. His pa knew what was coming. So why did he look so...happy?

"Just tell me," Ricky said.

Jonas put his hand on Ricky's shoulder again. "It wasn't a woman who died in that fire. Several folks remembered it. It was a different sheriff, but they even had a file on it they were able to pull. It was some kind of big cat that died in that cabin. Maybe a mountain lion."

"Why would a wild animal be inside the cabin?" Ricky asked. It was too unbelievable.

Daisy must've sensed his upset. She came to his side and wrapped her arm around his waist.

Jonas shrugged. "Maybe it had chased some game inside. You said the cabin was abandoned, was outside of town. Maybe the cat took it over as its home."

"But...the screams," Ricky protested weakly.

"I've heard of cats screaming so loud and so high-pitched that it sounds like a woman's voice," Jonas said quietly. "It wasn't a person."

Ricky couldn't speak, overwhelmed with the information Jonas was revealing to him.

"Are they sure?" Daisy asked, voicing the question that Ricky couldn't.

"Yeah. You can talk to the sheriff yourself, if you want."

He wanted. It wasn't that he didn't believe his pa, but he had to be sure, before he let the hope swirling through him right at this moment get loose.

Daisy stood at Ricky's side when the sheriff verified Jonas's story. It sounded too far-fetched to be true, but then she knew that nothing was impossible with God.

They were back on the boardwalk, his brothers and papa approaching from the side, when it finally hit him. He sagged at her side, shoulders going limp, and the grip he'd had on her hand suddenly let go.

She turned to meet his fierce embrace. As his arms went about her waist, she put her arm around his neck, squeezing him just as tightly as he was holding her. He was trembling, quaking against her as all the fear and dread and uncertainty flowed out of him.

"I didn't kill anyone," he said into her hair.

"You didn't," she agreed, her words muffled in his shirt.

And to think she'd almost let bitterness get in the way of loving this man.

Audra had been right. All she'd had to do was let the past go, and forgive. And the moment she'd seen Ricky in that fire, knowing he'd come after her, she had. The man that Ricky had been, the drunken gambler, was gone. She'd never even met that man. She couldn't judge him for what he'd done before he'd accepted Christ as Lord of his life.

She'd also made up with Audra. She still didn't appreciate the woman's pushiness and that would probably never change. But with Daisy about to set up her own household, they would likely settle into a slightly more distant relationship and do just fine as mother and stepdaughter.

Over the past two weeks, the twins had followed Daisy around like wide-eyed, amazed puppies. They touted her bravery in going back into the barn to rescue the pups at every turn.

Uncle Ned had called her *bravery* something else entirely, but then he was Uncle Ned.

And it had all worked out in the end.

"You're free," she whispered, stretching up on her tiptoes to buss a kiss on his cheek.

He let go in the emotion of the moment and pressed a fervent kiss to her lips, one that lasted long enough that his brothers started whistling.

When he broke away, she was hot and flustered by the attention—in the best way possible.

"We're both free," he said, looking down at her with those intense gray eyes.

And she knew he was right. He'd come into her life when she least expected it, and freed her from the fear of living without her arm.

And in God's divine plan, they'd both been set free to live—and to love.

* * * * *

Dear Reader,

Thanks for reading Ricky and Daisy's story. At the end of *The Wrangler's Inconvenient Wife*, Ricky needed to be redeemed, and when he met Daisy and events started rolling, his journey started. It culminated in him ultimately having to face his greatest fear, and overcome it with God's help and the love of a good woman. I'm also blessed to have a partner to travel with me through the hard parts of life and the blessings—my husband, Luke. I wouldn't be writing without his support! If you love the Wyoming Legacy series, don't miss Davy's story, coming soon!

I would love to know what you thought of this book. You can reach me at lacyjwilliams@gmail.com or by sending a note to Lacy Williams, 340 S. Lemon Avenue #1639, Walnut, CA 91789. If you'd like to find out about all my latest releases in an occasional email blast, sign up at http://bit.ly/15lA19O.

Thanks for reading!

Lacy Williams

Questions for Discussion

1. Did you relate more to the hero or heroine in the story? Why?

2. Do you think Daisy's stepmother handled things the right way as she tried to help Daisy heal? Why or why not?

3. Ricky started the story overwhelmed with guilt for the accident he'd caused and its repercussions. Do you think his guilt was deserved? Why or why not?

4. What was your favorite moment in the story? Why?

5. Ricky's relationship with Beau was important to him. Tell about a close friend and how they have affected your life in a positive way.

6. What was your first impression of Daisy? Did it change over the course of the story? Why or why not?

7. At first, Daisy tried to hide from and avoid life, including her friends. How do you handle difficult times in your life? What would you deal with differently if you had a do-over?

8. What was the theme of the story? What parts of the book really showed the theme?

REQUEST YOUR FREE BOOKS!

2 FREE INSPIRATIONAL NOVELS
PLUS 2
FREE
MYSTERY GIFTS

Love Inspired
HISTORICAL
INSPIRATIONAL HISTORICAL ROMANCE

YES! Please send me 2 FREE Love Inspired® Historical novels and my 2 FREE mystery gifts (gifts are worth about $10). After receiving them, if I don't wish to receive any more books, I can return the shipping statement marked "cancel." If I don't cancel, I will receive 4 brand-new novels every month and be billed just $4.74 per book in the U.S. or $5.24 per book in Canada. That's a saving of at least 21% off the cover price. It's quite a bargain! Shipping and handling is just 50¢ per book in the U.S. and 75¢ per book in Canada.* I understand that accepting the 2 free books and gifts places me under no obligation to buy anything. I can always return a shipment and cancel at any time. Even if I never buy another book, the two free books and gifts are mine to keep forever.

102/302 IDN F5CN

Name	(PLEASE PRINT)

Address	Apt. #

City	State/Prov.	Zip/Postal Code

Signature (if under 18, a parent or guardian must sign)

Mail to the Harlequin® Reader Service:
IN U.S.A.: P.O. Box 1867, Buffalo, NY 14240-1867
IN CANADA: P.O. Box 609, Fort Erie, Ontario L2A 5X3

Want to try two free books from another series?
Call 1-800-873-8635 or visit www.ReaderService.com.

* Terms and prices subject to change without notice. Prices do not include applicable taxes. Sales tax applicable in N.Y. Canadian residents will be charged applicable taxes. Offer not valid in Quebec. This offer is limited to one order per household. Not valid for current subscribers to Love Inspired Historical books. All orders subject to credit approval. Credit or debit balances in a customer's account(s) may be offset by any other outstanding balance owed by or to the customer. Please allow 4 to 6 weeks for delivery. Offer available while quantities last.

Your Privacy—The Harlequin® Reader Service is committed to protecting your privacy. Our Privacy Policy is available online at www.ReaderService.com or upon request from the Harlequin Reader Service.

We make a portion of our mailing list available to reputable third parties that offer products we believe may interest you. If you prefer that we not exchange your name with third parties, or if you wish to clarify or modify your communication preferences, please visit us at www.ReaderService.com/consumerschoice or write to us at Harlequin Reader Service Preference Service, P.O. Box 9062, Buffalo, NY 14269. Include your complete name and address.

LIH13R

Love Inspired HISTORICAL

*As a widower, Sheriff Colt Garrett has his hands full
with a rambunctious son and daughter. Could feisty
schoolteacher Allison Grainger be the missing piece in
their little family?*

Enjoy this sneak peek at Penny Richards's
WOLF CREEK FATHER!

"I think she likes you," Brady offered.

Really? Colt thought with a start. Brady thought Allie liked him? "I like her, too." And he did, despite their on-again, off-again sparring the past year.

"Are you taking her some ice for her ice cream?" Cilla asked.

"I don't know. It depends." On the one hand, after not seeing her all week, he was anxious to see her; on the other, he wasn't certain what he would say or do when he did.

"On what?"

"A lot of things."

"But we will see her at the ice cream social, won't we?"

Fed up with the game of Twenty Questions, Colt, fork in one hand, knife in the other, rested his forearms on the edge of the table and looked from one of his children to the other. The innocence on their faces didn't fool him for a minute. What was this all about, anyway?

The answer came out of nowhere, slamming into him with the force of Ed Rawlings's angry bull when he'd pinned Colt against a fence. He knew exactly what was up.

"The two of you wouldn't be trying to push me and

Allison into spending more time together, would you?"

Brady looked at Cilla, the expression in his eyes begging her to spit it out. "Well, actually," she said, "Brady and I have talked about it, and we think it would be swell if you started courting her."

Glowering at his sister, and swinging that frowning gaze to Colt, Brady said, "What she really means is that since we have to have a stepmother, we'd like her."

"What did you say?" Colt asked, uncertain that he'd heard correctly.

"Cilla and I want Miss Grainger to be our ma."

Don't miss WOLF CREEK FATHER
by Penny Richards,
available January 2015 wherever
Love Inspired® Historical books and ebooks are sold.

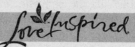
Keira wished she could keep her hands from trembling
as she handled Tanner's saddle. What was wrong with
her?

Seeing him again, his brown eyes edged with sooty lashes
and framed by the slash of dark brows, the hard planes of
his face emphasized by the stubble shadowing his jaw and
cheeks, brought back painful memories Keira thought she
had put aside.

He looked the same and yet different. Harder. Leaner. He
wore his sandy brown hair longer; it brushed the collar of his
shirt, giving him reckless look at odds with the Tanner she
had once known.

And loved.

She sucked in a rapid breath as she turned over the saddle
on the table. Tanner seemed to fill the cramped shop.

Keep your focus on your work, she reminded herself.

"So? What's the verdict?" Tanner asked.

"I don't know if it's worth fixing this," she said, quietly.
"It'll be a lot of work."

Tanner sighed. "But can you fix it?"

"I'd need to take it apart to see. If that's the case, two
weeks?".

"That's cutting it close," Tanner said. "Is it possible to get

it done quicker?"

Keira would have preferred not to work on it at all. It would mean that Tanner would be around more often.

It had taken her years to relegate Tanner to the shadowy recesses of her mind. She didn't know if she could see him more often and maintain any semblance of the hard-won peace she now experienced. Tanner was too connected to memories she had spent hours in prayer trying to bury.

"I'm gonna need it for the National Finals in Vegas in a couple of weeks." Tanner continued.

"I heard you're still doing mechanic work, as well?" She was pleasantly surprised she could chitchat with Tanner, the man who had once held her heart.

"Yup, except last year I bought out the owner. Now I'm the boss, which means I can take off when I want. I took over the shop in Sheridan after a good rodeo run. The same one I started working on before—" He didn't need to finish. Keira knew exactly what "before" was.

Before that summer when she left Tanner and Saddlebank without allowing him the second chance he so desperately wanted. Before that summer when everything changed.

A heavy silence dropped between them as solid as a wall. Keira turned away, burying the memories deep, where they couldn't taunt her.

But Tanner's very presence teased them to the surface.

She looked up at him to tell him she couldn't work on the saddle, but as she did she felt a jolt of awareness as their eyes met. She tried to tear her gaze away, but it was as if the old bond that had once connected them still bound them to each other.

Will Keira agree to fix Tanner's saddle?
Pick up HER COWBOY HERO to find out.
Available January 2015, wherever
Love Inspired® books and ebooks are sold.